7/20/92

To Terry,
And I now you
know the first part
of my story!
Hopefully you
will see this on the
screen. Love you,
Mary Carey

How Long Must I Hide

WEST TEXAS' OWN NEWSPAPER

The Abilene Reporter-News

"WITHOUT, OR WITH OFFENSE TO FRIENDS OR FOES WE SKETCH YOUR WORLD EXACTLY AS IT GOES."—Byron

VOL. LVIII, NO. 79. ABILENE, TEXAS, THURSDAY MORNING, AUGUST 18, 1938 —SIXTEEN PAGES PRICE FIVE CENTS

WITH SIX OF EIGHT DEAD—

Guard Charged In Slaying Of Convict

QUESTION: WOULD ABOLITION OF POLL TAX DISQUALIFY PENSIONER VOTERS?

Intense Search For Stamford Felon Ended

Roy ... Only One In Escape Still At Large

HUSBAND HUNTED—

MARY PENS 'PRAYER FOR A FLEEING CONVICT'

—REACTION RECOUNTED

AT $500 A WEEK—

Name Hines Policy Racket 'Protector'

TAMMANY CHIEF

JAMES J. HINES

Witness Tells Of 1932 Conference

Defense Counsel Asks Mistrial On Testimony

KIDNAPED COUPLE BACK HOME

Large Crowd Hears Terrell

'Did Not Vote For O'Daniel,' Candidate Says

Mann-Woodul Race To Fore

Former Ignores O'Daniel Endorsement, Latter Cites Reasons For Runoff Plaks

Injuries In Car Accident Fatal

R. L. Collinsworth Of Pumphrey To Be Buried Today

O'DANIEL'S 'OPEN MIND' ON HORSE RACING CAUSES STIR

New Law Against Bookmaking, Need For Revenue Seen As Aid To Ponies

Contract Awarded On Haskell Hospital

Oklahoma Firm Is Low Bidder

Back Trade Bill, Druggists Urged

Ranch Employe Drowned, Fear

Boy, Ill, Waits For 'God To Raise Him'

Mann Will Speak Over KRBC Today

Other Cities In Area On Route

Rayburn Guest Of Colorado Solon

Search For Outlaws Turns To Oklahoma

Information Sought On G-Man's Victim

Hand Mangled

Discovered Slain

The Weather

CLIMAX AT NOON TODAY—

Cavalry Of Browns Scores First Major Gain In Mock Warfare

SALUTE TO SCURRY COUNTY

Front page of the Abilene Reporter-News, August 18, 1938 with banner headlines about the slaying of the prison guard and the escape of husband, Roy. At the upper right is the poem, "Prayer for a Fleeing Convict" that Mary left in her typewriter.

How Long Must I Hide

Mary Carey

Eakin Press
Austin, Texas

This is a true story of the two years Mary Carey spent as a fugitive from the law. Other names in the book have been changed to protect the innocent.

SECOND PRINTING

FIRST EDITION

Published in the United States of America
By Eakin Press, P.O. Box 23069, Austin, Texas 78735

ISBN 0-89015-412-0

TO THE UNDERDOG

If reading this book keeps one person
from committing suicide —
— GREAT IS ITS SUCCESS!

Mary Carey as a newspaper reporter, in late 1930s

FOREWORD

This is a great and true love story. All the ingredients are here—youth blinded by faith, courage, hope and ambition . . . danger and adventure . . . an unavoidable and dominating fate working against the lovers . . . misguided loyalty . . . and then disgrace, family rejection, and finally disillusionment. Throughout the story there is an overriding foreboding of tragedy. In the end, after love has burned itself out, Mary Carey played an active part in a righting of wrongs.

Although Roy, her husband, was in the penitentiary, Mary was in a sense also a prisoner bound by love and feelings of guilt that she and her pregnancy caused her husband's crime.

All of these events occurred a number of years before I was District Attorney of Dallas, so I have no personal knowledge of what transpired. But as a District Attorney, I was very much aware of the struggle to improve the Texas Penitentiary and Prison Farms and of the conditions which existed during the period of this narrative. These conditions were very bad but fortunately are much improved now.

The economic harshness of the early years of the 1929 Depression plus the cruel savagery of a convict status combined to erode the character of Roy while providing the proving ground for Mary's courage, loyalty and devotion.

It is too bad that the Depression had to happen. It is too bad that the convict status had to happen. It is great that Mary came through with all flags flying—a true love story.

Will R. Wilson, Sr.
Former Attorney-General of Texas
September 14, 1983

... as they think
they think that some
men are doing all the
agitating While in reality Brutality
is the sole agitator. it doesn't
take much Brutality to make a life time
man quit and when they can just
Break an arm or leg to get out from
under Mismanagement, then that's easy
M. I am writing this in the
Dark and It will be O.K.
I got your telegram today.
We haven't made sure
Connections With the farm yet but we
Will and I can let you know.
Your story will be a little late
Cause I must get my notes from
the farm. although with a little
More time I can do it here.
Telephone Dr. Buttler and
ask is he going to take George
Drody and Melvin Barrow out of
the Morgue here in The Walls
They need medical attention
quick.
Clyde Thompson has been in
there 16 Months or More —
Telephone or write him % Prison Boar[d]

Copy of letter mailed to Mary Carey by husband,
Roy from prison farm in East Texas.

Table of Contents

PRAYER FOR A FLEEING CONVICT

This is the poem published in the August 18, 1938 issue of the Abilene Reporter-News that the Author left in her typewriter when she left to become a fugitive with her escaped convict husband.

Somewhere, God somewhere!
Somewhere in those moaning pines
a hunted man with a haunted soul
Quivers when a bloodhound whines;
Jumps when a leaf is stirred by the air.
Cowers as those thirsty bullets tear
that have gotten the rest.
Or does he know?
Know that his blood-steeped pals are dead?
Of eight, he's the one,
And the only one.
As closely he's pursued and pressed;
    His life their goal.
    They demand their toll.
Somewhere, God, somewhere
Condemned by law and man
He's starving while he's hiding.
Bruised and bleeding.
And justly so,
For other blood was shed.
But God, dear God,
Before he's dead
Let him feel this tenderness:
One baby's smile,
one mother's love,
One heart still held within his hand.
These things no law could reprimand.

Introduction

When describing the seventy years of Mary Carey's life, *incredible* becomes an inadequate expression. Her almost unbelievable escapades as a fugitive, crusader, reformer, journalist, homesteader and author range from Texas to Alaska, and indeed around the world.

As a twenty-five year old fugitive from the law (Mary never considered herself a fugitive from justice) she fled with her convict husband who had escaped in a spectacular prison break in which seven of the fleeing convicts were killed.

When Mary married, her husband, Roy, aspired to become a doctor. He was an assistant to a pharmacist when the drug store where he was working closed its doors. Mary was only nineteen at the time and the great Depression of the thirties was in full swing. Neither Roy nor Mary had the money to pursue their life's ambitions. She wanted to study journalism and become a foreign missionary.

Less than two years after they were married, Mary became pregnant. Two weeks before their daughter was born, Roy came home to find Mary in tears. There was no money to consult a doctor, no clothes for the baby, and almost no food in the house, just some dried black-eyed peas that had been their diet for the past several weeks. Mary was even fearful that the child would suffer birth defects because of her own malnutrition.

In an agitated state of mind, Roy took an old pistol and robbed a store. He was caught and sentenced to twenty years in prison. Mary remembers that the court-appointed attorney was inebriated at the time of the trial. Both became bitter, believing that he did not receive a fair trial because they had no money for adequate representation. In addition she felt she was partly to blame because of her fears for their unborn child.

Roy had been in prison five years when he masterminded a prison break. A nightside reporter on the *Abilene Reporter-News,* Mary slipped away from a detective who had been assigned to watch her apartment, and joined Roy. For two years she was a fugitive, fleeing with her husband to California and back, and facing death so many times that just surviving was a miracle.

''It's tough when the world turns thumbs down on you,'' Mary wrote, ''Especially when you feel in your own heart that you are not a criminal and that the sins you committed were to help the man you love to become an honest citizen. I had to prove to the world that Roy was a good man.

''He was when he went into prison. But prisons, like depressions, can radically change lives. I finally had to admit that I had failed in my attempt to bring back the old Roy that I knew. It was difficult to know when to stop . . . to re-evaluate . . . to quit.

Seven years of Mary's life were spent trying to help Roy and to bring about much needed reform in the Texas State Prison System. Incredible as it may seem, Mary had already divorced Roy when she started helping Harry McCormick, a noted Texas police reporter, develop newspaper exposes and bring about prison reform and rehabilitation. Harry knew and wrote about such notorious depression days desperados as Raymond Hamilton, Clyde Barrow and Bonnie Parker.

Fifty years have passed since Mary's story began. Although many of the people mentioned in this book are now deceased, there is yet a generation of Texans who will recall many of these exploits.

In 1945, Mary was married to Richard Carey, a World War II veteran who had flown fifty two missions in the southwest Pacific and received many military honors, including the Presidential Citation. With her name changed, Mary felt free to teach school and pursue her ambition as a newspaper woman. She received a bachelor of science degree from McMurry College in Abilene and a bachelor's degree in journalism from Texas Tech University in Lubbock.

When Richard Carey returned from overseas to Sheppard Air Force Base in Wichita Falls, Mary taught school there. Later when he became a charter employee of Texas Instruments in Dallas, she taught journalism in North Dallas High School, and still later when he was transferred, she taught in Houston.

Richard died of a heart attack only six weeks before he was due to retire in 1962. Personal tragedy again stalked Mary Carey. After fulfilling a teaching engagement in a creative writing conference at the University of Indiana in Bloomington, Mary impulsively drove alone to Alaska. Here she began a new life as a teacher in a fly-in village, and a part-time newspaper correspondent.

Mary was the first reporter to fly over Mt. McKinley, the nation's highest peak, and became the only woman in the world to land on Mt. McKinley in winter. And that feat, was, of course, in pursuit of a story. She homesteaded in the foothills of Mt. McKinley in an area which has now become a park.

At one time, Mary wrote four newspaper columns, "Takeetna Topics" in *The Fairbanks News Miner,* "Alaska Recipe Round-up" in *The Anchorage Daily News* and "Talkeetna Ticky-Tac" and "Mat-Su Menu of the Week" in the *Palmer Frontiersman.* She won many first place awards with new newspaper writing, her first being at a Corpus Christi, Texas writer's conference. At one time she penned a column, "My Job Is Different," in rotogravure section of the *Houston Chronicle,* as well as being a faithful contributor to the newspaper's weekly magazine.

Mary has also written for many national magazines. In 1955, she won a $5000 National True Story Award and has also written for Argosy, Cavalier, Outdoor Sportsman, True Detective and Startling Detectives. She has written for many religious and children's publications.

Mary declared "war" via the news media in two states and won. In Texas it was for prison reform. In Alaska, it was for the completion of the Parks highway which now connects Alaska's two largest cities, Anchorage and Fairbanks.

Mary has published four books, including *Alaska, Not For a Woman,* her story of her Alaska adventure.

Today, seventy-year-old Mary Carey works in her gourmet garden in summer, goes on an international gem hunt each fall as president of the Anchorage Gem and Mineral Society, spends December in Texas and writes books when the snow is deep back in Alaska. She is still active with the National Press Women and is a charter member of the Talkeetna Historical Society in Alaska. One of her most coveted awards is the National Leadership Award given her by the National Federation of Press Women in 1980.

OTHER BOOKS BY THE AUTHOR

★ Alaska, Not for a Woman

★ Fireweed Philosophy

★ Let's "Taste" Alaska

★ Green Gold in Alaska

Get Set! Prison Break Ahead!

For five long years I had tried to get my husband out of prison the right way . . . and failed.

Wildly I clicked the receiver for the telephone operator. I had been disconnected. Excitement ripped through me like a tornado through a Texas wheat field. I didn't want it to happen this way. Not a prison break! But . . .

"Hello! Hello! Operator," I pleaded, "are you there?" I've been disconnected."

"What number were you calling, please? If you wish I'll try it for you."

"No. Not me. I mean it was an incoming call."

"Was it long distance?"

"I don't think so, Operator, but it was urgent. You see I'm a reporter here at the *Reporter-News* office and . . ."

"Then I suggest you hang up and give your party an opportunity to replace the call," came the acid reply.

I was defeated. The party had left the line . . . intentionally. I heard the receiver click, but I couldn't believe it. This was not the type call to try to have traced.

Dumbly I stared at the telephone and my note pad, oblivious to the clicking typewriters and tattling teletype near my rewrite desk at the *Abilene Reporter-News.* As in another world I relived every word of that call.

"Are you Mary Gregg?" a man's voice had queried over the phone. "You are? Then you must be the wife of Spider Gregg. If you are, I have a message for you," came the 220 jolt over the wire.

"Who are you and where are you?" I fired back.

"I said I have a message for you," the informer repeated emphatically, ignoring my questions. "It's from Spider. He said that if I couldn't contact you by phone to send this message as a telegram; but he hoped it wouldn't go down in print. I suggest you use pencil and paper. Are you ready?"

"Yes," I gasped, afraid to ask further questions.

"WE ARE PLANNING A 'R.B.C.' REUNION," came the telegraphic message. "SAME GROUNDS. BRING TRANSPORTATION AND BIG PICNIC LUNCH. DATE YET UNDETERMINED. STAY PUT! DETAILS FOLLOW. YOU ARE TO TRANSPLANT MY AMERICAN BEAUTY ROSE THE NEXT GOOD RAIN AT THE HAM."

"At the Ham? I've got to talk with you."

"I'm sorry this message is a little late" the voice continued, never bothering to answer my pleading, but there were a few delays.

The telephone receiver clicked in my ear. Message delivered.

I recognized a part of the code, but I was stunned. I couldn't believe what I had just heard nor the words scribbled on the pad. They didn't make sense. My husband couldn't be planning a prison break. Not now. Not when he was so near parole?

I was trapped. I could never forget. The day Roy Gregg was sent to prison flashed before my eyes.

Again I stood on the steps of the Eastland County jail, waiting for my husband . . . a final glimpse of him. This was the day he would be transferred from a local cell to the Texas State Prison. The transfer truck stood waiting.

As the double doors of the jail burst outward, I saw him, handcuffed between two policemen. Only our eyes met. As the linked trio descended the steps, with a full accompaniment of big hats, cowboy boots and guns, an armed sentinel, who had stood motionless near the rear of the caged truck, fitted a huge key into the dusty lock of the barred door. Light spilling into the gloom revealed a blinking mass of chained humanity.

Seemingly oblivious to it all, my youthful lover homesteaded on the steps as we drank in each other with our eyes. I knew he had to see his baby, so I uncovered her face and held her up for his approval. Would he ever know this action had caused me to break with my mother and father?

I could still hear my mother's voice. ''If you ever see Roy again you and the baby are no longer welcome at my home. He must never see his baby. He has brought disgrace to the whole family,'' mother screamed hysterically. ''You must never see him again. Never! Never! Never.''

A cop cleared his throat. Roy had hesitated a moment while descending the steps, beaming with justifiable pride, embracing his new-born with his eyes. They were not shackled.

''Get moving, Gregg,'' one of the big hats commanded with a nudge from his pistol. ''Your chariot is waiting.''

As Roy's handcuffs were unlocked the door to the cage swung open and he was pushed inside. Only dust and a strong locker-room stench escaped the truck as its human cargo was crowded closer together. Arm and leg chains clanked. The door was slammed shut and locked.

As that portable prison cell on wheels groaned down the highway my heart screamed defiance.

''Roy Gregg is not an animal! He's not even a criminal! He did it for me and our unborn child. It wasn't him. It was the Depression. It was the Depression that did it.''

The ten-day-old baby in my arms squirmed and rooted for an empty breast. I crushed her to me.

''Take me! Take me,'' I screamed as the bars through which I caught the last glimpse of my husband's face pulled me after the truck like magnets. In prison there would be shelter and food of some kind. That's more than I would have on the outside. How could I care for my baby by myself?

Shifting the now protesting lump of circumstance to my left arm, I picked up a battered suitcase with my right and drifted in the wake of the prison transfer truck.

A mother at nineteen, limp and listless, weak and homeless, I was caught in the undertow. Ignorant of worldly things I drifted. Farther and farther I drifted toward that incessant whirlpool, the "Hell Hole of Texas," as the inmates termed it, a literal junkpile of humanity.

But all that horror was over now. No one could beat me down and grind me into the earth again. My husband would be with me — or would he? What I had just heard over the telephone, was it true?

I looked around me in the newsroom. No one seemed to be watching. How long had I sat there in a stupor looking at the note with the strange message? I couldn't just sit, looking at it forever. I couldn't use my typewriter. I couldn't think. I had to get to where I could try to decipher the message.

The newspaper had a library. It was seldom used at night. I could go there, if my legs would carry me. I could pretend I was going there for reference.

I don't know how I made it, but I did. Going to the back of the room I pulled out a book, then sat facing the doorway. When I was sure no one had followed, I pulled out the note. Concealing it behind the open book I tried once again to grasp the message.

The words "PLANNING A "R.B.C." REUNION" struck at me like a rattlesnake. Since Roy had been in prison R.B.C. had always meant Raymond, Bonnie and Clyde, the ruthless bank robbers who had terrorized the Southwest. He couldn't mean them, they were dead. "SAME GROUNDS." Now I got it. My husband was planning a prison break in the same area where Clyde Barrow and Bonnie had come for Raymond Hamilton and his buddies. How well I remembered that break.

"BRING TRANSPORTATION AND BIG PICNIC LUNCH." Just because Bonnie and Clyde brought guns and a get-away car, Spider needn't think I would. I hated that name for Roy and I didn't understand it until later, much later.

"DATE YET UNDETERMINED. STAY PUT! DETAILS TO FOLLOW." This was not code, but the next sentence stumped me for a few minutes.

"BE READY TO TRANSPLANT MY AMERICAN BEAUTY ROSE THE NEXT GOOD RAIN AT THE HAM."

We had no rose, but my hair was red. Suddenly the book was laid wide open. I was to bring guns and a get-away car to the Eastham Prison Farm the next good rain there. I was to transplant myself, whenever and wherever he directed.

I knew what he needed. Enough rain to start little streams to flowing. Enough rain to make water stand in long, shallow pools. Enough water to help an escaping convict throw bloodhounds off scent.

Yes, Roy knew all the tricks, like doubling back on his own trail and then jumping as far to one side as possible. Walking fences. Wrapping shoes in rags soaked with oil of mustard. But these were old tricks. Tricks good enough to give an escaping convict a little start, to baffle the bloodhounds a few minutes.

But for me to bring guns and a get-away car?

Secretly I prayed that the convicts had not managed to get hold of a gun. How could the man I loved ask me to bring guns and a get-away car? He must be out of his mind. Could he have forgotten our child? It was unthinkable.

Gradually the library came back into focus. I would have to warn Roy. I would have to send a telegram letting him know that I would have nothing to do with such a plan. What could I say? Could I code it so that the guards would not understand? When could I send it? Tonight? Tonight when I got off work so he would have it in the morning I might say:

"SORRY, CAN NOT ATTEND REUNION. CAROLYN VERY SICK."

How could I tell such a lie? Especially about our own precious daughter? God, forgive me, I prayed. I could use a little strength and guidance, too. I just could not take part in such bloodshed, not even for my husband, despite my great love for him. We had a child to think of.

For five years I had worked to better myself. I worked hard. Four years I worked all night as a waitress in the old Grace Hotel Coffee Shoppe in Abilene, Texas, while I attended McMurry College during the day. I had become capable of making a decent living for myself, and for our daughter.

My mother, who lived just fifty miles away, kept Carolyn. Of course she did it for less than anyone else would have done, and gave her infinite care. But I had paid for this "T.L.C." to the best of my ability. I owed no one anything. It had to be that way. It was a part of my plan. So long I had worked and waited for the day when I could be living with my husband and daughter. But my parents would never have agreed, so I kept it to myself. I realized I would have to shoulder most of the load for a while after Roy and I were together. But I hadn't planned it this way. Not a prison break!

Less than two months ago I had finished college. Now I had a full-time job as a newspaper reporter. I'll admit I was on the rewrite desk, but this wouldn't last long. I could write! Soon I would be given a big assignment and my stories would be published with by-lines. This would be a dream fulfilled. Surely I must be insane to even think of such desperate action. True, the world had wronged my husband and me. We would prove its mistake, but this would take time. A prison break would be the worst thing he could possibly do. That would ruin everything. I had to get moving.

"Wait! Roy, wait" was my silent prayer as I returned to my desk. "Give me more time. What's happened? You were doing so well. I just can't figure it out. Why are you out on the worst farm where they keep the incorrigibles? What happened to your good prison job in the hospital?" I asked in dismay, knowing there would be no answer.

Again I was at my desk. It was mid-summer and a heavy, unrelenting heat made it difficult to breathe. The windows were open, but the night was still, too still to ruffle the litter of unweighted sheets of yellow copy paper in front of me. I couldn't think. I drifted toward the teletype machine, hoping it would bring me back to reality.

It was August 16, 1938, and the machine chattered of the proposed Munich Conference between Hitler and Prime Minister Chamberlain of England. Japanese troops were on the march again in China. President Roosevelt was asking Congress for more arms money for America. But the machine carried no news from East Texas. No news from the Eastham Prison farm.

No news was good news. The *Abilene Reporter-News* would go to press on time . . . if the world would stay asleep.

But I knew that at the prison farm the convicts would be gotten up before daylight and the hoe squads run out on the mile-long turn-rows at the crack of dawn. I had to send that telegram! Would I be caught if I tried sending a personal message from the news office? To the prison? Get fired before I got my first check?

I watched the teletype so closely that one might have thought I had placed my last nickel on the nose-diving stock market.

"Hey, Mary," one of the reporters called. "Let's take a coffee break."

I must have looked reluctant because Charley called to Ted Randel, another reporter on the night shift. "Take a look at the way Mary's glued to that teletype. You'd think it was going to write her a check for a million bucks."

I must have been a little hard to bring down to earth for he continued:

"Don't you know the world's too dead for a story? The Depression's so rough that even the gangsters have given it up since Clyde and Bonnie got theirs."

"Come on, come on," urged Ted, getting up from his desk. "Since when do you need urging for a cup of coffee?"

I grinned and tore myself loose from the machine to join Charley and Ted in our regular midnight coffee session. They were my friends, these reporters, real pals. Especially Ted. He had broken me in on the job. Since then he had shown me in a dozen little ways that he was fond of me. Our midnight coffee session in the all-night cafe across the street had become a sort of ritual.

After all, I was the only girl on the night shift and I guess a touch of feminity does add a little to a cup of coffee. They were so nice to me that I couldn't refuse. We had met our deadline.

If coffee drinking hadn't been second nature with me on that night drag, I couldn't even have done that. I picked up my cup before that cooling off period respected by black coffee drinkers, and burned my tongue.

"Well, look at that," chided Charley. "A guy on either side of her and here she goes thinking about somebody else and burns her tongue. Come on, Kid, give! What's happened to you? You're out of this world if I ever saw it. Always did figure some guy would come along and melt that ice some day."

I tried desperately to pull myself back to normal. I resorted to a little wisecracking, but it fell flat. I kept wondering what I would say in that telegram, and whether it would reach Roy in time.

We finished our coffee and started back to see if there was any last minute news to be done before the presses began to roll. Lightning flashed! I stopped dead in my tracks, electrified. Did this mean rain?

Ted's arm locked in mine and I heard him say, "Hey, what's the matter? Didn't you ever see lightning before?"

No. Not this kind of lightning, the kind that meant a prison break. But was it really going to rain, or was this merely summer heat lightning? And if it did rain in Abilene, how could I tell whether it was raining in East Texas?

I had to send that telegram before daylight. It had to reach him. I was caught in a centrifugal force. Something I couldn't fight whirled me as in a vacuum, shutting out reality. It was like riding in the eye of a death-dealing tornado, ripping above the unsuspecting world and threatening to strike at any minute. "Please, God, don't let it rain before I can get that message to Roy."

Maybe I should change the telegram. Would I dare say, "YOUR PAROLE IS COMING THROUGH, POSSIBLY WITHIN THE NEXT TEN DAYS."

What if it didn't, or he failed to believe me? Perhaps I could pretend I had never received the message at all and say:

"AM ON MY WAY TO STATE CAPITOL. THE GOVERNOR ASSURES A PAROLE, AND POSSIBLY A PARDON FOR YOU."

Dazzling streaks of lightning seemed to bolt me.

The three of us ran across the street and up the back stairway. The night editor was bending tensely over the teletype which was clicking wildly. He looked up and began to bark orders.

"Stop the presses! Stop the presses! Tell them to stand by for an extra. Fine bunch of reporters you are! All gone for coffee while a young war is erupting down on the Eastham Prison Farm. Man! They're killing them off like flies!"

Eastham Prison Farm! A break! My legs went limp like a ripped parachute and I would have crashed except for my eyes holding to the swaying lines of the teletype.

"Pull the lead story, Charles. Get to work on the new make-up, Ted." The night editor was giving orders rapid-fire.

"No names coming through yet," came his commentary, "that hole must be way back in the piney woods. That break was made this morning and there's been shootin' enough for a battle before we ever got wind of it. One of the cons nabbed a guard and rammed a knife through him with five hundred men looking on!"

"Let's get her moving," Ted cut in. "They'll get them all killed before we can get out an extra. Fine thing, wait for a paper to go to press then come through with a banner spread."

If everyone on the staff hadn't been in such an uproar, I know that some one would have noticed I was petrified. Time had stopped. Eternity had begun.

"Some names coming through," yelled Charley.

Afraid to watch, yet knowing it inevitable, my eyes devoured the tape as it clicked off, telegraph like:

TWO OF THE CONVICTS KILLED IN THE BREAK HAVE BEEN TENTATIVELY IDENTIFIED AS JOHN KENNON AND ARTHUR BOSWELL. GUARD JOHN GRAYSON, WHO WAS STABBED BY AN ESCAPING CONVICT REMAINS IN CRITICAL CONDITION. EXACT NUMBER AND

NAMES OF ESCAPING CONVICTS ARE NOT YET AVAILABLE. THE BREAK TOOK PLACE EARLY THIS MORNING AS THE HOE SQUADS WERE BEING LED TO THE COTTON FIELDS.

How well I knew those cotton fields, how the convicts hated that early flowering cotton in East Texas that was ready to pick in the fiercest heat of summer. How they were run out on the turnrows before daylight and picked until dark. One cup of water during the morning and one during the afternoon, with salt. Just enough to keep them working.

Many times I had seen those mile-long stretches called turnrows. I had looked over the terrain when I had gone down there to see my husband.

ROY GREGG! Was I imagining it? Was I reading it with my eyes or dreaming it with my heart? The long roll of yellow paper ground out of the machine with these words:

AMONG THOSE BELIEVED TO BE YET AT LARGE ARE ROY GREGG, LEONARD BROWN, FRANK JACKSON, JOHN CLAY AND RAYMOND MARLOWE. BLOODHOUNDS ARE ON THE TRAIL OF THE FUGITIVES AND THE TEXAS RANGERS HAVE JOINED THE SEARCH. O.B. SIMPSON, GENERAL MANAGER OF THE PRISON, HAS EXPRESSED CONFIDENCE THAT THE REMAINING CONVICTS WILL BE ROUNDED UP BEFORE DAYLIGHT.

'Wake up, Mary,'' I heard Ted say teasingly. ''A big story breaks and you stand there like a zombie. Go rewrite the old lead story and I'll handle this prison break. It's a real 'he man' story with blood and guts. Fems can't handle stories like this. How come you escaped the 'Pink Tea' division? Women belong in the society section. How come you a regular reporter, and on the night drag, too? Some dames get all the breaks, but there's not enough iron in you for this story. Hey, Charley, how many inches for Mary on the old lead? And how much copy do you want on the prison break?''

Ted's orders seemed to be coming from another world. I made my way back to my desk and sat down, but I have no idea what I wrote. My mind was in East Texas with Roy, pushing through tangled underbrush, sloshing down small streams, gasping for breath, listening to the bay of the bloodhounds, ever nearer and nearer . . . ready to swim the swollen Trinity River.

Could he do it? He had been a good swimmer once. Five years in prison might have changed that. Was he wounded? Did he have a gun? I hoped not.

I don't know how I lived through the next two hours. A sort of breathless prayer filled my heart . . . "Don't let him die, God, don't let him die!. He's not a real convict. He's different from most of them. He only robbed because I was expecting a baby and was hungry. He didn't hurt anyone. He wouldn't hurt anyone, ever. He just didn't stop to think. He was desperate. He had to have money for the doctor . . . for food and baby clothes. He didn't do it for himself. He did it for us.

The next thing I knew the newsboys were on the street yelling "Extra! Extra! Read all about it! Big prison break! Read all about it!"

Then Ted was tapping me on the shoulder. "Come on, Honey," he said. "I'll give you a lift home."

It was very unusual for Ted to call me "Honey." He only did it when I got a tough break or failed to get a story.

"The extra's out," he gloated, "and we've got our continued story. This will really sell newspapers. It's kind of like reading about a race and wanting the underdog to win. Well, nobody's been killed in the last two hours, anyway. Big price they're paying."

There just wasn't any talk in me. I hadn't said ten words all night except to answer "yes" or "no."

I reached for my purse and Ted held my arm as we descended the stairs. Suddenly I was glad to have such a man for a friend. I needed a little steadying.

Neither of us said a word as we drove through the silent streets of Abilene toward my rooming house. Finally Ted pulled up to the curb under the branches of the mesquite tree that wove lacy patterns outside my window. He put his hands on my shoulders and turned me around to face himself.

"What is it, Mary? What's troubling you? And don't tell me there isn't anything."

I shook my head. "There's nothing wrong, Ted," I lied, hoping I was keeping my voice calm.

"Out with it," he coaxed. "Everybody has to have some one to confide in. You've pulled that widow stuff on me long enough. It may work with some of the other boys, but I always knew there was someone holding your heartstrings."

Eyeing me sharply he continued, "Remember that night when it was two below zero and I came by for you? You didn't have the heart to leave me out in that storm while you were getting on your hat and coat, so I sneaked a look at a little book of poems I found on your table. They were written by you and dedicated to a prisoner. How come you don't let people know about your achievements? You know I like your poetry. And those poems you always wrote for your college paper, wasn't I always the one who prophesied you would be poet lauerate of Texas some day?"

"But how did you know about the poems." I asked.

"Remember the landlady calling you and asking if you wanted your fire lit in the morning? I spied the book and took a quick peep. Always did want to get up enough courage to ask you to let me read it. I'd love an autographed copy."

I fumbled for words but he cut in, "Remember this morning when the name Roy Gregg came over the wire? You went and sat down, then. You worked too mechanically. The names Roy Gregg and Mary Gregg kept circling in my mind."

"Gregg's not an uncommon name," I retorted.

"But a curvacious young widow dedicating a book of poetry to a prisoner isn't. Seems he came to life."

I knew I was defeated. The dam broke and tears flooded like a West Texas creek in a cloudburst.

"Always did want to let you cry on my shoulder," Ted chided. You haven't fooled me much with your front."

He spoke again and his voice was very low. "I love you, Mary, you must know it by now. I want to marry you. I know that pretty little girl of yours is living with her grandmother. She deserves parents. Don't you see. I want to be your little girl's father, help her grow up. I want to love her too."

"Sympathy certainly does deal a vulnerable hand," I finally

managed to reply. "There's no need making love to me just because you feel sorry for me. I'm a big girl."

"But how big, Darling? Things like this don't go unnoticed. You know the old saying. 'To find the fugitive, watch his gal.' You've got too much at stake. Sooner or later the cops will wise up and track you down. The prison officials know where his letters go. They may have a tail on you now."

I looked out into the fading darkness and the coming day seemed to cast moving shadows beneath my friendly trees.

"You can't hide it, Mary. It's too big a story. I don't like to ask it, but why don't you let me do a feature story on you before the truth leaks out. It's inevitable. If the whole town is to know, let's make it good. I'll make a heroine of you, denouncing all evil. Why shouldn't the world know you have worked all night for four years and attended college days to better yourself and make a decent living for your child. You really are a heroine and the world should know it. Don't let them give you a black eye, Darling. You don't deserve it. You can't let them drag you down. You can't let a fugitive ruin your life. You've just finished college. You're just beginning your career. You can write, stories as well as poetry. Don't throw it all over!"

I didn't seem to be hearing him and he shook me ever so slightly.

"Don't you see," he continued, "That pretty little girl of yours doesn't deserve a fugitive for a daddy. You've got to think of more than yourself, or your husband. She needs parents. You can't take a chance on throwing everything you've worked so hard for away. You've always been so ambitious, yet so distant. Surely you realize I love you. I know this is no time to tell you, but I have no choice. We could wait."

How could I answer him? My lips parted, but no words came. I loved Roy, not Ted. Roy Gregg was the father of my child. That love was the strongest thing in my life. I couldn't fight it, I didn't want to.

It was daylight now and the milkman looked toward the car as if he thought I was just getting in from an all-night party. I hoped he couldn't see my tears. I didn't want to cause a scandal in the neighborhood. I had to get into the house. I had to turn on the radio.

"You don't have to answer my question now," Ted replied with compassion. "I know you are in no position to answer. I didn't mean to push. Just had to let you know how I feel. Especially since you are in trouble. I know I don't have any business offering advice, but I wouldn't leave the house today, if I were you. You need sleep. Don't worry about the boss. I'll tell him you called and said you didn't feel like working."

He was just trying to be nice. I knew I wouldn't have a job if the boss learned the truth. I knew people would stare at me, like some sort of strange animal.

"Thanks for everything," I said, fumbling for the handle of the car door.

"You might at least let me try to be a gentleman," he teased as he walked me to the door. There was no parting embrace. Ted understood, but I knew I had hurt him deeply.

Eight Try, Seven Die

When I reached my room I locked the door, pulled down the shades and turned on the radio. A Bob Wills tune for early risers was playing when an announcer broke in:

"We interrupt this broadcast for a bulletin just received from Huntsville. Two of the convicts from the Eastham Prison Farm have been shot while resisting arrest. The slain fugitives were identified as John Clay and Raymond Marlowe. Three of the escaped convicts remain at large. They are Roy Gregg, believed instigator of the break, Leonard Brown and Frank Jackson. The condition of John Grayson, the guard who was stabbed through the abdomen, remains critical. Stay tuned for later developments."

Roy Gregg was still alive! That was all that mattered. All day the radio provided fragmentary news, but not one word of Roy Gregg. I was hungry but didn't dare leave my room for fear of missing some news. I was thankful for the few pieces of fruit I kept in a bowl on the table to supplement my cafe diet.

Day dragged into night. Three convicts were still at large.

The dogs had lost the trail but the area was being combed by guards, Rangers and patrolmen. Highways were blocked.

Real torture ensued as one by one the radio stations left the air. A late dance band clung on here and there. Maybe they would interrupt the broadcast for a new bulletin. I prayed they would.

In the small hours of the morning my thoughts were with Roy. Would five years in prison change him? I wondered.

I remembered when we had first met . . . how handsome he was, and how sweet he had been to me. It was love at first sight for both of us. We could not live without each other. That was just three months after I graduated from high school. He was from a fine, religious family. We were both young, and so in love. We were a promising young couple, people said.

Promising? The word stuck in my throat. Promising? Strange this should be happening just two months after I had finished college. Fate took and twisted the encouraging word into a futile question, promising what?

Frantically I twisted the dial as the radio broadcasting stations began leaving the air. I had to have someone to talk to, but I was left in silence. I turned to the only friend I could talk to, my typewriter. The keys assembled a little prayer:

> Somewhere, God, somewhere,
> Somewhere in those lonely pines
> A hunted man with a haunted soul . . .

I could talk to my typewriter. It continued setting down the prayer in my heart. It always recorded my inmost thoughts.

News was sure to come with day, and it did. As the day broke sharp and clear, came the first bulletin:

''Early this morning,'' the radio blared forth, ''Bodies of two of the escaping convicts involved in yesterday's spectacular prison break were found in the Trinity River. Only one fugitive, Roy Gregg, remains at large. Hope is expressed that he, too, will soon be apprehended. The Texas Rangers who have joined the search are leaving no stone unturned.''

Hope dared breathe in my heart, but it differed from that of the announcer. I never realized the odds against stolen freedom were so great.

How had these men died? Their bodies were found in the Trinity. Drowned men's bodies sink for several days before they float, don't they? If they had drowned, would Roy also have drowned? My womanly intuition would not have it so. The drownings I questioned. I learned about them later.

Except for reporting the condition of the guard, John Grayson, who had been given a blood transfusion and remained in critical condition, no news of importance came through. The same gruesome details were reported over and over. There were a few interviews with guards who had witnessed the break. "Lifers and incorrigibles," that's how they referred to the convicts on the Eastham prison farm. "Most dangerous men in the whole system."

I wanted to scream my defiance as they pictured my husband a hardened criminal and put a price on his head. He was dangerous, probably armed, to be shot down like a dog. How wrong can the public be? My husband had never hurt anyone. How could they picture him like this?

In my mind's eye I saw his perpetual grin, punctuated with provocative dimples, his high forehead with blond waves spilling over. His wide, gray eyes so capable of holding me in their spell, even with prison walls between. Could this be the man they were speaking of?

Strange the indelible picture the one word "convict" can stamp on the public mind. Never once was he spoken of as a young father, a husband . . .

Maybe God had let him live for a reason. He wasn't a criminal, not in the real sense of the word.

I braved the daylight long enough to run outside and grab the newspaper as I heard it thud against the house.

Screaming headlines proclaimed the break. Gruesome, horrible photos of the bodies of Leonard Brown and Frank Jackson on the bank of the Trinity River, partially submerged, made me sick. A mass burial was planned, but hope was still held that Roy Gregg's body would be added to the pyre.

I tried to fight back, but my strength was sapped with emotional strain. Two days I had stayed holed up like a caged animal, fighting with my own conscience. Why had Roy been the only one to live? Would I help him, even if I could? Was he still caged in the river bottom? Could he escape the iron ring they had thrown around the area. Was he even alive? Again his message came to me:

STAY PUT! DETAILS TO FOLLOW.

I had little choice. A get-away car and guns were not needed for dead men. Getting to Roy was impossible, too. Why should I even think of such a thing?

This reminded me of something. Was I being watched? Darkness had fallen. I turned out my light and raised the shade a little bit. I gazed into the darkness across the street. There was a park bench there at a bus stop. I had a strange feeling that eyes were glued on my window. Two or three times a match flared in cupped hands. I strained to see the partially lighted face. I remembered wondering if the man wasn't smoking a pipe. It didn't glow like a cigarette. Was it the same man every time? Why did he sit in the deepest shadow? I promised myself I would strain for a closer look the next time a match flared, but consciousness slipped away from me.

It was daylight when I sprang to my feet, still fully dressed. This was the third day. Could it be the third day, really? My radio was still tuned in. It had been on all night. I twisted the dial. No news came. Surely Roy must have made a clean break by now. How far could he have gotten? It was less than three hundred miles from the prison farm to Abilene. Three hundred miles . . . three days . . . maybe even now. Strange how he was the only one who managed to stay alive. Now it was hope rather than fear that I seemed to feel.

My body was stiff and I was still groggy. A cold shower would help. Then I could think. I turned the radio up a little to make sure I didn't miss the news.

The shower helped considerably. No news was the best news in the world. I felt more serene. The problem of meeting escaping convicts with a get-away car and guns was solved. If Roy lived, we would try it my way, on the legit.

I had been saving for the time when I could be with my husband and child. One hundred seventy-six dollars wasn't much of a showing, but it was hard enough to squeeze out of my small cafe wages while paying for my schooling and taking care of my daughter at the same time. It was a fortune during the Depression.

I couldn't have saved even this much without my mother's help. I paid her, to be sure, but the amount was pitifully small. She, my father, and my sister, who taught school, gave Carolyn far greater care than I could ever have done. She had, not a rich, but a fine home. This was another thing to think about. They had become too attached to her, especially my mother. This, for reasons I shall explain, worried me greatly.

First my family had wanted to keep Carolyn until I finished college. This I appreciated. In fact, it was a necessity with my going to school days and working nights. Then they wanted to keep her until my job was well established. Now they seemed to believe that, since I was working a night shift, they should continue keeping her. Recently our friendly feud had reached a semi-finalized agreement. To my family, teaching seemed the most fitting profession for a woman. Now, that I had a degree, I should apply for a teaching position. Then, when I became a teacher and would have the same school hours as Carolyn, then, they felt, I could take proper care of her.

I knew Carolyn was safe, but my heart ached for her. If I helped an escaping convict, how would I ever get her back? I wouldn't. If I had the opportunity I would send Roy the money I had saved.

Although early, the sun was flexing its summer strength when I peeped through the glass in the door of my little room, which had become my prison cell. My heart hammered.

Coming up the sidewalk was my girl friend, Oletha. She and I had grown up together. We had always shared our innermost secrets and emotions. After Roy and I married and moved away from the old home town, she had spent weeks at a time with us. We helped her find work. When one ate, we all ate. In fact, we had even been rich enough at times to take in a cheap movie. Maybe Roy had gone to her. She was the only one he could have trusted under the circumstances. I wanted to rush to meet her, but I thought of the man across the street and waited, straining for a reassuring smile from Oletha.

Your Lover Lives

''He's waiting for you,'' were Oletha's soft words when I opened the door. To me she looked like an angel, standing in the doorway with the early morning sun haloing her golden blond hair.

My fingers flew to my lips as I motioned her in and closed the door.

''Don't even trust the walls,'' I whispered, ''they may have a dictaphone planted.''

''I've come to see if you want to go shopping with me,'' she said loudly and cheerily as she gave me the wink. Always did hate to go shopping by myself.''

''I'll powder my nose and be ready in a jiffy.''

''I'll help you pack,'' she whispered.

''No, that would be a dead giveaway. I'll have to leave everything just as it is, and walk out just as I am. I've saved some money that I've got to get to him.

At the moment I wasn't thinking of my trusty typewriter nor the little prayer I had finished and never taken from the cylinder. Little did I realize then that the next morning that prayer, a poem, "A PRAYER FOR A FLEEING CONVICT," would be headlined in the *Abilene Reporter-News* and elevated to first story position. In fact, I have never seen a poem in first story position, before nor since. Strange how quickly the world jumps to conclusions.

I felt sure I would be followed; but the fact that I would be branded "fugitive" when I failed to return to my room by nightfall never once entered my mind.

I snatched my purse as we walked into the hallway of the public rooming house. Then I did something I just couldn't help doing, any more than I could help going to Roy. Maybe this was my second big mistake. I don't know.

I called my mother's house. Luckily Carolyn answered.

"Mommie . . . Mommie!" her sweet voice reached me over the wire. I tried to talk happily and not let her know how my arms ached to hold her, how much I wanted to kiss her.

"Hello, Darling," I tried to sound cheerful. "How's Mommie's girl?"

"I have a new doll, Mommie. I named it Carolyn, after me. It's beautiful, Mommie. When are you coming home to see me and my doll, huh, Mommie?"

'Soon, Darling," I breathed into the phone. Oh, how I wanted to hold her in my arms and kiss her again and again. Why should I be so sentimental about it? I would see her again, soon.

"I'm a big girl now, Mommie. Pretty soon I'll be five. Can I have a birthday party, huh, Mommie, can I?"

"Sure, Darling," I tried to answer reassuringly. Never once thinking I would not attend. "Where's your grandmother?"

"She's out in the garden picking beans. Do you want me to call her?"

"No, Darling, no. Mommie just wanted to call and tell you she loves you. Be sure to be a good girl and help your grandmother with the dishes."

"Will you come to see me before my birthday, Mommie? Grandma and Grandpa were talking yesterday and they said that if you didn't come home by tomorrow we were coming to see you. That will be nice, won't it Mommie?

"Yes, Darling, yes," I choked, afraid the wires had been tapped. "That would be wonderful. Then we could plan your birthday party. But why don't you ask Grandma and Grandpa to wait until Sunday, when I'll be off work." I stalled for time. "Good bye, Darling."

"Wait! I think I see grandma coming back to the house now," Carolyn called cheerily as I heard her drop the receiver and run to the window.

"Good bye, Darling," I half screamed, not sure whether Carolyn had yet gotten back to the line.

I was blinded by tears as Oletha grabbed my arm and hung up the receiver.

"Isn't it a beautiful day for August?" she chortled, as we hit the sidewalk.

"I hope it doesn't get too hot before we finish our shopping," I said loudly enough for the fox ears across the street to hear.

"That's a pretty salty smile," Oletha winked. "But keep up the good work. And dry up before someone gets a look at you. Keep smiling. Say something, loud and happy like."

"I know just the place for a cup of coffee," I complied. "I doubt that the stores are open yet."

Oletha started to turn her head, instinct told her that we were being followed.

"Don't look around," I cautioned quietly. "I know he's there. Been outside my window two days and nights now. Sits across the street under the little willow tree in the park. He's about worn that bench out. Never got a good look at him, but I know he smokes a pipe."

"He's too far back to hear what we're saying, isn't he?" she asked in a breathless sort of manner.

"Yes, so tell me what I want to know. Is Roy O.K.? Was he hurt? Keep talking and don't look so serious. Take your own advice, keep smiling. Laugh, clown, laugh. He could have someone stationed on some of these corners. Look casual!"

"He came to my door last night," she began. "He was afraid to come in. My family had gone visiting, but I told them I didn't feel like going. I was afraid to leave the house. I had a feeling he'd had time to get this far.''

''Was he hurt?'' I urged.

''He wasn't shot, but his left foot was an awful mess. Could hardly walk on it. Said the guard he was supposed to take had a black devil of a horse. He said that when he grabbed for the guard's gun that rodeo bronc reared and came down doing a tap dance on his left foot. The guard managed to get his finger on the trigger of his shotgun and it exploded, right over the horse's ear, while they were wrestling for it. He said that dancing devil took off like greased lightning. He didn't get the guard's gun, but at least the guard had to spend his time holding on.''

Thank God, I said to myself.

''You know Roy,'' she continued with that whimsical grin. ''He said he would like to have stayed and seen the show, but when he looked around he was the only spectator. All the cons who were not running fell flat on their faces in that cotton patch when it started raining buckshot. He said a scared jackrabbit started cuttin' through that patch with him, but he left it so far behind it just sat down and cried.''

''Same old Roy,'' I chuckled for the first time in days. ''No one else but Roy could have seen anything humorous in a rain of buckshot.

''I tried to get him to let me doctor his foot,'' Oletha continued, ''but he said just start at his head with a chunk of beefsteak. There was some cold roast in the icebox. I grabbed it and a loaf of bread. He carried it out under the grape arbor and while he was eating that I tried to pack him a little lunch. When I got back, all the meat and most of the bread was gone. He grinned and asked me for the main course.''

We were nearing downtown. Our shadow lurked a block back.

''We'll get our coffee at the corner drug,'' I suggested. ''There's a booth where we can see the street. I'd like a look at our shadow.''

About the time the girl brought coffee, I saw him. He hesitated near the door, and on a second thought walked across the street and started browsing in a news stand. He always managed to face the drug store while fingering magazines. He finally bought some tobacco and fumbled with his pipe. I could have enjoyed making him hunt excuses to hang around all day just to see how versatile he really was, but there was more exciting business on hand. I had what I wanted, a good look at him.

"When we've finished with our coffee, we'll go to the Citizen's National Bank and I'll check out what money I have."

I started laying out our plans. "Then we'll walk into a dry goods store just to make sure our shadow doesn't think I've been to the bank with something other than a sale in mind. After that we'll go to the Union Depot. You buy two tickets home while I make phone calls."

We went through with our plans. Our tail with the pipe stuck close behind. When we got to the railroad station Oletha went to the passenger window and bought two tickets.

I went to the phone booth and called taxis from two different companies. From the first company I ordered a cab sent to the loading zone just south of the depot. At the other I asked for George. Luckily he was there. George had known me for a long time and had often driven me to school, and recently for hot news stories. I could trust him, I thought. I had to trust him.

I ordered George to go to the college and wait for me at the bookstore. He didn't ask questions. He knew that I meant McMurry, although there were two other colleges in Abilene at the time.

I joined Oletha and we started for the train. Good old Sunshine Special, always on schedule. As we boarded I looked back and saw our shadow at the ticket window, undoubtedly checking to find our destination.

We walked toward the front of the train. There was no one on the platforms between cars. This was just the set-up. I grabbed Oletha's arm and whispered, "Now listen carefully because everything depends on this. I'm going to duck into the washroom in the next car, but you go right on and stand by the door at the front end. Just as our shadow enters the rear door, you go out the front as if I'm leading you to a forward car. He'll think he's following us both, I hope. Now, let's go!"

I made the washroom on the double, waited a few seconds

and then peeked out to see the detective come through the car and follow Oletha to the next one. Then I ducked back toward the rear of the train and swung off just as the conductor was yelling, "Board," and the train began to move.

A few feet south of me was an underground walkway for the safety of pedestrians who wished to cross the tracks. I shot through it and came up near the far loading zone. A cab was waiting. I jumped into it and told the driver to take me to McMurry College. "I'm late for class," I urged to try and speed him up a bit.

To me he seemed to drive much too slowly for comfort, yet I still didn't see anything suspicious looking back of us as I stole a few furtive glances.

"Just drop me at the Ad building," I directed as I handed him the fare before we came to a complete stop.

Straight through the building, out the back door and to the bookstore I scampered. George was waiting. I could have hugged him.

"Set sail," I commanded. "When the cab gets to Avenue A, double back on Sayles Boulevard and head south."

"Hey, what's all this doubling back stuff, Mary?"

"George, I'm counting on you. Please don't ask any questions. Keep driving fast, but not too fast. Remember the old highway that parallels Highway 80 (later to become Interstate 10), a mile or so south of it? Well, head for that."

He nodded and ground the cab into gear, but I could see that he was brimming over with curiosity.

"It's a big story," I told him. "I can't tell what it is, but if you'll stay with me until dark and ask no questions I'll give you fifty dollars."

"For fifty bucks, Baby, I'll stay with you a lifetime." To hell with my job, that's a fortune."

I kept my eye out for anyone following us. No one seemed to be. I slumped down in the seat and drew a long breath. This was an all important step. Time was more precious now than money. Money, saved so slowly, spent so rashly.

George drove quickly and skillfully. We were soon on the old road which paralleled the highway. I was turning over in my mind the fact that before the day was over two people would know something of our secret, Oletha and George. I could only pray that George would not get suspicious.

How many people would have to know something about Roy and me before this night was over? Who might want the reward money? Would the fifty bucks look very big to George, compared to the reward for Roy's capture?

As the cab sped forward I thought back to the night . . . over five years before . . . when I had watched and waited in vain for Roy to come home, the night he had committed the crime that sent him to prison. We had been married fourteen months then, and I was eight months pregnant.

Roy had tried to make a living out of the small filling station, but the Depression was still holding on and no one had any money. He used to fix flats free, so he could pick up new business. But there wasn't any business, no money at least.

I was hungry. Hungry and afraid the baby would not be normal for lack of food. Eight months pregnant and I hadn't even seen a doctor. There were no clothes for my baby. I tried to make a little dress from an old sheet and orange embroidery thread, because there was no money, not even enough for a nickel skein of pink or blue. Then I cried. Roy caught me crying.

My crying did something to Roy. I was sorry, but it was too late. All day he stared into space. Once I saw him take an old busted Colt from the empty cash drawer. He said it wouldn't shoot, but he might be able to hock it for something.

He left and never came back. The next day I learned that he had held up a garage. He was caught and thrown into jail. There was no money for a lawyer. The one the state appointed was thick-tongued from drinking. The state had just passed the law making robbery with fire arms a capital offense. Roy got twenty years.

All that had been five long, agonizing years ago. Suddenly I came out of my reverie. "Do you know how to get to Ross from the next crossroad?" I asked George.

He nodded and I continued, "I want to stop just short of there at an old wooden bridge that spans a fishing stream."

''All this to go fishing?'' George asked with a questioning grin.

''I made a date with a guy I used to go fishing with in my younger days,'' I joked back.

''And he had a hell of a time keeping it,'' was George's leading remark. I knew he suspected.

''Now don't go knocking yourself out with any heavy thinking,'' I put in. ''I'm here for a story. Just sit tight in the boat until I get back. You should know by now that a reporter doesn't start hollering 'EXTRA' before he gets a scoop. You've helped me chase down leads before. Just raise your hood, like you are tinkering with the motor, and keep your shirt on. I'll be back. Let's stop by that old wooden bridge.''

Imperiled Rendezvous

It was almost dark as George eased up to the old wooden bridge that seemed to beckon to me with crossed arms, like an old friend.

I was out of the taxi, almost before it stopped. I slid down the embankment, climbed over the fence and headed downstream, my feet flying to keep pace with my pounding heart. Ahead was a grove of pecan trees, their branches hanging low over the water.

This was the spot! This was where Roy and I used to lie on our backs during long, lazy afternoons, gazing at the sky cut into delicate blue patterns by the branches overhead. This was the spot where we used to have picnics, and fry fish, if we were lucky in catching them. This was the spot which had lain hidden deep in our hearts for five years. Our secret spot, far enough from the road and civilization. Our secret rendezvous of love. And now, at long last, we were to meet here again.

I stepped beneath the pecan trees. The branches enfolded me, concealing me from everything but the sliver of moon just peeping as it, too, started its new venture across the sky.

"Going someplace, Sweetheart? came a quiet voice from behind me. With a little cry I whirled around and threw myself into his arms.

For a moment we clung together in silent desperation, suspended in space, suspended in time, nothing real but the ache of our arms, the fierceness of Roy's lips against mine. We were together under the sky with the pale moonlight washing over us. I can still see Roy's eyes, deep and burning with the hunger of five years. I can still feel his caresses and still hear his words, which were always different from the conventional forms of lovemaking.

"Five years is a long time to wait for a kiss. Every time one of those bloodhounds let out a yapp I jumped twenty yards closer to your arms. Make this kiss as hot as the bullets that singed the seat of my pants."

His banter ended in a provocative grin as his lips found mine. An agonizing thrill shook me as I clung to him. This moment was worth any cost. Hundreds of dreams melted into one.

"Together again," he murmured as he kissed me back to consciousness. The moonlight etched his features, as he raised his face to look at me, showing his hollow cheeks in dark shadows. Around his mouth were deep lines of pain and bitterness which I had failed to notice during his banter. He had been through five years of hell. It was written there for me to see.

It was all a mistake, a cruel, stupid, unfair mistake. Roy was not the incorrigible the papers pictured. He wasn't even a criminal. All the world had made a mistake and we must prove it, yet I felt every confidence Roy could do it. With a feeling of uneasiness I remembered George at the bridge, and wondered how long we had kept him waiting.

"Our taxi is waiting at the bridge," I said, forcing us back to hard reality.

"TAXI? You can't mean you have a cabbie waiting for us? You don't expect me to ride a taxi?" Roy's voice was explosive. He raised himself on one elbow to stare at me.

"I told you, a get-away car!"

"I know, but . . . Well, since what happened to the others,'' I stammered, ''I just thought things would be different.''

''What do you mean, different?''

''Just you and me, so I told the taxi driver I was on a newspaper assignment. I don't think he'll recognize you. That newspaper photo didn't look like you at all. Besides, we need a quick ride to Sweetwater. That way you could get a head start. I'd go along, and then double back to Abilene with George, the cabbie, just to make sure. Then I could say I was real hungry. Since I am paying him well he would have to stop and this would kill more time. I promise I won't let him out of my sight for hours. That would give you a real start.''

''How long, Baby?''

''Maybe long enough for you to get to the border, if he doesn't stoole. I don't believe he will, honestly.''

''There'll be no cab for us. Understand? Did you bring the ''PICNIC? He'll walk. We'll borrow his cab.''

''No, Roy, no. I just can't let you take that route. Either you go on the legit or I'm through. I'll bring Carolyn to you as soon as you feel it's safe. You can trust George, honest. He's helped me lots of times when I was trying to get a story, like he thinks I'm trying to do now.

''We've got no friends. Get that into your head. It's you and me against the world. Our own mothers would turn us in to the cops. You go up there and get that hackie rollin'.''

Ashamed of my mistake, I climbed to my feet to obey. I could at least stick with Roy a little longer. Seven men had died for this freedom. I couldn't desert him, not yet.

I found George waiting, as I knew he would be. I told him that the story had fallen through but that I was going to stick around awhile and see what broke. He offered to wait, but I said I had no idea how long it might be. I thought it best for him to go back to Abilene and wait at the taxi office until I called.

I handed him the $50 which I hoped would take us an extra hundred miles. I felt it pinch, but tried not to look too concerned as I remarked, ''Hang by the cab stand as closely as possible. This way you won't be gone long enough to lose your job, I hope. If the story does break, I'll beat it to the nearest telephone and get you back here on the double.''

"How could a guy refuse service to such a generous and charming young lady? Mysterious too," he added. "Never a dull moment when a red-headed reporter gets on a rampage. I'll stick around. You can count on me." With a fond wave of the fifty bucks he was off.

Would he stick around the cab stand, without cops, I wondered as I walked back along the stream? He had been my friend, but Roy said we had no friends now. Anyway, I had tried a little stalling. Maybe it would work. Even if he did suspect I was to meet Roy there, maybe he would believe what I had said about waiting, and take his time about calling the cops. He hadn't seen anyone. I had never lied to him before. It was a chance I had to take. I felt sure Roy's judgment was better than mine, but how could he get away from here, in a hurry?

"How will you get out of here before George gets back to Abilene?" I asked with a dismal note in my voice as I again reached Roy. "With your foot like it is you can't do much walking, and our dough is short. I had that ride paid for, $50. Now we have only $126.00, but we could . . ."

"What you mean, Baby, is how do WE get into Abilene before they start looking for us here."

"Me! Abilene! I can't go there. I'm too well known."

"So you're chicken. You don't have to come along unless you have the guts. We're just a short way from Ross. We've walked it many times to go fishing."

"What do you mean?" I cried in desperation.

"That's what I wonder. Does a guy live through hell, just for this? Go on home. Blabber to your parents. Keep your precious baby and your money. I went to prison for her, didn't I? Before she was even born. You were blubbering then, too."

I was beyond speaking.

"Make it easy on yourself. Let your parents turn me in. Nice reward, Baby."

"Roy! You're out of your mind! I'll go with you, at least until you are safe. But I can't go through Abilene."

"Yes, Abilene. That's the shortest cut to Sweetwater. We don't have time to go around. That's another thing I've learned. Go where you least want to go. Unless you are far enough ahead of the searching party, get right in with them. They'll do the looking ahead. Maybe we can get through Abilene while they are still looking for just one person. We've got to make tracks."

"But what about Carolyn?" I asked under my breath.

"We're not going to a Sunday School party. We're riding a freight. If you had brought a rod we could go in style."

"A freight? You must be teasing. I have money. Not much, but enough . . ."

"As I remember," Roy began with no apparent attention to my plea, "quite a number of freights come through here every night on the T&P. It's less than two miles from here to the tracks. With luck we won't have to wait long."

I insisted on examining Roy's foot before we started. It was well mangled, quite swollen and blue. There was little I could do except for bathing it in the stream and binding it up again, in the same dirty rags.

"Don't worry about it, Darling," Roy remarked as we cut through the fields. "Got wings in my feet now. Nothing matters, now that I'm with you.

"Those clothes you're wearing, Honey, nice and clean, but someone forgot to press them."

"You know, that colored gal wasn't home when I borrowed this suit off her clothes line or I would have asked her to press it for me."

This sounded like the real Roy I knew. A big grin sunk all the way into his dimples as he continued. "Did have a striped suit, but the stripes went around instead of up and down and it didn't make me look tall enough. A guy's always got to look his best, you know. Some day I'll put a new suit on that line in place of this one.

I was thinking of the pride Roy had always taken in his clothing and was glad he hadn't changed there. He broke into my chain of thought.

"I think I'll drop a sack of groceries there, too. That gal could really cook. Did a bang-up job with what few groceries she had in her kitchen. Couldn't you dream up a hamburger now?" Roy joked. "I've dreamed of such things by the hour."

"I was foolish not to bring food," I repented.

"Don't worry too much about it, baby. I know a patch between here and the railroad that has the best watermelons in the world. You should have seen them last night, dancing in the moonlight. Just one fence away, if I remember correctly. Now they might be a little cooler, after the dew falls, if you care to wait."

I never realized how much fun a watermelon patch in the moonlight could be. For a few minutes we were like kids again, pretending our greatest fear was of a farmer's dog.

The spell was broken by four distinct whistles from a train in the distance.

"That's our chariot, Baby," Roy said as he dropped the half eaten melon. We'll have to hurry, but we can make it. Stops several minutes for water. I watched it last night."

We reached the siding just as the pipe to the water tank came back up with a clang.

"Wait a minute," Roy cautioned as the engine let off steam. "She hasn't highballed yet. I'll find our pullman."

With that he made a quick dash and looked in the third boxcar before he seemed satisfied. Without realizing it I had followed him down the track.

"Here I am!" I yelled as the train whistled twice and started to move.

Roy picked me up and tossed me bodily aboard, then swung himself into the big, empty boxcar.

"Most of the hobos are on top to catch a breath of air," he explained. "If we keep rolling we ought to have a private car into Sweetwater."

The moonlight was beautiful outside, but he pulled the door almost closed, or rather slid it almost closed. It seemed stuffy already.

"We can open her a little when we get rolling," he said by way of explanation. "Don't want to take a chance on any visitors swinging in."

"Say, what's 'highball'?" I asked as we settled down.

"You've been to college, baby. Didn't they teach you what highball is?" Roy never missed a chance to twist any question I asked him.

''I mean on a freight, you dope.'' I said in a very determined manner. ''I very distinctly heard you say to wait until she 'highballed'.''

Roy laughed. ''I see I'm going to have to finish your schooling, little girl. We may as well take the first lesson now. Don't you know trains can talk?''

I waited for I knew he was fixing to answer his own question.

''Suppose we start with three easy words, forward, backward, and crossing. If forward's too big a word for you we can just say 'go.' That's when she highballs. Two short whistles, not snorts, mean a highball. A highball and you're off to the races.''

''Sweet of you to put it so even a college graduate can understand,'' I said with irony. ''Now if you'll just be as explicit with the other two, I'll do my best.''

''Now sometimes a train has to back up, then she blows three times.''

''And a crossing,'' I yelled in delight, ''that's four.'' I was surprised that I had never thought of the meaning before, having heard the whistles all my life didn't make as much an impression as the four, long distinct blasts I had heard from the freight as it approached the crossing a few minutes earlier.

''Darling!'' Roy applauded. ''You can go to the head of the class now.''

Fugitives

There was something about Roy's wholesome fun that made even a freight train ride glorious, despite the fact that the whole world was looking for me. Perhaps this is what I had waited for during those long five years.

When they took Roy away they took the sparkle from my life. He had been given a dirty deal, but he hadn't changed. Sure, he had made a mistake, breaking out, but the world had made a mistake putting him into prison. It was now up to Roy to prove that mistake. All he needed was a little time. Surely the world would forgive him when it saw how much he wanted to go straight.

For ninety miles we feasted on hugs and kisses as telephone poles slid dizzily by. The setting doesn't matter. When fulfillment comes to the soul that has long been deprived, there is no time nor place. I scarcely realized we slid through Abilene, so recently my friend, so quickly my enemy.

"We'll quit her as she slows." Roy was instructing. "I'll jump out and lift you down."

Before I knew what was happening, Roy slid from the boxcar and was running alongside. He pulled me out into his arms and had taken several steps before I realized he was running with the train.

''Oh, let me down,'' I cried as I thought of his sore foot.

''Through this coupling,'' was Roy's only reply as he climbed between two cars on the siding and held his hand for me. We're in the yards in Sweetwater.''

Taking a quick look around Roy picked our route across the maze of tracks. ''It's almost daylight,'' he commented, ''and a dress might be a little conspicious in a railroad yard.''

Breathless, I did not say another word until we were clear of the yards and had crawled a fence into a lonely looking pasture. We kept going until we came to a clump of juniper cedars which grew profusely around Sweetwater and the rolling plains of West Texas.

''We'll wait here until daylight,'' Roy said as he dropped to the ground. ''Try to get a little rest. I wouldn't mind just a little more time with my sweetheart, and another picnic. Did you notice that grocery store, not two blocks from the tracks? Good girl! When it opens, you do the honors. We're rich. Be sure to get bologna and cheese and milk and candy bars and fruit.''

''Seems we haven't eaten for a year,'' I admitted. ''Let's try to get a little sleep and forget about it until morning.'' We slept.

When we awoke Roy asked, ''See that long grade, where a freight will have to slow? I could grab it there, then you could walk back into Sweetwater, take in a couple of double features at the movie, and then catch a bus home. They still come through real often, don't they?''

I assured him this was true.

''The later the better. You could catch a bus back for Abilene after dark. Just before you get into town, tell the driver you want off. Don't tell him beforehand. Just pick a spot fairly close to home, where there is a cafe or service station, call a cab and don't stop until you are back in your room. Maybe you will get back, even before you are missed, since this is Sunday.''

My heart did a cartwheel, but I said nothing. I only hoped

my family had not gone to Abilene. Too late to worry about it now.

When we judged it was about time for the grocery store to open I headed for town. Maybe I didn't look too bad. We had found a little water in a creek and had washed up. I applied a little make up. Roy promised to soak his foot until I could get back with some first aid equipment.

Everything seemed more or less right with the world as I bought groceries. It was fun picking out goodies for my husband. Just like real people, almost. I also picked up some things which would not spoil so that Roy could have them after I left.

I checked out, unnoticed, and headed for the door. I eyed a news rack — an *Abilene Reporter News* rack — and gasped, Headlines: ''WIFE OF FUGITIVE DISAPPEARS'' jumped at me. Furtively I glanced about me, dropped a nickel into the slot and shot from the store. I had to read that paper. All the way back to Roy, after leaving the main part of town, I stole glances. There was my poem, and the feature. Thank heaven I had refused to give Ted permission to use my photo when he proposed making me a heroine. What could he or anyone else make of me now? Evidently the private detective, who had trailed me, reported that I had headed east on the train — probably to try a rendezvous with my husband — accompanied by an unidentified woman.

I was in tears by the time I reached Roy. The paper was more important than our hunger.

We read and reread. Neither of us said a word for a long time.

''Nice poem,'' Roy said, finally, ''but a dead giveaway.''

''How could I have been such a fool as to have left it in my typewriter? The police had searched my room. There was little doubt about it. I had never seen a poem given first story position in a newspaper, but it was of little consolance. Roy finally spoke.

''I hate to tell you this, Baby, but if they catch you now you'll get five years for harboring a criminal.''

''And if they catch you?''

''As you noticed, the guard who was stabbed is in very critical condition. If he dies, I'll be wanted as an accomplice, for murder. They're sure to pin it on me, as sole survivor."

For a long while neither of us spoke. Then we ate, in silence. I did what I could for his foot. Sterile bandages and disinfectants would help, if it wasn't already too late. It looked terrible.

At last I broke the silence. "At least they think I am headed the other way, and with another woman."

"And they probably think I'm still holed up somewhere in East Texas," Roy concluded. "Maybe you could sneak back. How could they prove you have been with me. No one has recognized us . . . I hope."

"I'm not going back," I said decisively. "I know what I'll face. No job. No child. Cops and a prison sentence. Together we might make it. I'll go home when the heat is off. No one can prove I was with you, not yet, anyway. Sooner or later I'll think up a good story and go back, when you are in Mexico or South America."

"Darling," Roy said as he bombarded me with kisses, "together we could make it to the moon."

"I'll catch that freight with you," I offered.

"Impossible! I would be taking a long chance by trying to catch it on that grade myself. Even if we could both grab it, a woman on a freight in broad daylight would be just the answer . . . the one the cops are looking for."

"Today we stay put, a little deeper into the woods," Roy commented. "Got to think this one out."

"Your move," I tried to say lightly. "Looks as though the 'King' has trapped the 'Queen.' "

"Unless our next move is the right one, it looks as if both the King and Queen are trapped, but we'll outsmart them yet. We'll go to the moon, on a freight."

"Are you sure, my dear King, that a freight is the conventional way of reaching the moon."

"Now you have it! It's not likely they'll be looking for a woman on a freight, but they don't know what a pal my gal is. Got it figured. Two freight lines, the Orient and the T&P have junctions here. We came in on the Texas & Pacific, but since it runs east-west, through Cisco and Abilene, I suggest we leave on the Northwest Orient . . . heading south."

"I get you," I cried almost delightedly, "it heads to the border, too, but to the Texas-Mexican border, at Brownsville, where it picks up citrus fruit from the valley."

"You're cookin'. As well as I remember, we're less than two miles from the junction of the two railroads; but we'll have to skirt town. If we could just make that Orient siding where the T&P sets off the empty refrigerator cars to be picked up by the Orient."

"We're on our way," I answered as I started gathering up the extra food and bandages, for which I was now very thankful.

We circled, rather than head straight for town along the railroad track. We must stay out of sight. Daylight might prove itself our greatest enemy. We skirted out-laying houses. There was no hurry. Before mid-afternoon Roy was limping painfully.

As we topped the long drag up a mesa the view was perfect.

"Look!" Roy exclaimed as he gazed into the distance, beyond the foot of the mesa where I was eyeing a windmill. "Our chariot is waiting."

As he pointed I shared the view of the waiting cars on a rail siding, at least half a mile away.

"We're in luck," he added with closer scrutiny. "They're empties, 'reefers,' refrigerator cars to you, Madam."

"How can you tell from this distance?"

"I can see the reefers, the ice comparts at each end are empty. The lids to the compartments are open."

I agreed, even though I wasn't sure. My attention was fixed on the windmill. Beside it was a round, galvanized, water tank which appeared to be about waist high. The kind most commonly used in West Texas for watering livestock.

We made our way down the mesa to the windmill. First we drank, then washed up a bit. I suggested Roy again soak his foot.

"Why not?" he agreed. "We have plenty of time before dark. Glad you brought our picnic along, what's left of it." Later I disinfected and rebandaged that swollen foot as best I could. Roy insisted this wasn't necessary, but picked up the old wrapping and twisted it around the new to keep it from getting dirty before we "got to our train," as he said.

A few minutes more of his painful walking, we finally came upon a dark row of empty refrigerator cars standing on the deserted siding. Roy squeezed my hand in congratulations. We climbed up the iron rungs to the roof of one of the cars. There we found two trap doors propped open, one on either end of the car. Those doors led down into the empty ice compartments.

Following Roy's directions, I eased through the trap, hung by one hand and with the other searched for a hold on the inside wall of the reefer. The walls were made of steel, but perforated with holes about the size of an egg. I found a hole and gripped it hard. Slowly I swung my weight against the steel wall and climbed down to the floor. Roy followed me. Our compartment was about five feet long, three feet wide and eight feet deep. The floor we sat on was made of small iron rods, which might not have been so bad . . . for ice. For a while Roy left one of the little trap doors at the top, which were used for chunking in hundred pound cakes of ice, open for air. As the gray light of day began to appear he climbed up and closed it.

It must have been about eight a.m. when we heard a train pull up, felt a bump as our cars were coupled to it, then began the rocking, switching and shifting back and forth. We were rolling at last! Roaring down the rails! Rolling toward Mexico!

Soon our troubles would all be over. How wonderful to have an opportunity for beginning again.

Roy must have felt my sentiment. He slipped an arm underneath my head to pillow it from the iron rods, kissed me as gently as a mother promising her child a wonderful, new tomorrow, and we both slept.

Trapped

That afternoon as Roy and I lay gasping on the floor of the car, there came the hiss and screech of brakes. The train lumbered to a stop, and hurried steps crunched on the gravel just outside our car. There was the clanging of iron against iron. My heart pounded with sudden fear, for I was sure that we had somehow been discovered and the police were breaking into the car to drag us out. I think I started to scream, but Roy gripped my arm.

"Take it easy," he whispered. "We've got a hot box on this car and they're working on it."

There was a lot of pounding, and after a while we began to move, first forward, then back, then forward again. Finally our car was still. Roy was quite disturbed when he felt us cut loose from the rest of the train. We heard the engine highball and take off without us. We had been left behind.

We didn't dare climb up and open the hatch, for fear we might look right into the face of a railroad officer. But after an hour the heat and our curiosity got the upper hand and we pushed open the trap door for a peek out. It was sizzling hot.

We were on another siding. Our car had apparently been left behind because of the hot box. But what brought a sob to my throat was a sign I saw beside the tracks. It simply read, Van Horn. That was the name of a junction on the stretch between Abilene and El Paso! Our train had been going in the wrong direction. It was headed west for California, instead of south for the border.

El Paso was a border town, true enough, but it was internationally known and well guarded for underworld characters. Besides that, it was the wrong way and we were fighting for time. We were farther away from freedom now than ever. I felt sure they were looking for me, too, by now. We were caught like animals in a trap. One look from our stifling hole and we were goners.

Roy must have been reading my mind for he changed the subject.

''Know what a hot box is?'' he asked.

I had been quite enthusiastic in learning how trains talked, but the spark had died.

''We're a cripple,'' he continued. ''Our wheels have boxes at the hubs which are filled with oil-soaked string. If they get too hot, the oil-soaked string catches fire.''

It didn't make sense to me at all, but Roy still talked with a cheerful strain, ''You know, hobos sure give train crews a fit in winter by robbing the boxes to build fire. You ought to see how that oil-soaked stuff flares up.''

I still showed little enthusiasm. I'm not sure whether I finally dozed off or passed out from the heat. I came to gasping.

''We'll be out of here in less than an hour,'' Roy consoled. It won't be long until dark now. The nap did you good.''

I wondered what good smothering to death could do, but quickly became ashamed of myself. Roy had suffered much more than I. Why should I be bitter when he tried so hard to be cheerful. How could moaning help? I thought of the prison break. I still had no idea how he managed to live when all the others were killed.

''Tell me about the prison break,'' I begged in an effort to get our minds off the horrible thought of another hour of waiting. Cotton filled my mouth and I thought I couldn't possibly wait another hour without water.

''You won't like it, Mary, not unless you have a good imagination. Fate can sure twist you around. I wanted out of the water that day, even more than I would like to get into it now. That was the day I turned into a fish. Are you sure you want to hear this? I can still feel the water running into my ears and strangling me as it forced it's way through my closed nostrils. I almost drown just thinking about it.''

''Go on, Darling,'' I begged, beginning to feel the water myself.

''Our farewell party was a hot one. When we hit that river it was raining buckshot. It splatted the water and thudded the bank on the opposite side as we scampered out like scared jackrabbits. When I hit the first clump of bushes I realized John Kennon wasn't with us and paused for a quick look.''

'' 'Go on, you fool!' '' I heard him yell. '' 'They got me, go on! I'll keep the yellow bellied S.O.B.'s at bay.'

''I heard him cry out as another round of buckshot riddled him. He had Grayson's shotgun, the guard who was knifed. It was too late to help John now. I saw him drag himself to his elbow for a last stand as I took off.''

I was shuddering and Roy looked as if he had opened the wrong box of memories. Quickly he put the lid back on and tried another.

''Oh, yes,'' he started off quickly, trying hard to shut out the last memory. ''I was going to tell you how I made like a fish.''

He seemed more like himself again as he began to joke about his short legs.

''You know, I just wasn't built long enough to outdistance guards with bloodhounds, especially with them bringing hounds in from the other side of the river from the Ferguson Farm.''

I remembered the Ferguson Farm well. Only the Trinity separated it from Eastham No. 2. I had crossed the river on an old ferry, hand drawn by trusties. I remembered well how it capered when the river was up and shuddered at the very thought of trying to swim it after a hard rain. You could see from one farm to the other, if you looked straight down those mile-long turn-rows. The buildings were squat and foreboding. Usually people went through Weldon when they visited the No. 2 farm, but I had to reach the farms anyway I could. This wasn't at all easy without your own mode of transportation. Sometimes I could catch a ride from Huntsville with relatives of inmates of the Ferguson or Eastham No. 1 farms, but no one frequented the No. 2 farm.

Easthan No. 2 wasn't put there for a sentimental public. That was where the prison system put lifers and incorrigibles. The Eastham No. 1 farm was just two miles from Weldon, which was little more than a clearing in the pines, which was hard enough to get to itself. From the Ferguson No. 1 farm I usually walked. I was thinking back to the disasterous event that landed Roy on the No. 2 farm when he continued with his story.

''Being built as close to the ground as I am kept me thinking how little trouble one of those lanky bloodhounds was going to have to stretch to get at my throat. Those rascals are all the name implies around that prison system, and I didn't have any red corpuscles to spare at the moment. We'd all planned to split and get together at a certain meeting place later, anyway. Makes it more interesting for the hounds that way. A new batch of quick yelps from the hounds let us know they had picked up our trail again, and it was good and hot. They were a little too close for comfort. We headed for the river again. We had to shake them.''

Again my sympathy was with my husband in East Texas as he battled the bloodhounds. Indeed my own miserable state slid into the background and I could almost hear the baying of the bloodhounds.

''By the time we hit that river I was wonderin' just how far we'd get down that side before we'd be jumped by the guards from the Eastham farm again. By now they'd know at Eastham No. 1 that there had been a break. They would join the guards from Eastham No. 2, or what would be worse, they'd probably get ahead of them. Prospects weren't good. Guards and bloodhounds from the Ferguson farm on one side of the river, guards from No. 2 back of us, guards from No. 1 in front of us.''

I could picture the guards closing in from all directions as he talked.

"Let's all jump in the river at different places, that'll make it more fun for the hounds. 'Spread out and come out in different spots,' I yelled."

"As we fanned out," Roy continued, I ran upstream looking for a good crossing. The river was pretty swift so I kept watching ahead for a nice clump of brush or overhanging branches on the other side to grab on to. I skidded my wheels enough getting up that slippery bank when the guards were shooting at us the other time. I didn't care for a repeat performance.

"Finally I spotted it," he said. "It had to be there, the hounds were breathing down my neck. Four of my pals had climbed out on the other side before I entered the water. I dived in and made for the overhanging branches down stream. I wasn't quite across the river when I heard the dogs hit the spot where the first man had hit the river. They ran back and forth yapping. Then they picked up the spot where the next man hit the river.

"The guards rode up on horseback and started yelling 'Halt!' and shooting across the river. I didn't know whether they had someone spotted or were just bluffing. The hounds weren't bluffing, I knew, and they kept edging on down the river. I was across and under the branches I had headed for, but was afraid to come out. A few yards on down the bank I saw an old log extending out into the water. There were reeds growing beside it. I eased toward it. I ducked underneath it and bobbed up like a cork on the other side.

" 'Let's get the horses and dogs across the river.' I heard the dog sergeant yell.

"They weren't two hundred feet from me. Another few steps and the dogs would have known where I jumped in, too. Neither the horses nor the dogs liked the river when it was swollen, but they urged them across. It was just a matter of minutes now until they'd be on me.

"I started 'crawdading' down that tree trunk." I heard him say as I felt his body reliving the motion, "I just edged my way down until there wasn't nothing but one eye and a nose in the angle where the water lapped the underside of the log. One guard and a dog was driftin' mighty close my way. Looked like they were goin' to land right under the branch I first hit, or what was worse, right on top of me."

I heard him draw a long gulp of air.

"They were close enough I thought the dog might smell me when I gulped in all the air I could and crawdaded on down to the base of the old log. Sure was glad to feel an old root I could hook my foot under. If one of those dogs got hold of me he was going to have to pull me out. I tried to open my eyes but the water was so muddy it didn't do any good, just made them sting. I was thankful, for if I couldn't see out, maybe they couldn't see in. I heard the guard trying to get his horse out on the bank. I didn't hear the dog. This made it worse. They always get right quiet when they are right on you. A little more swearin' and the guard made it out of the water. Must have hit one of the branches, judgin' from the way he let it out. My lungs were bustin'.

I heard muffled sounds under the water," he continued, "as the dogs picked up the other trails. They really let it out. I was hanging on to the bottom of that log like a cork about to pop from a bottle. I knew I was going to shoot right out into that hound's jaws.

" 'Come on!' the other guards yelled from upstream. 'We've got a red-hot trail.'

" 'But this here dog's actin' funny,' " the guard yelled back.

"I could just feel that hound hopping out on the log."

" 'Bring 'er on in,' " the others called. " 'We're right on 'em.'

"I was still hanging to the under side of the log but was sucking water into my bursting lungs when I heard the sergeant finally call that dog. My foot gave way and it seemed like I was clawing my way through a long, black tunnel. When I came to I was hanging just above water with one arm wrapped around that log. I don't remember, or will never know, how long I just hung there."

I felt him relax a little as he continued.

"I heard shooting, but the guards and dogs were too far away for me to understand why they were yelling. I edged a few feet from the bank, staying close to the log, and caught hold of the bottom of a reed and lodged myself in a sitting position. I was too beat to think or even move for a spell. When I did come to my senses I knew that those guards and dogs or other guards and dogs would be back along the river when they found some of the men missing. I wondered who had been caught? If the bloodhounds had chewed them up or if they had been shot. Maybe I'd best think a little about myself. There just wasn't any place to go. I looked around and saw a dead reed I could reach without touching the bank to give the dogs a scent. I reached out and cut it off with my shiv, which was the only weapon I had along, and finished hollowing it out. I tried breathing through it and it worked. I could lay under water and suck air through it into my mouth."

He moved restlessly and looked toward the hatch of our prison. It didn't seem quite so light around the edges.

"Well, I guess that's about all there is to it. I was afraid to crawl out on the bank, afraid the bloodhounds would pick up my scent, so I just stayed. Every time I heard anyone near the river I edged back under the log and used the old Indian trick. Hooking myself down I could stay under a long time. The river was like Grand Central Station all day. By nightfall the dogs must have lost the trail of the ones who weren't caught for I heard them being brought back to the kennels. Good thing it was warm. I stayed under water nearly all day."

"Water," I gasped. "I believe I could drink a barrel of it right out of that muddy river."

Roy climbed to the top of our trap and pushed open the hatch. He motioned for me to follow. The air was cool and I took deep, grateful gulps of it. But now as I walked I found myself trembling. I was weak from hunger and thirst. My blouse and skirt looked as if they had been wadded into a ball. I wanted to look pretty for Roy. I certainly didn't now, but nothing really matter except our thirst.

There was a big, black water tank down the line where

trains took on water. We headed for it, thankful for the benevolent, cool encasement of nightfall after our day's inferno.

Water never was so good before. After we had drunk gallons, it seemed, and washed our face and hands, we slid off into the desert on the right hand side of the track.

A few hundred yards down the tracks were the lights of the village. The lights were pretty, but towns were not for us. I was beginning to wonder if they ever would be. If anything would. Roy had insisted that I throw away the paper, the one with my poem, which I wanted so much to keep. This was a different world.

''Doesn't the Sunshine Special still come through Abilene about six in the morning?'' Roy asked.

I nodded assent.

''Then it should put in here about 1 a.m.,'' he calculated. ''It looks like our best bet.''

''But that's headed for California,'' I cried. ''It doesn't even go down into Mexico.''

''O.K., then, if you're so set on striking out south, why don't you take off? There's only about fifty miles of rattlesnakes between here and the river, but there's a thousand miles of trackless desert on the other side of it. If the Sunshine Special goes out of Texas,'' he said grimly. ''It's good enough for me.''

''But it's a passenger train,'' I said in dismay. ''We don't have enough money for that kind of trip.''

''I don't mean on the inside,'' Roy answered. ''We'll ride the blinds. Now lie down and try to get some rest.

I was afraid to ask what ''riding the blinds'' meant. I felt I would find out soon enough.

So Near and Yet So Far

We lay down side by side. The moon hung low on the rim of the desert off to the north. I reached for Roy's hand in the darkness. I was tired and hungry and scared. My husband had spoken crossly to me for the first time. I wanted him to take me in his arms and comfort me and tell me how much he loved me. But Roy seemed far away. He just lay there on his back without moving his eyes and staring into the darkness.

I was doing a little thinking of my own, and a little lamenting. How cruel that Old Mexico should be only fifty miles away, and yet so inaccessible. I knew Roy's foot was hurting him more all the time, and he couldn't have walked five miles. A thousand miles of trackless desert on the other side. I knew he was right, but El Paso? Of all the places I'd rather not be, that was it.

Roy's hand felt hot. I was afraid he had fever. He began talking, but he didn't seem to be talking to me. He talked slowly, haltingly, almost to himself.

''We worked in the cotton fields all day, with only two cups of water for each man. We were run out on the turn-rows before daylight and picked until dark. I planned the break a long time before the rain came. Every guy there knew just what to do. I was head of one hoe squad and Steve Clancey was head of another. When I decided the time was right, I slowed down my squad and Steve speeded up his so the two squads got jammed together. Then when the guards rode their horses over to break up the jam, we had all of them in one place and jumped them. We did it right, only that wild, devil of a horse reared and came down on my foot.'' He broke off and almost fell asleep, but a sharp pain brought him back with a loan moan.

I crept closer to him and put my hand on his shoulder. ''Darling, try not to think about it,'' I begged. That's all over. Forget it.''

''Forget it!'' he hissed. ''I'll never forget it so long as I live. I didn't tell you about the next day, when I caught up with the rest of the gang. 'Marlowe and Clay shot to death while resisting arrest.' That's how the papers put it, wasn't it?''

He let out a sob and continued. ''I saw them resisting, with their hands over their heads, begging for their lives,'' he cried as sobs racked his body.

''Please, Darling, forget it,'' I begged.

''Forget it? What did the papers say about Leonard Brown and Frank Jackson? The papers said they drown, didn't they?'' Then he spoke lower, ''Yes, that's what the papers said! They both drowned. But I saw them drown!'' his voice broke forth in a high crescendo. ''But it wasn't like the papers said.'' He broke into a fit of hysterical laughter and I was afraid that the strain had been too much for him.

''Roy! Roy! Roy, Darling, it's all over. We're together! Let's forget about it.''

''Forget it! Men who have lived in prison don't forget. I'll never forget it! I'll get even. Somebody's going to pay. They'll pay!''

''No, Roy, we've got to mark it off. There's you and me and Carolyn . . . that's all that matters now.''

''Aren't you the Pollyanna?'' he sneered. His tone was filled with contempt, almost as if he hated me. ''There's only two kinds of people in the world, guards and prisoners. If you don't fight, you're ground down until you live on your belly like a snake. None of that for me. From now on I'm looking after Number One, and I'll beat the life out of anyone who stands in my way."

This man I loved was suddenly a stranger to me. I shrank from him. He was eaten by hatred for the whole world and everybody in it. He seemed disinterested in the future . . . the future happiness that I had wanted for us.

I shuddered, and he must have sensed the stark fear I felt at what he had said.

Abruptly he softened. "Sorry, Baby," he whispered. "I'm sort of shaken. Those five years were hell, without you."

His arms reached for me and I went into them. But his love-making was rough, savage. I felt as if he were finding some kind of release through me, as if he were still hating instead of loving.

I remember thinking, "This isn't Roy. Not the man I loved. Not the man who was taken from my arms five years ago. What has prison done to him?"

From far across the desert came the melancholy wail of a train whistle. That was the train we were waiting for, the next step in our flight. But now I wondered where we were fleeing to, what we were fleeing from. The train whistled again, closer this time, and I fought down the doubt and fear that had began to swell within me.

"That's our train, Roy," I said gently. He looked up, startled, then climbed to his feet. He staggered as he tried to put his weight on his injured foot, and I sprang up to help him. With his arm over my shoulder he hobbled up and down with clenched teeth, forcing the injured foot to bear his weight. After a few turns he thrust me aside and walked alone, flexing his muscles for the ordeal that lay ahead.

Five minutes passed and then we saw the train's headlight, its ghostly white finger probing the tracks in front of it. Roy pulled me down behind the water tank as the engine whistled four times to signal that it was slowing for the Van Horn junction.

"We don't board the train until after it has stopped and

started up again,'' he said. ''That way the crew is all inside the train and won't see us.''

''Now!'' Roy shouted. We both jumped up and ran along beside the moving train. As a coupling came abreast Roy grabbed the air hoses and swung himself up between two cars. Planting his feet firmly and leaning back against the heaving, accordion-pleated material that coupled the two coaches, he grabbed me and lifted me up so that my feet cleared the ground but dangled just above the flashing, grinding wheels.

''Grab those bars and pull yourself up.''

With my last strength I pulled. I don't believe I could have made it without the stimulation given by those menacing wheels. Slowly I hoisted myself up until I could plant a foot on the narrow ledge extending from each car.

''Hold tight,'' Roy gasped. ''Stay with your feet spread, one on each car, and don't move. There's only room for our feet. One mistep and you're off into space.''

The train gathered speed. My feet grew numb and the cinders cut my face. As we approached Guadalupe Pass the night wind became bitter cold and lashed at us, buffeting us back and forth.

We roared through the pass and began the long, winding decent to El Paso. The train gathered fearful speed, and the cars shook and lurched beneath us, threatening at any moment to hurl us under the wheels. It was like being on the end in a nightmarish game of snap-the-whip.

Hours — and centuries — later I felt the speed of the train slackening. Roy started shouting instructions into my ear.

''Get as close to the edge as possible,'' he instructed. ''Then jump out as far as you can. Keep your legs in a running motion. Remember, you have to jump while the train is still going. If you don't pump your legs and lean back when you land, the ground will come up and smack you.''

I was frightened beyond words. I clung desperately to those lurching cars.

''Let me edge myself in front of you,'' Roy said. ''When the train slows a little more, I'll jump. You follow.''

He peeked around the edge of the car toward the front,

then jerked quickly back. "Flashlights up ahead on the siding! That means yard dicks! They're looking for us. Gotta jump, now! Remember, keep your legs running and lean back."

He threw himself from between the cars and out into the night. I leaned out to watch him, and in the little slices of light thrown by the car windows I could see him running.

It was my turn. I felt as if I couldn't move. But I had to. Cops were up front. Closing my eyes, I threw myself forward with all the strength I had. I tried to pump my legs into a running motion as I flew through the air, but something pulled my body forward faster than my legs could move. The ground came shooting up to meet me. My last sensation was rolling over, head first, down the embankment.

Now It's Murder!

I was crying when I came to, and Roy was bending over me and stroking my head. He wiped a few spatterings of blood from my face and arms.

''I carried you across the highway from the tracks,'' he said. ''We can't go any closer to town now. There's a tourist camp down the road a bit. We'll tell them we had an accident with our car and want to stay there till morning.''

We made our way to the tourist cabins. The attendant growled at being awakened before daylight, but Roy's story seemed to soften him. The last thing I remember was sinking into bed between wonderfully white sheets.

When I opened my eyes again it was daylight. Roy was sitting on the bed with his foot in a pan of hot water. On the rickety table there was bread, bologna, milk and cookies. I fell upon them with a ravenous appetite.

After I had eaten I examined Roy's foot. ''That's blood poisoning! Look at those streaks, I'll get a doctor.''

''That's what you think. Take a look at this!''

Roy tossed me a paper he had bought while I was asleep.

His picture was on the front page. The guard who had been stabbed was now dead, the paper read. Roy was the only one of the original seven fugitives who was alive.

"It's a murder rap if they get me now," he said grimly. "I didn't kill the guard, Len Brown did, but they'll hang it on me."

In spite of Roy's protests, I knew something had to be done about his foot. I walked over to the little general store run by the attendant of the cabins. He had a dusty box of Epson salts on the back shelf and a roll of bandages, too, though they had been around so long that they hardly looked sterile. I bought this meager equipment and returned to the cabin to heat some water on a small gas plate that stood in a corner.

All night I kept salt water as hot as he could stand it on his foot. Some black-looking clots finally began appearing where the skin was broken on top of his foot. Later some thick, discolored pus came out. The red streaks climbed no higher. For this I was thankful.

By daylight I had hope that we had won the battle, though the foot would be terribly painful for a long time yet. I fell upon the bed and immediately drifted off into blessed sleep. Hours later it was dark again, and I felt myself being roughly shaken. Opening my eyes, I dimly saw Roy's face close to mine, his fingers pressed to his lips in a warning gesture. He took my hand and led me silently from the cabin into a waiting car, whose motor was left running.

Roy again motioned me not to speak as we pulled away from the tourist court.

"But Roy!" I cried as soon as we were on the highway, "Where did you get it?"

"Isn't she a beaut," Roy teased. "You don't think a guy could stay in prison five years and not be a good poker player, do you? I knew we'd need a little money when we hit the outside."

"Stop teasing," I begged. "This is no time for such foolishness. I know you didn't have that much money. Now where did you get this car?"

"Well, I could have rented it, couldn't I?"

"You could have, but you didn't. If this car is stolen we're getting out of it right this minute. I didn't come with you for this sort of thing. We're staying on the legit!"

"But Darling, he cut in, "You forget circumstances alter all cases. You saw my picture. What chance do you think we'd have getting out of this town on the legit? Every exit will be watched. Do you want me to burn?"

It's hard to fight when you know you face the stark truth. I swallowed hard when I thought of what the courts had done before, giving Roy the maximum for a first offense. Many hardened criminals have received shorter sentences for greater crimes. Roy belonged to no syndicate, and we had no money to hire a lawyer. I blinked back the tears.

"Don't take it so hard, Mary, he softened. "I promise it won't happen again. There's no other way out. Seven cons and a guard died for my freedom! Remember? You're fleeing with the most wanted man in the Southwest. You can't play the game according to your Sunday School book."

"But it's the worst thing we could do." I fought back desperately. "Besides all that, they'll catch us before we can get out of town. They're probably looking for this license number right now."

"Give me credit for a little more judgment than that, baby. I borrowed this sweet little buggy from a couple who had just climbed out and entered a theater. I watched them buy tickets, to make sure. It's not likely they'll be out of the show before two hours have passed."

"But even at that," I continued in desperation, "As soon as they do come out and turn it in we're goners. You know we can't get across the border in a stolen car, and there's just one good highway from here to California. We won't have a dog's chance. As soon as this license number is turned in to the cops, we're done for."

"Maybe not quite that soon. The license plates have been changed. I picked up a pair off a wrecked car in the junk yard. We ought to be able to get out of here, anyway. Now you just sit up right straight and proud, like we owned this shiny little toy. Now slip over here close and put your arm around me while we head out the Las Cruces highway. No one ever looks twice at turtle doves.''

My heart turned to lead, but I did as he said. Nothing exciting happened before we got to Las Cruces, but Roy skirted town carefully and hit highway 80 again at the outskirts and we headed west toward Deming and Lordsburg, New Mexico, and Tucson, Arizona.

We traveled for three hours, stopping once at a lonely station for gas and oil. We drove several extra miles feeling our way around Deming and Lordsburg. We had to stick with the one highway. I became more nervous by the minute. Surely they were looking for the car by now. I urged we abandon it, but there was no way through here but by car, or rail. I'd had enough of freights and blinds to last me for a lifetime. Roy said the quicker we could get through this ''one way chute'' the better. It was the first time he had driven a car or even ridden in one in five years, and this was so pleasant in comparison with the other modes of locomotion we had tried. We stuck with the car a little too long.

A few miles from Tucson, we turned one of the infrequent curves along this route and spotted a highway patrol car parked just on the other side of one of those too frequent drainage dips along the lower route to California. It was too late to turn around when our lights hit the car. There were five men in it.

''Guess this is it,'' Roy remarked in what seemed a casual tone in comparison to my jumping heart. ''May fool them with the changed license plates, but they may be wise by now. Nothing to do but pass them. Hang tight. If they follow we'll give them a run for the money.''

We had hardly passed the car when it eased out onto the highway behind us, lights off. Roy speeded up gradually and got a little start. When they realized Roy had speeded up, they too, stepped on the gas, lights on.

When they turned on that siren I nearly jumped out of the car. Roy told me to get on the floor board.

''They might start shooting,'' he cautioned.

A few seconds more and I felt the brakes screech and the car veer wildly. I was slung against the door as we turned off the highway. Roy had found a side road and was tearing down it at break-neck speed, lights off.

The cops realized we had turned, however, and were still in hot pursuit, lights on.

"They're gaining," Roy reported. "Get ready to quit the car when you feel me hit the next corner."

A shot rang out. A second and then a third. The car began careening wildly. I'm not sure how Roy managed to keep it upright. Before I realized we had stopped, Roy pushed me from the car and catapulted me across a fence into a clump of bushes. Grabbing my hand he started dragging me out of range, in case there was more gunfire.

By this time the police car had slid to a stop back of ours. We looked back. Nothing except a cloud of dust was visible. As we looked back we ran head-on into an irrigation ditch and plunged into waist-deep water.

"Come out! Come out or we'll shoot!" came the menacing command from the police car.

I was ready to come out but a restraining hand held me back.

Surrounded

"Come out of that car with your hands up!" was the next command of our pursuers.

"They think we're still in the car," Roy whispered. The dust fooled them. They're afraid we're armed. Follow me, but stay bent over so they can't skylight you."

With that we crawled out of the ditch and headed down a row of tall, irrigated cotton, crouched over.

"They're not in here," we heard one of the officers yell as we covered another hundred feet. "Get the spotlight to work!"

"Flatten out," Roy commanded, "and lie still."

"Let's go after them," one patrolman suggested.

"They're probably armed," cautioned another. "We'd make good clay pigeons."

"Call into Tucson for more cars," the first voice was commanding. "Two of you go on up the road to the other end of the field. No, wait. Let's make it hot for them!"

A shot rang out, then a fusillade. Bullets started raining in the field. They zinged over our heads and spatted into the ground in front of us and behind us. Rifle shots whistled over and into the far corners of the field. I was as flat as a sheet of paper.

''O.K.,'' a voice finally broke in. ''That's enough. You two go on up to the other end of the field. Bob and I'll stay here. Redding, you stay here with the radio.''

As the car started, we did. I learned what Roy meant when he said his pace down a cotton row made a jackrabbit sit down and cry. He dragged me along in that crouched position until my legs ached and my lungs burned and I grew dizzy and sick at my stomach. Just when I thought I could go no further, Roy stopped short. Both of us dropped to the ground and lay there gasping like animals brought to bay by hunters.

''We're cornered,'' I whispered hoarsely. They've surrounded the field. They'll find us at daylight.''

''We won't be here at daylight,'' Roy said. ''We've been running parallel with the road, about a hundred and fifty yards to the side. I figure we're out of hearing and seeing distance in the dark, so we can start cutting across. Try not to hit the stalks too hard. Stand up and run, now!'' he gasped.

Run we did. Fortunately for us, there was a road on only two sides of the field. We were out of the field, had slowed to a fast walk, had crossed the second field and were ready to cross the third when we saw several headlights coming at a distance.

''They're getting help,'' I said with dismay.

''All we can do is put as much distance as possible between us and the road,'' Roy said between gasps for breath, ''and pray for daylight not to come. They'll surround the whole area.''

We were running again. My heart seemed about to burst each time before we stopped for breath. My lungs were on fire.

''I can't go another step,'' I gasped.

''They'll have bloodhounds here within an hour,'' Roy said, ''so let's keep moving.''

''Bloodhounds!'' I needed no more urging. We walked quietly, careful not to shake any cotton plants and reveal our position, for we knew cops could be anywhere by now.

Suddenly Roy pulled me down beside him, ''Someone's coming.''

We lay crouched for what seemed hours, holding our

breath, fearing that any minute a cop would stumble upon us. Finally Roy whispered, "Edge over toward that irrigation ditch at the end of the field. We'll have to get across that highway before daylight and that isn't too far off. We'll have to follow the irrigation ditch until it does cross the highway. They do ever so often, I notice. We'll crawl through the culvert it flows through to the other side of the highway, otherwise they'll skylight us."

We slithered into the ditch and inched down it. Finally we found a place where a ditch flowing from the other side of the highway joined the one we were following at a right angle. One of the patrol cars was approaching. I wanted to stop but Roy kept leading me on, close enough for that flashing search light to hit us, I thought. Then he motioned me to get low in the water as the car moved slowly across the culvert.

We edged into the main ditch and were almost swimming, as we headed straight for the culvert. As we started under it we could see the next patrol car coming.

"We'd best wait under the culvert until it passes," Roy advised. "Might pick us up with the spotlight on the other side."

But the car didn't pass over the culvert. It just rolled up and stopped. Roy put a finger to my lips as we edged back toward the center of our rounded bridge, where it was completely dark.

"I told them last night this radiator needed checking," one of the cops spoke up. "They can issue me a new cap for this."

We heard him walking toward the edge of the culvert and remained breathless, with just our noses above the water. We saw him dip his cap into the water and heard him return to the car.

"It won't be long now," one of the men in the car remarked. "A rat couldn't crawl through this blockade. At daylight we'll twist them out."

The cop with the cap growled as he returned to the ditch a second and third time. We could have touched him with a long fishing pole.

Apparently satisfied, we heard him slam down the hood and close the car door. As he shifted gears we started wading.

The car still seemed fairly close when we emerged on the other side. Scurrying out of the ditch we lost no time in getting out of range before the next patrol car arrived. A few hundred yards away from the road we left the ditch and started climbing a little, bald mountain.

On reaching the top we sat down to rest and watched what looked like about a two-mile area surrounded by slowly moving lights. Intermittently a spot of light shot here and there over the fields. We were out of the surrounded territory, but not far enough away for comfort. We had to make tracks.

Daylight was beginning to streak the sky as we lost sight of the lights. A few houses appeared here and there. A train whistled in the distance.

"That may be our way out," Roy said. "If we could just hop that train while they think they have us surrounded in that cotton patch . . . if we could just make it."

We quickened our pace and headed straight for town. We knew that Tucson was a big town and we also knew we were still several miles away.

"We're going to have to take a chance one way or another," I put in. "Why don't we just try to get to a telephone and call a taxi?"

Roy thought it a good idea.

Before long we came to a dairy on the outskirts of town. The lights were on and men were working away inside. Being less afraid of a cow than we were of the highway, Roy decided to walk up to one of the fellows loading his milk truck and ask if there was a telephone he could use.

"Say, fellow," Roy asked, "is there a telephone here we could use to call a cab. Had a little car trouble and it's a long walk into town."

"Especially with a sore foot," the milkman remarked, noticing Roy's now shredded bandage. "Looks like you've had too much already."

"If you don't mind riding in a milk truck," he continued, "this is my last case and my route is on the other side of town."

We were crawling in. It was my first milk truck ride. The milkman seemed in a talkative mood.

"Now if you'd been on Highway 80 you wouldn't need a ride into town," he teased. "They got some escaped convicts from Texas rounded up out there in some of those cotton patches. I saw the bloodhounds they brought in from the state prison on my way to work, about forty minutes ago. Brother, I'd hate for those rascals to get after me.''

I was glad it wasn't too light yet because I'm sure I turned whiter than his milk, but it didn't seem to bother Roy.

''They must be tough hombres,'' Roy put in. ''Maybe if you'd wait around awhile we'd get to see what a real desperado looks like. I hear they grow 'em tough in Texas.''

''It doesn't matter how tough they are, those bloodhounds will flush them like quail. Those cops will use them for target practice.''

I couldn't stand any more. ''You can let us out anywhere downtown,'' I said in an effort to change the subject. ''We can take a cab.''

''Well, I go across the tracks, holler when.''

I was afraid Roy was going to hunt himself another laugh, but the words about crossing the tracks struck home.

''Since we live in that direction, we'll ride a little further,'' Roy said simply, much to my relief.

We were within sight of the tracks when Roy asked him to let us out. I had nothing to say, although I certainly wished for another means of locomotion. There was no train waiting, that we could see, so we headed up the tracks, west, we thought. As we cut through someone's yard, Roy jerked some jeans and a blue denim shirt from a clothes line.

''First cover we find, you slip these on over your dress. A woman is too easy to spot in a freight yard. You need a hat.''

It seemed good daylight to me now, but I huddled behind the next hedge, at Roy's suggestion, and drew on the pants. I had to hold them up around the waist, so he gave me his belt. Down the line we saw many tracks and many cars.

''Looks like a freight is being made up,'' Roy remarked. ''I could wish for something faster, but when they find out we've made it to town, they'll turn this place inside out and everything leading from it. They'll probably expect us to try to pick up another auto. They don't know our de luxe mode of traveling,'' he grinned. ''The sooner we're out, the better.''

''That's the caboose,'' Roy continued. ''It must be almost

made up. We'll go down the track a way so we can catch it when it pulls out. We'll have to catch it on the fly. Can't mount it with everyone looking.''

''Catch it on the fly?'' I sheepishly asked, remembering my recent train experiences.

''Yes, the train will be between us and the men working in the yard. Now listen while I tell you how. See those box cars near the front of the train. As it passes we will catch one of those. There are iron rungs, ladders to you, on the outside of each car, one at the front and one at the back. If you catch the one on the front of the car, the most it can do is slap you against the side of the car. If it jerks you loose, you at least fall clear of the wheels.

You will have to catch on first. The lowest rungs are a little over waist high from the ground and I may need to help you get your feet up to them. Whatever you do, swing onto those bars with both hands for all you're worth.''

Sounded like a simple way to commit suicide, but it had come to a point where it didn't matter much.

''It's headin' this way,'' he said with real cheer in his voice. ''Now just remember what I have told you. Be running as fast as the train when you grab those bars and it won't slap you back against the side of the car.''

We stayed off the siding until the engine passed us. Then Roy started heading for the tracks. I was a step behind him.

''The first two cars are oilers,'' he yelled. ''It's that first boxcar we want. Do exactly as I told you. Been lots of hobos never grown old who flunked this lesson.''

It was rushing toward us, Roy grabbed my hand and we started running along the roughly graveled siding.

''Here it comes,'' he yelled. See those iron bars. If you miss 'em, grab the ones at the front of the next car. Don't try for those at the back.'' He was beside me and yelled, ''Grab!''

I grabbed, almost as high as my head. My feet swung wildly, hitting back against the side of the car, but not hard enough to hurt me in my state of excitement.

''I've got your feet,'' Roy yelled, ''Grab a rung higher with one hand.''

This I did and then moved the other hand up as I felt my foot placed on something solid, more or less.

Roy, who was running alongside yelled, "If you don't mind would you step up a rung off my hand so I can get my feet up, too."

This brought me to my senses and I climbed on up the iron ladder as the train picked up speed. When we got to the top he instructed me to keep hold of the iron rungs until we got to the cat-walk running down the top of the car lengthwise.

Cat-walk! It didn't look to me like a mouse could walk down that board with comfort with the train in motion.

"Just crawl up there and sit down," he coached. "I know you can be seen, but don't worry about it. Just look at the 'Soldiers of the Depression' sitting on top of those cars near the back."

It was a very long train. I could see the "Soldiers of Fortune," or should we correct that statement to keep in tone with the time and say "Soldiers of Misfortune," victims of circumstance, sitting in twos and threes on top of the cars all the way back. Fortunately the nearest ones were three cars back of us.

"You didn't see this," my acrobatic husband yelled above the roar of the train as he produced a crumpled felt hat from his pocket. "I scooped it up off the siding as you watched the rungs. Better get those curly locks tucked under it before somebody decides to try to take my gal away from me. I'm not looking for a fight. I've had it."

The hat looked surprisingly clean. It was rather tight for my full head of hair, but that just helped hold it on. Our clothes were perfectly dry now. I held my breath while we rode with that milkman for fear he would notice we were a little damp, but darkness is a most welcome companion during moments of embarrassment.

"A person would never know your hair is red, in the dark," Roy continued, "Because it is always black in shadow, even in daylight, but sunlight sets it afire. I don't need anyone to help put out the flame," he teased.

Things went smoothly for awhile. I was even beginning to think the desert lovely, with its tall, slender Organ Pipes and its giant saguaras. Here and there prickly pears matted its white floor while in the distance blue and violet mountains made a perfect backdrop.

The sun was hardly an hour high, but it was already bearing down. We thought we were headed for the west coast when we started, but now that the sun was with us, we could tell that we were headed north, toward Phoenix. But as far as the direction was concerned, it really didn't matter much, so long as we were putting distance between us and Texas. Our problem was to keep moving. I was trying to remember when we had eaten when Roy disturbed my thoughts by stretching his neck.

"Why are we stopping out here in the middle of the desert?" he asked. "There isn't even a siding here to pull on to for a passenger to pass. Something's wrong!"

Shot Off a Freight

Alarmed, Roy stood up for a better look toward the back of the train.

"Holy smoke! Look at those hobos scram!" he exclaimed. "There's two special dicks heading up each side of the track. They're holding a gun on some 'bos now. Wonder if any of them noticed a girl on the train? Let's get moving."

Two hobos headed for the desert but stopped right quick-like when the detectives fired in their direction.

"Let's head for the tender," Roy called as he started crawling down the rungs between our boxcar and the first oiler. I followed suit and stepped across the coupling as he did and we started scooting around the fat sides of the big, black oilers. An iron rung running parallel to the sides of the tank and about wasit high helped us to hold on.

I thought Roy had lost his reason entirely when I saw him climb right up on the water tank, tender, as he called it, which was back of the engine. He opened a little round, iron door, motioned me to follow, and jumped in. The water, up to my chin, was warm, but not hot.

We had ducked the fireman as he walked back down the track while we were on the far side of one of the oil tanks. Roy peeped out the door of the tender. He described the show:

"One of the dicks is holding the hobos they have rounded up at the point of a gun while the others shake down the train. They're about ten cars back. If they climb up and look in this tender we're done for."

A steam bath with a hat on wasn't my custom, but I was living in a different world now, a warm one. We heard them coming on up the track. They were close enough now that we could hear them talking.

When they seemed even with us one of them was saying, "Looks like we've missed them, but they're here all right. A snake couldn't have crawled off this track into the desert without us seeing it. They must be in the rods under one of the cars."

"Check underneath the cars. Check the reefers of every car on the way back," one of them was directing. We'll flush 'em out. Keep your guns ready!"

We heard them start back down the train, working it systematically.

"What are we going to do?" I whispered.

"They'll find us sooner or later," Roy whispered back. "If they're fool enough to all work back toward the rear of the train at the same time, we could crawl out and make a run for the desert when they're out of good range. They can't shoot straight with those pistols. We'll put a shotgun out of range and we'll zigzag until they can't draw a bead on us with a rifle before we get to those big tree cactus. Your being a girl, they'll probably try to talk us out without shooting. If we have to run for it, don't stop."

They must have been twenty or more cars back when we heard someone walking toward the tender from the rear of the train. The steps drew nearer and we heard someone swing up to the side of the tender, climbing toward us. It sounded like just one person. Roy motioned me back with his hand.

The second the iron door opened, Roy was ready. He grabbed what must have been the train's fireman, head and shoulders, and pulled him in with us. As Roy grappled with him he hollered for me to climb out. The water was so deep that all they could do was go into a clinch. Just as I got to the top, Roy did manage to get in one good punch at the fireman and he went under, spluttering.

Roy was right behind me now. As he emerged the fireman made a lunge for his legs. Roy gave him a swift kick and he went under again. My heart was in my throat. What if he was knocked out. He could drown.

''Think you'd better see if he comes up?'' I asked.

Roy laughed. ''Quit your thinking and scramble down.''

Evidently the engineer had heard nothing of the commotion for just then he let off steam.

''Run in front of the steam,'' Roy yelled. ''It's a blind.''

''We were hardly out of the steam when the fireman hit the top of the tender hollering bloody murder. Evidently he was slightly irritated for he hit the ground and started running after us.

''By that time we were well noticed. One of the special detectives fired a few shots into the air and yelled ''Halt!.'' We kept running and so did the fireman. He was really gaining and I believe he would have caught us, especially me, if the engineer and everyone else hadn't been yelling for him to stop.

''Stop, you fool, so they can shoot!'' the engineer's voice boomed from the cab.

But before the engineer could stop him we were across the right of way and headed for the first tall saguaros. There were no fences. They're not needed for rattlesnakes.

By not thinking to flatten out, the firemen shielded us from the rear. A few rifle shots whizzed around us, and some whistled over our heads. How I zigzagged! We worked in and out like a shuttle among the tree cactus, never slowing down.

By the time the cops had reached the vicinity where we had entered the desert we were well out of range, thanks to the saguaros.

Stocky, middle-aged men with heavy guns don't last very long in a desert, even in pursuit of fugitives. I don't believe even the best of them followed us a good half-mile before they stopped for consultation.

We stopped to catch our breath, too. We were well into the deep cactus country and it was doubtful whether they could even catch a glimpse of us any longer, but we could see them well enough to know what they were doing. They went into a little huddle, scattered and then started firing at random into the desert.

"Come out!" their spokesman commanded. "Come out! We've got you covered!."

Roy put a restraining hand on my back.

"Come out while you can get out alive!" he yelled.

Roy laughed aloud. Their little barrage didn't last long. We just lay on the desert floor and called their bluff. None of the bullets came very close, although they did have some high powered rifles that sung out of hearing into the desert.

We lay still as we saw all the officers, the crew and the hobos crawl back on the train. Evidently they made all the soldiers of fortune crawl into an empty box car. There must have been over thirty of them. The detectives climbed into the caboose with the brakemen.

We wondered if they would drop some of the officers, when they got out of sight, to try to fool us.

"Will they get bloodhounds?" I asked.

"Maybe so," my husband answered, "but it might not do them a whole lot of good. The dogs won't like this desert any more than the cops did. The trail will be hours old before they can get dogs out to this godforsaken place. With the sun like this, a scent won't last too long. Being too hot and dry makes it as hard for dogs to trail as being too wet.

"Step on rocks whenever you can and don't let your clothes brush against anything green," Roy admonished as we again headed into the desert. "Green stuff holds the scent longer."

The glue holding the straps to the soles of my sandals had given away and they slapped with each step. Roy's injured foot was bare, but it looked much better. Most of the discoloration had vanished. Only the little toe, which was evidently broken, remained puffed. We had only been on the desert a few minutes, but our well-soaked clothes seemed almost dry.

We had to stop for repairs before we could go farther. Roy

tore strips from one trouser leg and tied the sandals to my feet. He then tore the other trouser leg off at the knee and wrapped and tied the cloth around his injured foot, more as insulation against the hot sand and rock than for any other purpose. I was thankful for the tight hat, which was still with me. My husband remained bareheaded.

Undaunted, my fugitive companion extracted his damp, but well made prison billfold from his pocket and remarked, "Where do we eat?"

I was in no mood for jokes. I tried to remember when I had last seen my purse, but it didn't matter much. I had given the lone ten spot left in it to Roy. The make-up I didn't need, to mix with sand, although I could have used a comb.

"Well, navigator," Roy broke the silence, "Have you any idea where we are?"

Having passed through this part of the country before, I expounded, "I think that mountain in the distance, in front of us and slightly to the right, is Superstition Mountain. It's about thirty miles east of Phoenix. If we keep heading for that mountain we are bound to come to that highway."

"Highways are what we don't want," Roy teased, "but I'm glad to know we are about to strike it rich. Isn't Superstition Mountain where the Lost Dutchman's mine is?"

His banter didn't help much so he continued, "We know that the railroad track we just left parallels the highway running into Phoenix, and it is to our left, while Superstition is in front of us. As long as we head for that mountain we're not lost. They'll guard every inch of the highway and railroad we just left. If there's any civilization on that highway coming down from those mountains, maybe we can get close enough to borrow a drink from a windmill."

I remembered a memorial at the base of Superstition Mountain and a tourist camp. I thought I could find them.

We walked . . . and walked . . .

The sun climbed the heavens like a ball of fire. Everything fled from the heat until there was no sign of life except a few lizards and here and there a rattlesnake curled in the shade of a cactus. Perspiration ran down our arms and dripped from the ends of our fingers. I trudged ahead without thinking, conscious only of the pain that racked my body. Around mid-afternoon we fell into a thin slice of shade made by a tall saguaro.

As soon as we could catch our breath Roy took his knife and cut a branch from the saguaro. It was porous on the inside, but the woody, chewy pulp was not damp enough to cool our parched lips.

Then Roy cut some kind of cactus that we had always heard harbored water. We found none. He pulled up some yucca and peeled the spoonlike roots. They were beautiful, a golden color and smooth like satin, but we gnawed on them in vain.

Thirst drove us on. We staggered to our feet again and headed for Superstition Mountain. Hour after hour we pushed forward, losing all track of time, but the mountain never seemed to come any closer.

We heard no sound of pursuit. Many beautiful lakes appeared in the distance, but we knew they were mirages. The desert seemed nothing but tortured space. Earlier I had been thankful for the hat and borrowed trousers I wore over my dress, but now I was too numb to feel anything but thirst.

I felt as if I were drying up, like a mummy crumbling to dust. There was no moisture at all in my mouth, none in my eyes. No perspiration came now. I burned all over. Visions of my five-year-old daughter kept coming to me, and in the visions she was crying and begging me to come home to her. I reached for her outstretched fingers but could not touch them.

I don't know when I blacked out, but when I came to again it was night and freezing cold. I shivered uncontrollably and even wished for the agonizing sun. Roy lay beside me, his gaunt face lit by the desert moon. He looked gentle in sleep and I thought I saw in him some of the tenderness I had known five years before. Lonely, I touched my parched lips to his, and he stirred, murmuring something.

"Darling . . . darling," . . . I whispered.

"Water," he moaned, then sat up. He looked about dully for a moment, then climbed to his feet.

"Come on, Mary. We gotta cover ground before the sun comes up."

I thought I couldn't move, but I did. I stood up and staggered after him through the desert, under one of the most beautiful, star-dusted skies that God ever made.

We walked the rest of the night, and Superstition remained in the distance. The first streaks of dawn filled me with horror of the mounting sun. Soon there was no shade, no escape.

We plodded another hour, maybe two. There was nothing left. All strength seemed drained and my legs no longer held me up. I had gone as far as I could. My numbed mind was beyond hope, or fear or love.

The Desert Deals a Deathly Hand

I don't know how long I lay blacked out, but the sun was still fierce when I came to a numbed consciousness which was most unwelcome in my tortured state. I closed my eyes and tried to black out again, but remained conscious. Roy lay prone at my side. Why should I disturb him? Perhaps he would never awaken.

Carolyn was with me every conscious moment now. She kept begging and begging me to come home. What had I done to my own little girl? Would she grow up thinking her mother never loved her? Could we just disappear from the face of the earth? Would she and her grandmother ever know how we tried, how we died?

I wished I could just write a note telling how much her mother loved her, how I died with visions of my beautiful little daughter beckoning to me, but there was nothing to write with. A mute prayer stuck in my heart, begging God not to let my baby hate her own mother for deserting her. This must be about her birthday, I wasn't sure. Days or hours no longer mattered. I only wished to die, and that quickly.

Roy groaned. The sun beat mercilessly on his upturned face. He had no hat. He hardly looked like a human being, and I was sure I didn't. I had worn the hat all along. At least I could pull him to me and we could both die with our faces in the shade, if I placed the hat across them.

I reached out to try to drag him to me. I lay under the thin, jointed fingers of some sort of cactus that afforded no real shade at all, but it seemed better to lie beneath something. Roy's eyes opened and he pulled himself to a sitting position when he felt my tugging. He scooted as far underneath the cactus as possible and leaned back into it's thorny arms, seemingly feeling no pain. I was sorry I had wakened him. I crawled to his side and he propped the hat to shade my face. Neither of us spoke.

After what seemed a long while, Roy began speaking, or rather rasping out words between parched lips.

"I'm sorry I got you into this, Sweetheart. Let's don't let nine people die for no freedom. That doesn't come out even, eight tried and nine died. You don't figure in on this deal, Darling. It's not right for you to die. The score's perfect without it."

I tried to follow him but numbers didn't make sense to me any more. There was just one word that had meaning to me and I was trying so hard to shut water from my mind.

"I did a lot of reading," I heard Roy saying, but he seemed very distant. "I did a lot of reading during the five years I was in prison. There was a tribe of Aboriginals in Australia who raised sheep and lived off nothing but blood and milk. They would bleed their sheep."

I thought his mind was wandering and tried to pay no attention to his gruesome story until I saw him bring his knife from his pocket.

"I'm going to slash my wrist," he said. "When I do you drink the blood. It will give you strength to get to help. Maybe you can get back to me. I don't have much to look forward to, anyway."

The very suggestion hurtled me to my feet in horror and I almost ran toward the mountain. He followed.

After a great length of silence he raised his arm and

pointed to a low line of trees. "There's our chance," he rasped in a half prayer.

We headed for the trees. They seemed nearer. Twice I fell to my knees, but Roy dragged me up again. We were near enough that we could tell they were desert Joshua trees, but even Joshuas require some water. I envisioned a cool pool under the tallest one, which we were heading for.

Our struggle brought us to the brink of a dry gully, cursed with some scattered rocks. Completely defeated I sank in the shade of the tree.

A sharp rattle attracted my attention. At the base of the tree lay the largest rattler I have ever seen, unwilling to even share the shade. It raised its ugly, diamond head above its singing rattles.

I almost laughed at the irony of what we had found. This wouldn't take long, and it would be easier, I thought as I saw it tense to strike.

It sprung, but its forward lunge was intercepted by the impact of a heavy rock. Another rock thudded into the midst of that writhing mass before I realized what had happened.

I was wondering whether my life was worth thanking Roy for saving when I took note of his actions. Before the snake was fully still, he was cutting its head off with that knife and skinning its thick body.

"Steak, rattlesnake steak," he remarked as he sunk his swollen mouth into the white flesh, shoving me a hunk.

I watched a moment, horrified, but nature took its course and I, too, began gnawing like a cannibal. After we had gorged we both fell asleep.

When we awoke, or at least when consciousness returned, nature seemed trying to compensate with one of those lavish desert sunsets. I was wondering if it could possibly be the same day, the day that had dragged into an eternity?

At first I thought I had been dreaming, because nothing seemed real, not until thirst came as a grim reminder. I wanted to believe it was a dream, all a dream, especially what we had just eaten, but it was a big snake and I saw no flesh remaining. I remember closing my eyes and telling myself that I was eating raw shrimp. The very thought of the cannibalistic instincts we had just exhibited made me shudder.

Mental bars had not effected the meat's nutritional value, however, and we both felt stronger. I was even beginning to feel a little hopeful.

"Superstition looks a lot closer," I remarked as I gazed at its splendid dark blues and violet. "And look," I cried as I pointed at a ten o'clock angle, "That must be Camel Back Mountain on the other side of Phoenix."

"We'll get to water tonight," Roy encouraged. "Why, we could walk from Tucson to Phoenix in two days and a night."

We kept a good pace in the cool of the desert night, but things look much clearer than they really are when viewed over a vast expanse of sand. We had walked well into the night when we sat down for a brief rest. We said little because any movement of our parched lips or swollen throats brought sudden added pain. Although both of us were in our early twenties, lack of food and water and nervous exhaustion had taken their toll, leaving us feeling about as young and talkative as the Sphinx. The light of the moon added to the white of the sand was soft and quite beautiful after the dazzling light of day. Roy had no bandage on his foot now but said the cool sand felt good to it.

We walked all night with hardly a word passing between us. Even words took energy which we did not have, so we plodded on. Superstition Mountain seemed only a stone's throw away. Camel Back was outlined in the distance. We dared not rest because of the coming of the dawn.

With the first bright streaks came those agonizing fears of the sun. Strength seemed to leave my body as if extracted by the sun's rays. I couldn't stand a repetition of the last two days. The first rays touching my dehydrated frame seemed to make me a flaming ball of desire . . . WATER. WATER. WATER. There was no other word or thought in the world except WATER!.

"Come on," Roy coaxed as he sensed my feelings. "Water can't be far now, if the highway is between us and Superstition. We've got to travel before it gets too hot."

He took my hand and pulled me along. We plodded another hour, maybe two, before I stumbled. Although quite young, the sun was showing its desert strength. I felt as if it were clubbing me to the ground with its rays. I buried my head in my arms as I sank to my knees on the sand.

Roy remained standing. Looking! Looking! Looking!

Safe with the Strangest Sort of Jesus

Roy's voice seemed to come to me from a great distance, as if through a long, black tunnel. He was saying something over and over again, but I couldn't understand what it was. Suddenly the earth seemed to drop from under me. I cried out. It was only Roy pulling me to my feet. He held me with one arm and pointed with the other.

"Look!" he cried. "Smoke! Smoke from a campfire."

I looked where he pointed. It was true. A thin spiral of blue smoke was climbing the cloudless sky.

"Someone built that fire, and they have water," Roy commented.

We rushed forward, stumbling, falling, climbing to our feet again, mumbling to ourselves all the while. We were afraid to guess at the distance of that smoke. We must have walked an hour when our hopes started fading with the vanishing smoke. The last wisp vanished as we climbed a little rise, but at the spot where we had seen the smoke rose a tall cottonwood tree.

"Bound to be water," was the almost unrecognizable voice

that forced its ray of hope through Roy's sandpapered esophagus.

As we pushed our way forward we saw lower trees. Willows, I fancied, willows by a river bank. I felt sure I could hear flowing water as we half ran and half crawled the last lap.

Babbling like lunatics we lunged toward the bank of a river. God was merciful.

We plunged our faces into the sparkling, clear water. We sucked up great mouthfuls and tried gulping it down, but our throats were too swollen. Swallowing was difficult. When we were able to slow down we held mouthfuls of the precious water and let it trickle down our sandpapered throats.

When we had drunk until we could drink no more we crawled into the river and sat down, waist deep, to absorb what we could through the pores of our dehydrated skin. The river flowed gently over a bottom of whitest sand. A million diamonds, I thought, as we splashed in laughing luxury.

Suddenly we became aware of the fact that we were being watched from the bank. My eyes followed Roy's and rested on a white-headed, brown-skinned old man.

''Madre de dios,'' he commented as he approached, making the sign of the cross over his chest as he smiled broadly. ''No es goot, no es goot?'' he spoke in a jumble of English and Spanish. I wasn't sure I understood him, but thanked God that he wore a smile instead of a gun.

''Cafe y frijoles,'' he said in Spanish as he pointed over to a dead campfire and some pots in the shade of the huge cottonwood tree.

''Coffee and beans,'' I yelled as I climbed out of the water. I think I beat him back to the campsite and filled a tin plate with beans as he poured coffee into tin cups. I was sharing my beans with Roy. We both ate from the same pewter spoon. The old Mexican scurried over to a dug-out in the side of the bank and returned with another tin plate and pewter spoon, grinning broadly all the while.

Never was food better. The coffee was cold and the only seasoning in the beans was salt and chili peppers, but it was heavenly. The peppers burned our raw throats, but we didn't care.

I thought I could have eaten a barrel of beans, but when I was half finished with that first generous helping there seemed to be no more space. I was so sleepy. The last I remembered was the old Mexican man pointing to himself and repeating, "Jesus, me Jesus."

"He's Jesus," I interpreted, and I halfway believed he was, as I fell asleep.

I awakened with strange bleating sounds in my ears. As my eyes popped open I saw Roy and Jesus, with the white flowing beard, on the other side of the stream skinning a sheep. Roy and Jesus . . . what a strange combination. A sheep herder and an escaped convict . . . Jesus and the criminal! But Jesus liked us and seemed happy with our companionship. Could it be that lonely here?

"We're going to have mutton," Roy called to me as I sat up. "Jesus has killed the fatted calf."

It sounded strange to hear Roy talk that way. I didn't mind his muffing the story of the prodigal so long as the fatted calf was a reality.

Jesus smiled broadly when I told him my name was Maria, the Spanish for Mary. He seemed to like me all the more because I could halfway speak his own language and was named Maria.

Jesus and Roy could not understand each other and most of their conversation was carried on by a series of motions. Perhaps it was better that way. There couldn't be but one story.

Trying to think of a logical way to explain our presence I thought of the lost mines of Superstition. I could think of the Spanish word 'montaña,' for mountain, but could not remember the Spanish word for lost.

"En la montaña," (in the mountain) I explained as I pointed and made a circle with my hand, shaking my head in a negative, puzzled manner.

"La montaña," Jesus repeated, "la montaña es del diablo. Hay muchos hombres que se ma tan por el oro."

"The mountain is possessed of the devil," I interpreted. "Many men are killed for gold."

"Es verdad," (it is true) I agreed in one of the few Spanish expressions I remembered.

"Los muertos no hablan," (the dead don't talk) he said with a plaintive smile.

I was quick to agree with him, thinking how nearly we had come to fitting his expression. Many stories I had heard of people who never returned from the mountain. I thought of the lives lost in the search for the Lost Dutchman's Mine. I felt the old Mexican could have told more, could we have understood each other better. I wondered if he had saved others?

We slept outside the crude dug-out on sheep skins and covered with the tattered blanket offered us. In the morning we discovered that Jesus' food supply was very menial, consisting of corn meal, with only a few weevils, a poor grade of coarsly ground coffee, salt and chili peppers, garlic cloves and one No. 2 can of tomatoes.

Having only two plates and cups, Roy used the tomato can to drink from, after we had tasted its rare delicacy. Jesus ate from the frying pan.

To earn our keep I cleaned Jesus' simple dug-out and patched both his and our tattered clothing. I washed everything I could find and tried to make my skirt and blouse halfway presentable once more. Roy found a few fish hooks and managed to catch some beautiful golden sunfish and a few channel cats. A shave with an old straight razor made Roy look years younger. I cleaned an old comb I found in the dug-out and used it to good advantage.

There was no road to our new heaven, only a burro trail. We felt fairly safe. On the third night I ventured asking how far it was to the highway that lead into Phoenix. Jesus informed us that it was six miles.

It was good not to have to run nor hurry. Jesus never hurried. We loved our beautiful stream, which our sheepherder told us was a dry river bed used as an irrigation canal with its waters flowing from the Roosevelt dam high in the ore-laden mountains.

It was a simple life. Looking back on it now, I think that in all the months we were pursued by the law, those were the only peaceful days we knew. Food and rest brought back our strength and cleared our minds. But the future still stretched grimly ahead of us. Where to run? How to hide? Mexico seemed too far away, too difficult to reach. The prospect of a wonderful new life with my husband and daughter dimmed. But we'd make the dream come true!

Doubt of the wisdom of our flight lay within me, but I throttled it. My decision had been made long ago. What the world thought made no difference. Roy was good and noble once, and he would be again. Nothing would ever force us apart.

We had been in the desert for a week when Jesus announced that his boss man was due to arrive soon with new supplies. There was no need of our walking to the highway. We could go a half mile down the burro trail with him to meet the boss man and ride back to town with him in his truck.

That night Roy and I talked things over as we lay under the stars. The boss man coming threw a new light on the subject. He might not be as trusting as Jesus, especially since he could probably read and write and was likely capable of deductive reasoning, if he found us harbored in Jesus' heaven. The news made us restless.

The heat would be off in the search for us now, Roy reasoned. Maybe the cops would have given us up for dead. At least there would be no highway blocks after all this time. We decided to leave early in the morning. Three hours of walking should bring us to the highway before the sun got too hot.

Jesus seemed disappointed at our leaving before the boss man came. Roy offered him $10.00, all the money we had left, for his charity, but he refused it. If he could only have known this was our only worldly possession . . . maybe he understood. He filled one of his two canvas water bags for us and mumbled a blessing over us. Jesus and his flock looked so peaceful as we headed into the desert again. He waved until we were out of sight.

Back to Civilization

We had plenty of time to cook up a little story, in case we needed it, as we walked toward the highway. We decided that the most feasible one, considering our well-worn look, was that: out of curiosity and a desire for unusual snapshots we had driven to Superstition Mountain and gotten lost. Many a poor soul had been lost there and looking at its jagged, bald upheavals, it didn't take much imagination to see how hard it would be to keep from getting lost if foolish enough to enter its vast, rugged expanse without a guide. Even those who knew the mountain, or a portion of it, sometimes disappeared and searching parties were sent out from Phoenix.

We must have made a strange looking pair, standing on the edge of the highway. Roy's foot was again bandaged, this time more to hide the fact that he had but one shoe. He had tried to tack the straps back to the soles of my completely frayed sandals, but they looked and felt very crude and uncomfortable. Roy was wearing the blue jeans I had worn because he had torn the legs from his trousers for bandages for his foot from time to time.

The jeans were as much too small for Roy as they had been too large for me.

The sun was getting pretty hot as we crossed the streak of asphalt that led into the mountains to the east and Phoenix to the west. We kept the water bag, after pouring out a portion of its precious content to keep it from looking suspiciously heavy.

We saw no sign of civilization and took our stance at the edge of the highway. A car came from the wrong direction. We left the highway and crouched behind some cactus until it passed. We heard another coming from the mountains. This would probably be going into Phoenix. Again we stood at the edge of the highway.

There was a lone man in the car and he screeched to a stop a few feet ahead of us. If for no other reason, I suppose the man would have stopped out of curiosity. His questioning look demanded an explanation.

Roy presented our little story and he seemed satisfied with it. When we told him we had been lost for two days the salesman raised an eyebrow and asked if we were not quite hungry and thirsty.

I explained that we had carried a generous picnic lunch and a couple of water bags with us. Roy shook the little bit of water left in the bag to substantiate our story, explaining how we had drunk sparingly, not knowing when we would find civilization.

Our benefactor was a salesman from the East. This made us feel better. Perhaps he had seen nothing in the papers where he had been in the last few days to make him suspicious.

He insisted on stopping at the first outpost and buying cold drinks, some fresh oranges, dates and candy. We ate with great zest, much to his pleasure.

Roy made our story so interesting that before we reached Phoenix the salesman wanted to drive us back to Superstition to pick up our car.

I quickly assured him that we could get the family car. This was another mistake, for he began wondering if our folks wouldn't be worried about us.

"We live in an apartment across town from her folks," Roy came to my rescue, "and the people in the apartment house are used to our being gone over the week end. They probably haven't even missed us yet. If the folks called they would just have thought we were out fishing or hunting good snapshots. We're great shutter-bugs."

Before there was time for another mistake to be made I said, "You can just let us out at the next red light. We live just around the corner."

The salesman offered to let us out at our door but I already had the car door open and was crawling out of the car as it stopped for the light. He waved a reluctant good-bye. In fact, if he could have had things his way he would have carried us right down to the newspaper office and had a feature story done on our being lost in the mountain. I think he fancied himself an unsung hero. Little did he suspect that our appearance in a newspaper office would have changed the tune.

When we crawled out of the car we found ourselves in a small shopping center. Roy did have a little change so he bought a newspaper. He held it well in front of us as we sat on a bench at a bus stop, trying to figure our next move.

Handing me our last ten spot he instructed, "Go to the resale shop across the street and get us some shoes. I can't go with my foot wrapped in a rag. It will attract attention, besides, the foot's okay now for a soft shoe."

While he sat with the paper before his face I went across the street to buy the things we had to have. I got a pretty good pair of secondhand shoes for myself for a dollar and bought Roy a pair of soft leather house shoes. Then I went to a dime store and bought a ten-cent lipstick, a pocket comb and a small box of powder. Being a woman, I couldn't resist these, even though I had been forced to buy secondhand clothes.

I returned to Roy and we cut over another street. In the rest rooms of a service station we put on our shoes. I fixed up my face with the first make-up I'd had in ages. Funny what a little lipstick will do for a woman's morale. I felt almost lighthearted as I faced my lover once more. We emerged looking less strange, but were eyed curiously by the attendant. We headed down a side street.

''We had best get away from this side of town,'' Roy advised. ''We might have attracted a little attention.''

A city bus with ''Five Points'' printed on its placard emerged from somewhere. We had no idea where we were going, but we stayed with the bus until it had passed through town. The oranges on the trees around the court house were the most brilliant I have ever seen. They were very large. Later we learned they were only for show.

The bus left the business district and seemed to be heading out a highway. Finally we came to a spot where five roads seemed to merge and traffic was controlled by one of those many sided lights.

Probably thinking that we had ridden long enough, or that we did not know the town, the driver glanced in the mirror and called, ''Five Points.''

We crawled off the bus. The sun was sweltering hot, but there were trees. I feasted my eyes on the palm trees and the green grass. We went into a drug store and bought Cokes. We were hardly noticed.

''This is our happy home,'' Roy remarked as we emerged from the air conditioned coolness of the drug store into the blinding sun once more. ''Let's look for a room.''

As we left the shopping district built around Five Points we found a modest residential section. Everything seemed air conditioned, but we knew we could not afford such luxury. Just a room must suffice, and a very modest one at that, until I could get work.

The depression still clung tenaciously on and there were plenty of 'For Rent' signs anywhere we looked. With our last few dollars we rented a room for a week on a quiet side street. We climbed to the second floor, opened the last door in a long hall and we were home. It was a small room, barely big enough for the two pieces of furniture in it. A peeling brass bed stood against one wall, and opposite it was a scarred dresser with drawers that rested crookedly on their runners. In one corner of the room a closet had been formed by nailing curtains on a high shelf. Above the dresser was a mirror whose wavy surface threw back a warped reflection. But it was a room with walls and a ceiling to keep us from the eyes of the world. We were safe here.

"Roy," I said softly, turning to put my arms around his neck as he closed the door behind us, "We're people now."

"So far so good, Mary" he said, walking over to the window and looking out. "Except we're broke."

"It won't matter too much," I comforted. "We're safe and I can find work. I'll have to. I managed all during the worst part of the Depression and I can manage now. I'm glad I learned to be a waitress while I was going through college. A waitress can always find work. Of course I'll have to start where they furnish uniforms because . . ."

"Forget it now, Baby," he said pulling me to him, "we've got to celebrate. This is our happy home."

Sure, Darling, I said holding him close and kissing him. "Tomorrow can take care of itself."

Later, as I lay on the bed with Roy quiet beside me, I stared at the ceiling and wondered what was wrong. I had gone through hell for this, turned my back on the world just to be with my husband, but now it seemed that I was left with something strangely empty. The wonder and beauty I had once known in being with Roy was gone. His caresses had been mechanical, without any deep feeling, without love, or so it seemed to me. Surely it was my imagination. It had to be.

All that I knew was that I felt terribly alone. Suddenly my arms ached for my little girl. Roy had done very little talking about her. I knew that there had been no time for such reminiscence, but she was our child, our responsibility.

What kind of mother had I been to Carolyn, leaving her with her grandmother, while I fled with Roy? I couldn't keep back the tears when I thought of her fifth birthday, with not even a word from her mother. If I only had the money to call her by phone, or if I could only drop a birthday card, they would know I was alive. I knew Roy would never agree to my taking such a chance. To whom should I be loyal, my child or my husband? Fine time now to ask myself such a question. The choice was made, but was it the right one?

I searched for the answer, tortured by doubts. I remembered Ted Randel's offer to marry me when I was working in

Abilene on the newspaper, his offer of safety and comfort and a respectable life for my baby. Should I have said yes to him? Should my love for Carolyn have outweighed my love for Roy? I closed my eyes tightly, I had to face this problem and come up with a solution.

I would talk it over with my husband. That was the way problems should be worked out.

With a sigh of relief. I turned on my side and rested my head on Roy's shoulder. "Pretty soon now we'll all be together, you and me and Carolyn. Won't it be wonderful having a family. You never really had a chance to know what it is like," I murmured. "As soon as I get a couple of weeks wages we'll take a bus to the border. You can disguise yourself."

"Huh?" he grunted.

"After we find work in Mexico we can send for Carolyn. You'll never know her, she's a young lady now, almost ready to enter school . . . well in another year at least."

"You crazy?" Roy asked harshly. "What are you talking about?"

"Carolyn," I said. "We could get her before we cross the border, now that the heat's off. I don't mind working a little longer. We'll save every penny. Three of us could travel as cheaply as two. With Carolyn along we'd look even more like a family and avoid suspicion. I miss her, Roy, it's killing me."

"Forget it," Roy snapped. "We're not getting saddled with any kid, so get it out of your mind. Just because they're not shooting at us, don't think they've forgotten. Take a look at the post office bulletin board tomorrow when you go to town. They don't put those pictures up and post rewards to encourage people to forget."

I felt as if I had been slapped in the face. It was his tone that did it, so cold, so distant.

"Roy, you talk as if Carolyn were a stranger."

"Well, I haven't seen her since she was a tiny baby," he mumbled.

"But she's your daughter, Roy! Your own flesh and blood!"

"We're traveling light," he snapped. "Now let's shut up about it."

Everything seemed to go to pieces inside me. All during our flight from the police, on the trains, through the cotton fields with bullets flying around me, across the blistering desert . . . in all that time something inside me, a faith in Roy, kept me going. If that faith vanished I knew my strength would be gone. I would be beaten, not by bullets or starvation, but by Roy.

I was just tired out, and so was he. The strain had been too much for both of us. Tomorrow would be another day. Tonight was just a bad dream. Everything would be right tomorrow.

Just Like Real People, Almost

I was downtown when the stores opened the next morning with the want ads in my hand. My clothes were so shabby that it gave me a false sense of timidity. I was beginning to think that I was going to fail in finding work, for the first time, as I was turned down in place after place. Maybe I just looked too terrible. Maybe they thought I was a Latin American, my skin was so brown. Fear was closing in on me. I no longer felt sure of myself.

The shoes I had bought the day before were white, and they didn't look too bad, but my skirt and blouse were faded and I felt sure they looked like I had been picking cotton in them. Perhaps that's where they thought I belonged, in the cotton field with the Mexican labor.

I walked in front of a linen place that had out a sign advertising all kinds of uniforms for rent. I didn't have the money to buy one, but maybe if I could rent one. We had less than half a dollar in change left. If I rented it and failed to find work there would be no food today nor tomorrow. I walked on.

In the next block there was a 'Waitress Wanted' card in the window of what looked like a working man's cafe. I hesitated in front of the cafe long enough to get a glance through the glassed-in front. The waitresses were wearing different kinds of uniforms. That meant they weren't furnished, like they were in classier places. I had to take the chance. I walked back to the linen place and rented a uniform and put it on. They wanted a deposit. I asked if it was all right for me to leave my clothes there. I would give them the thirty-five cent laundry fee and pick up my clothes tomorrow, when I came by for another clean uniform. They agreed. I didn't tell them I didn't even have a job.

I walked back to the cafe that had out the sign, drew a deep breath, lifted my chin and walked in like I belonged. "I'm ready to go to work," I told the manager as he eyed me with evident surprise. "I saw your sign, so I just came ready to start."

Evidently he doubted my ability, even as a waitress, but since I was ready he said he would let me finish the day. If my work proved satisfactory I could return tomorrow. It was almost lunch time and I wasted no time in showing him that I knew what I was doing. I stacked the dishes high on my trembling arm and tried harder than I ever tried in my life to remember every order perfectly. I let no small service slip by me and received some show of gratitude from customers in form of tips. If they only knew how badly I needed them. After luncheon was served and the tables and counters cleaned, I sat down to lunch with another waitress. I was ashamed to eat all I really wanted, but what I did eat gave me strength for the dinner run.

I was extremely happy when the dinner run was over and the manager asked me to return the next morning at six. I had enough tips in my pocket to rent another uniform and to buy food for Roy. He could at least have a good evening meal and food tomorrow while I worked. Soon we would have clothes and money for a little apartment. We would begin saving money for our trip to Mexico.

When I had worked in the little cafe for two weeks the manager threatened not to pay me again if I kept forgetting to bring my social security card. I knew I could not go on working in the same place, for I could not use the card with the name Mary Gregg, and I had no other. I would just have to fail to show up for work after I got my pay and look for another job. I didn't like doing things this way, but life was different now.

With the pay, I got decent looking clothes for myself and some slacks and a sport shirt for Roy. I also bought some dye and used it on both mine and Roy's hair. He was no longer a sandy blond, and there was no red left in my hair. Being a brunette did change Roy's appearance. I cut my own hair with a razor blade. My once shoulder-length locks were now short cropped and very black. It looked fairly natural, with our highly sun-tanned skins.

On each new job I made up a new lie about no social security card and worked until they refused me further pay without it. It was always the same story, in many cities, in several states. Roy was afraid to show himself during the day and seldom did at night. We were afraid of our shadow, often moving without notice at night if we thought we were being observed too closely by anyone.

Twice I became so desperately lonely for my little girl that I sneaked in long distance phone calls, just before we left a state, to hear her voice. On other occasions I slipped out a letter or two or sent presents to Carolyn, just before we changed addresses. I never posted any return nor signed a letter. I was always afraid the mail would be watched or my own family would turn Roy in if they found out where we were.

As the months passed, my lies grew smoother and easier, but my mind was never at ease. I now tried to work at only the best coffee shops because my apron pocket grew heavier there. But as my pocket grew heavier I grew thinner.

Trouble had set in, hard and fast. Roy was rapidly becoming an introvert and he seemed to grow more and more afraid of the outside world. He had too much to think about, too little to do. We could never get money together to go to Mexico as I had planned. Work was hard to find, and Roy was afraid to try for it . . . without a social security card.

We were hopeful, to say the least, at first. But if an idle brain is the devil's workshop, he certainly had a free range and the tools of hatred to work with in Roy's head. I tried every kind of hobby our finances would afford, but he took little or no interest in any of them.

Once, when we were moving to San Francisco I asked if he didn't think it would be safe for me to return home and try to get my mother to let us have Carolyn. We had been away for five months now and the ache in my heart for her was almost unbearable. I could not control my tears. Tears always seemed near the surface now.

"Stop crying!" Roy shouted as he sprang from the bed. "I can't stand a blubbering, bawling dame."

He dressed and stalked out of the room, slamming the door after him. I was utterly and completely alone.

The next morning I awoke early, I slipped out of bed without disturbing Roy and went downtown to look for work. I was elated over finding work in one of the best restaurants in San Francisco with little trouble. I started at once. The tips were good. By the end of the day I had seven dollars.

When I got back home and entered our room Roy whirled around and asked me where I had been.

"Why, I--I got a job, Roy. I made seven dollars."

He relaxed at the sight of the money and a half-apologetic smile spread over his face as he took it, put it in his pocket. When I realized that he thought I had run away because of our quarrel over our daughter I felt a little sorry for him. I tried to tell myself that he was just afraid, tortured and all mixed up.

His apology seemed sincere. He said he would try to make things more pleasant.

In the days that followed he seemed to be trying. He was usually more cheerful. True, he was very moody, but I thought that being alone too much while I was away at work to blame for this. I urged him to get outside more. Surely the heat was off by now, and he was looking sallow and hollow cheeked.

Sometimes, when Roy was in a good mood, he would go out with me. Often we walked through Golden Gate Memorial Park. He loved the Golden Gate and Oakland bridges. We would watch cars crossing the bay on them by the hour. When a fog hung low over the harbor, Golden Gate seemed to rise right out of the clouds. Somehow we liked it better when there was fog, for then we couldn't see 'The Rock.' Always our dream ships would carry us out toward Alcatraz, and there they would hit 'The Rock.' It got to where Roy wouldn't even look across the bay on a clear day because of this grim reminder.

Often we spent hours in the Golden Gate Art Galleries, browsing through the old masterpieces which were always so realistic and restful, especially the pastoral scenes. Sometimes we would look at the grotesque modern art. Much of which gave us nothing but a sense of undefinable blotches of undetermined unrest. When we really sought amusement we would watch the facial expressions of pesons leaving the halls where masterpieces were exhibited as they entered the realms of the moderns. Brazen blotches of color would jump at them, or an obese nude distorted with exaggerations or inexplicable nothings caused some surprising facial contortions in the viewers. Some looked puzzled, others would become disgusted or amused, whichever way it seemed to strike them. Others pretended to understand modern art and would remain to discuss the boldness of line, the individuality of expression or it's abstraction.

Being a recently graduate art major kindled my interest in such observations. My values were so mixed that I am sure any criticism I could have made would have been of no note, but I finally drew a parallel in my own mind which satisfied my own questioning.

I couldn't help but think of the admirers of modern art like the persons I once read about in an elementary reader at school. As I remember the tale, some shysters had tricked the king into paying extortional sums for a robe which was to be made of the most wonderful material in the whole world, a material so extraordinary that only the pure in heart could see and appreciate it.

Not wanting to display his own worldliness the king kept pretending to see the material as the tailors measured and pretended to cut and sew. All the people of the kingdom were told of the wonderful robe the king was to wear, which was to be made of material that only the pure in heart could see.

As the royal procession passed through the streets the king held his majestic pose as grown-ups raved to each other about the splendor of the robe. Finally the king passed a little child who cried aloud to his mother that the king was wearing no robe. That's the way I feel about most modern art, nothing there!

Roy could not appreciate the modern art either, but when he was in a good mood he really got a bang out of watching other people look at it. But I was worried about Roy. Sometimes he took no interest in anything and at other times everything amused him. He was growing thinner by the day and showed no interest in my plans for the future. He seemed to have no thought of Carolyn nor of security.

Then there was always the money problem. I made pretty good wages, enough to support the two of us in a small room, but Roy was always demanding more money. For a time I thought he might be drinking it up, but I never smelled whiskey on his breath. Then I wondered whether he might be playing the horses, but at least he would win sometimes if that were the case, I thought.

I must find some way to jar Roy back to reality. He was living in the past, a tortured world of memories. He talked to himself so much now that I became quite worried about how the other people in the rooming house looked at us.

One day Roy was gone when I got back home. I walked down the hall to the bathroom to bathe and get off my uniform while I tried to decide what to do. The walls were the kind that are anything but soundproof. As I walked toward the bath I heard what sounded like confidential voices behind closed doors. I eased into the bathroom and closed the door, almost. I listened.

"He was raving today like a maniac," I heard what sounded like the agitated voice of the landlady. "I tell you, Mable, I don't blame you for being afraid of him. Of course he's never bothered anybody, but I tell you there's something wrong. Why does he stay holed up in that room all day while his wife works?"

Mable kept trying to get her say in and finally cut in with, "I tell you he just raves about shootings and getting even until it curdles my blood. Do you reckon he has killed someone and is hiding out?"

"I don't know" the landlady answered, "But I can tell you

this, when my husband comes home from work tonight, if he doesn't call the cops I'm going to. I'm going to turn him in for disturbing the public peace."

I slithered out of the bathroom. It was growing dusk outside and I knew that both the ladylady's husband and Roy might show up any minute. I reached our door and closed it ever so quietly. I started grabbing our scanty wardrobes from the hangers.

"And he's always raving about a prison break," I heard Mable call as an afterthought as the landlady was leaving her room.

"That settles it," the landlady said decisively. "He could be an ex-convict, or even an escaped convict. I'll not wait for my husband to get home. I'll call the cops this very minute and have them waiting when he gets back. It's about time for his wife to get in from work and I don't want her to know what's going on. That's just the thing to do," I heard her say as she clomped down the hallway. "I'll give him a warm reception."

There was very little to pack, and I always kept things ready for flight at a moment's notice. My hand was on the doorknob by the time the landlady reached the bottom of the stairs. I was peeping to make sure that Mable's door was closed when I realized I still had on my cafe uniform. I ripped it off and pulled a dress over my head.

As I tiptoed for the back stairs I could hear the dial clicking from the open door of the living room. I held my breath as I reached the bottom of the stairs and opened the back door. I had used the telephone in the living room several times and knew that if she heard a noise at the back all she would have to do to see me was lean back in her chair and peep into the hallway. I was gone by the time she finished dialing.

I didn't have time to wonder where I was going to find Roy for I ran smack into him as I rounded the corner of the house at full speed. He started to speak but I didn't give him a chance. A packed suitcase and full speed ahead made it unnecessary for him to ask questions.

Flight by Night

I was thankful it was so nearly dark as we rushed down the sidewalk. Perhaps even now the landlady had heard us and was opening the door. What was worse, there might be a cop's car just around the corner that could have been alerted. I hoped she had trouble in getting them to believe at the police station that her call was important. There was a drug store nearby and I wasted no time getting to it and calling a cab. We waited outside in the semidarkness for it to arrive.

"The landlady's turned you in to the cops," was about all I had time to whisper. "We'll have to make tracks."

"Hotel Mark," I ordered as we crawled into the cab. I knew there would be other cabs at the hotel waiting for we couldn't take a cab directly to any destination for fear we would be traced. Roy and I had always planned to go to the "Top of the Mark" for an evening of entertainment if our ship ever came in. At the rate our money had disappeared recently we couldn't afford one such extravagance, however much Roy had dreamed of it during his imprisonment.

I was thinking how pretty the lights would look from the

top of the hotel as the cab started up the hill behind the old trolley that always fascinated me. Once we had ventured to the "Top of the Mark," as spectators, and the city stretching below us and the bridges spanning the bay were breathtaking. I wondered how it would look tonight?

"Let's grab another cab," I said to Roy as the first one pulled off. We walked a few steps and Roy motioned another cab alongside as the first one turned the corner.

"The Oakland Bus Terminal," I directed the new driver. As we crossed the bridge I drew a slight breath of relief. Getting across a span of water, however short the distance, made me feel further away from our immediate danger. Maybe the landlady hadn't ventured out to our room. Maybe she had told the cops to lay low until Roy arrived. I hoped so.

We hesitated for brief planning before we entered the terminal. "We'd better take the first bus out," Roy said, "Regardless of where it's headed for."

There was a bus scheduled to leave for Phoenix within the next seven minutes. We looked queerly at one another. Life there had been better than what I had faced recently. We couldn't go too far because of our financial status, but Phoenix was within reach. Maybe, if Roy saw Superstition Mountain again it would bring back old memories. When he remembered how dearly we had paid for the freedom he was now squandering . . .

We were at the ticket window. I raised my eyebrow and Roy nodded yes as we bought two tickets to Phoenix, one way. As we climbed aboard the bus I was remembering the old Ford Grill, one of the first places I had worked. I was wondering if they would take me back. I didn't think it wise to go back to the same place but I was remembering, Ham, the bartender, and Arkey, a waitress, who was from Arkansas. They had been real friends and I was so desperately lonely. I was remembering the boss, Peter Marcon, too, and how he sympathized with me when I told him my husband was ill and unable to work. I remember how patient he had been in teaching me the different kinds of Italian foods that were served there.

I had never worked where Italian food and wine were served and sometimes got my orders mixed. I didn't know the difference between a martini and an old fashioned when I started there. The good natured bartender would point out my cocktails for me in the least conspicious manner. I could never have made it without Ham.

I thought again of Arkey and Peter and how they had helped me, each trying to hide the fact from the others. Nothing but beer had ever been legal in Texas and I was exceedingly ignorant about intoxicants, coming from a family of total abstainers. Once I ordered ravioli from the bartender and muscatel from the cook.

All these things ran through my mind as we again crossed the desert, this time on bus. I was wondering if Death Valley could be any worse than the part of the desert we went through when I thought of Jesus.

"Maybe we could visit Jesus, sometime," I mused aloud, but Roy was asleep. Nothing seemed to bother him any more. He didn't even bother to ask why the landlady turned him in. I was beginning to think that maybe I should do the asking. Why was he taking so many chances recently. I was beginning to think his mind was affected with too much thinking.

What else could make him so moody that I was even afraid to approach the subject. Not that I expected him to go out and get a job and dress me in furs, but I did want him to be interested in what I was doing and help me plan for the future. He seemed to have lost all interest in me and Carolyn.

Surely when he saw Phoenix and remembered how hard we had struggled for life and this freedom so insecurely won, surely he would straighten up.

I couldn't help but return to the old Ford Grill. I felt a desperate need of friendship. If there had been anyone in the world I could have talked to it would have helped, but I had to bear it alone. Just the sight of old friends made me feel better. I didn't even have to ask for a job. Peter just asked me if I had come back to work and I said "yes" with all my heart.

When I got home that first night from work I found Roy had either hocked or sold our radio I had bought especially to keep him company while I was away. He wouldn't talk about it. Before pay day came Roy was waiting for me to get off work.

Once he even came into the cafe and asked me for my tips. I was quite alarmed. Maybe they would be looking for Roy out in this part of the country if they made the association in Frisco when the landlady turned him in.

One day I saw the police talking with Peter a little while before time for me to get off work. They hung around the front of the cafe or loitered near the courthouse across the street.

I had a feeling they wanted a look at Roy. Maybe they were suspicious. I held my breath for fear Roy would show up. My boss had been so lenient in dealing with me, but he had told me in no uncertain terms to bring my social security card, or else he would have to hold up my pay.

When I left the place I didn't head for home, for I had a feeling I was being followed. I was always careful to give the wrong address when I went to work any place. I didn't want to do anything that would alert my shadow, if I was being followed, to the fact that I was alarmed.

Wondering what to do, I walked into a grocery store. I bought an armload of the biggest, bulkiest groceries I could find for the least money. This would give me good reason for taking a cab. I called one and gave an address a couple of blocks from home. When the cab was out of sight I chucked my bulky sack as I turned a corner and fairly ran. Fortunately Roy was in the room asleep.

''We're going to take our first plane ride,'' I said as I shook him. ''We've always wanted to ride on a plane and I think I was being followed on the way home. I gave them the slip. I don't think they suspected I knew I was being watched. Maybe they'll wait for me to show up to work in the morning.

I saw plainclothesmen talking with the boss and sneaking looks at me. I know they were dicks because I was just coming out of the kitchen with an order when I saw them pull open their coats. There were two of them, but only one followed. I had a feeling the other one was waiting for you to show up.

''Your imagination's sort of getting the best of you here lately, isn't it, Mary? I didn't see any cops the last time we ran. Are you sure you aren't seein' things?''

''I don't know, Roy,'' I confessed, ''but I am sure I was being tailed. Besides, the boss acted so funny and looked at me so strangely that I am almost positive they were talking about us in the cafe."

"Couldn't have been there for a thousand other reasons?" Roy asked nonchalantly.

"I don't know," I replied, "But I do know I can't get paid again. I was lucky to get it today. I had a feeling he wasn't going to let me have it this time until I produced my card. He won't take any more excuses."

"Where to this time?" he asked with a sigh as we began throwing things in the bag.

"Let's make it Los Angeles," I suggested. "We can make it our first plane trip. We will be there in no time."

"Take all our money, won't it?" Roy asked with an alarmed look on his face.

"Yes, honey, but you could go to work, too. Honestly, I don't think they'd think as much of your working as hanging around where I work. We could both work a couple of weeks without cards. Maybe we could save enough to go to Mexico."

"Work!" Roy exploded. "And get caught again? You think I'm crazy? Look, honey, someday I'll give you the things you deserve. Someday the big breaks will come my way. Don't think I'm not planning for it, I am, but it won't be for small change. It'll be in the big "G's" and you'll be loaded with rocks."

I didn't follow him. Maybe I didn't want to understand. All I knew was that we must get to another place, and in a hurry. I had a feeling we were doomed. In a way I was afraid I would find out the truth. I was not the type person to admit defeat, but somehow I felt it inevitable.

Face to Face with the Inevitable

In a new town and with a new job I tried to make myself believe things would be different. I tried to shut my eyes to the truth, but Roy had been in the cafe where I was working that very day, asking for my tips. It was like trying to fight an unknown foe. I couldn't remember my orders and was making a terrible botch of my work. I had tried so hard to ignore all the little signs that pointed in one direction, silently praying that I was wrong, but that night I couldn't duck the evidence any longer because it was right before my eyes.

My strength and courage had left me and I was dog-tired after the long day at the restaurant, so I took a taxi home instead of enduring the hour's trolley ride across Los Angeles. When the cab rolled to a stop in front of our rooming house I looked up to see that the window of our room was dark. That was strange. With a growing sense of uneasiness, I paid the cabbie, ran into the house and up the stairs to our room.

I fumbled with the lock for a moment, then stepped into total darkness and felt along the wall for a light switch. At the flick of the switch the room flooded with light and I saw Roy. He was sprawled on the bed, fully dressed, his head propped up by two pillows. His eyes were staring ahead with a strange, glassy expression, and his lips were parted with a loose grin.

"How ya, Sweetheart," he muttered. "How's everything?"

"Roy, what's the matter with you?"

"Huh? Matter with me? I'm fine, Baby, just fine!"

Running to the bed, I grabbed him by the shoulders and pulled him to a sitting position. The grin never left his face, and his eyes continued to look past me at something only he could see.

My eyes swept the room for some clue, and finding none, I ran to the dresser and began to pull out the drawers, one by one. In the bottom drawer, underneath Roy's shirts, I found it. There in a little box were half a dozen "decks" of white powder and a hypodermic needle. Now I knew beyond a doubt that Roy's trouble was dope, although I had never seen it before. How could I have been so blind?

Despair washed over me as I swung around to face him. For a moment I felt sick, deathly sick. "Roy . . . Roy . . . Roy . . . I moaned. Why? Why did you have to do this?"

"Because I like it," he said gaily.

Nothing seemed to bother him. He was completely befuddled by dope. I knew now that this wasn't the first time, but he had never been this "high" before.

This explained his moodiness, his restlessness at times and his complete abandon of caution at others. This was my unseen foe, and I had been a fool not to recognize any of the symptoms. But how can you recognize a thing you have never seen before?

"But how . . . where did you get the dope?"

"I got connections, baby. I know a few boys here in town. Five years in prison is a lot of schooling. I could make connections in any big town in America. You learn a lot in prison, baby."

So this was what he had been doing while I was at work. I felt sure he must have been on it some while we were in Phoenix, but it was worse now. When had it started? Where? How long had he been hiding it from me? What a cruel and senseless waste of man! What a bitter end for my dreams!

"I never knew," I sobbed, "I never knew you took dope. When did you start? Where?"

"Remember when I used to work in the prison hospital, baby, when I had the good job in the walls? You'd be surprised how much this stuff can make you forget. Lifts you right out of this world. That was the only way I had of getting out of prison while I was in."

"Oh, Roy," I moaned, "How can a man do such a thing to forget his misery."

"It's easy, baby, it's easy."

"But when you broke out of prison," I insisted, "You seemed all right then. You were more like the sweetheart I used to know. Surely you couldn't have been taking it then? You couldn't have while you were on the desert!"

"Yeah, that's it, baby, I was broke of the habit, and I can do it now, anytime I want to."

I wondered about that, but now that his talk was making sense I had to push to get what information I could while he was still in a talkative mood.

"But how did you get it, while you were in prison, I mean?"

"Some of the boys in prison used to have it smuggled in, I'd sniff it from time to time. Makes you feel real good. Then when I landed that hospital job, I didn't have much trouble. Even made a little money on the side."

"But you said you were broken of the habit," I insisted. "How?"

"Remember when I got ranked, Baby, ranked and sent to the farm? That was when Clyde Barrow made his break. Bonnie was waiting for him at the time, baby, just like you were waiting for me."

I shuddered at the comparison. How well I remembered their ruthless flight, the bloodshed and cold blooded murder.

"She wrote poetry, baby, like you, except not so good. Remember, they even found a poem on her when she and Clyde were ambushed. How many hundred bullet holes did they say they found in that car?''

''Please, darling,'' I cried in desperation, ''How did they break you of the habit?''

''Clyde wasn't so bad,'' he continued, determined to tell the story his way. ''I was in the same cell block with him for a long time. He wasn't so bad, just a little tough. It's the cops and guards that make people bad. Bonnie might not have been any worse than you, she just loved her man.''

''Stop!'' I cried. ''I don't want to hear any more. I'm not like Bonnie and you're not like Clyde.''

''That's just what I am trying to tell you, baby. People are never bad until the world starts to pushing them around. They aren't ever desperate until they are cornered, like animals.''

I couldn't stand any more. I got up from the bed where I had been sitting and started to leave the room.

''Hold on, baby,'' he called. ''You asked for it and now you're going to get it. Pull up a chair and make yourself comfortable.''

I sank into the only chair, exhausted. There wasn't any use trying to fight his talking spell and I knew it. If I left he would probably talk loudly enough for other people staying in the house to hear. This must be what happened before, while I was working. He must have had so much he was talking to himself.

''I'm right by you, Roy, and you don't have to talk so the neighbors can hear.''

''Like I was telling you, baby,'' he continued in a somewhat modified tone, ''I've been broke of the habit and I could quit it myself, just like that,'' he said with a snap of his fingers. ''I'm not an addict.''

''But how? I tried again.

''I never will forget that day Clyde broke out of prison. I was working in the prison hospital then. Whitey was in the death cell. Whitey and Clyde were buddies. I could have been in on that break myself, but you remember how close I was to getting a parole then. I felt sorry for Whitey. He was going to burn. There ain't nothin' that hurts so much as a guy gettin' burned. The lights flicker and then get dim as they throw on the current . . .''

''Please don't,'' I cried.

''But you wanted to hear how I got broke, baby. I'm telling you. Whitey's hand was shot up in his last bank robbery, that's why I had been dressing it. That's why I got to him. I was the hospital attendant. That's why I had you send me ten bucks a month, to keep a good job,'' he added.

I was silent and he continued.

''I had been dressing Whitey's hand for a long time. Then Clyde told me about the break and told me he had a pistol he wanted bandaged in Whitey's hand. He even told me where they had buried the loot from their last bank robbery. I could have been one of their gang, but you had been working for my parole so long I hated to muff it.''

I squirmed restlessly in my uncomfortable chair.

''There ain't much to it,'' he said. ''You read in the papers how Whitey was shot from the wall just as he got to the top. It was a tough break, but if they had all been killed I was to go dig up the loot when I got out on the legit. Pretty good set-up, huh, baby? If Clyde hadn't left that place alive we could have dug up sixty grand for me wrapping that bandage. If he did come out alive he was going to stake us when I did get out. How could I lose? I could have gone to medical school.''

''Except for the fact that Clyde was killed, after he dug up the loot. The bills were marked and part of them were found in the car.''

''Yeah, I know, but what if Whitey hadn't been shot off that wall? We had it made. I couldn't stand to see a guy burn. You know, that would have been something, him escaping.''

''Is that why you lost your good prison job?'' I asked. ''They kept telling me how well you were doing. You were filling prescriptions and everything. Remember when you told me about the math professor who visited you from Sam Houston State College? You had worked out a remarkable formula for breaking dope addicts whereby you didn't have to mix every shot separately. Is that how you mean? You mixed it with water, didn't you, a little more and a little more water each time? Didn't they find your formula mathematically perfect?"

"Yeah," Roy grinned. "At first they thought I was going to kill some of those dopies, but I got a way of working out formulas."

He laughed until I had to sush him up.

"They took away all my overtime when they found that pistol bandaged in Whitey's hand. That's why I had to break out. I couldn't stand it on the farm. I had a soft job and they threw me out to chop cotton right when the sun was getting hottest. That's when I got sick. I would have died. They cut off my snow and I felt sure I was going to die. That's when I saw the big black widow spider on the cotton leaf just before I passed out. I knew what they did to guys who fell out. They put the whip to them and told them to die and prove it. They said I still had that black widow in my hand when I got to the hospital. I had to coax her to bite. That's where I got my name, Spider Gregg, that's what they all called me after that."

He rambled on with his story as I tried to think of other things.

"It was nice in the hospital, while the others were in the fields, but I got out too soon. I wasn't ready for those hot fields, so I ate a little cotton soaked in soap. That gives you a high fever for a while, but it doesn't keep you in the hospital long, either. A lot of guys were mutilating. I could have severed my heel string or chopped off a few toes, but I wanted to break. Clyde Barrow chopped off two of his toes once. That's how he got back into the walls."

I couldn't stand any more about Barrow so I got up from my chair, indicating I had had enough.

"You're right, baby," he concluded. "I didn't have any snow while we were on the desert. I'd been broke for over two months. Down there you have to die to prove it. I'm not an addict."

I looked at him lying there, drugged, and I knew what an empty boast that was. He was caught, he was addicted, he could never lay off without the worst sort of agony. But maybe . . .

maybe with my help! Even in my deepest despair I wanted to believe there was still hope for Roy, hope for us.

At what stage does one give up marriage? When does one stop loving, stop hoping? I suppose it depends upon the woman, but for my part I couldn't stop loving Roy, not even then.

The next day, after the dope had worn off, Roy and I had a long talk. He cried in my arms and promised he'd never touch the stuff again. He made such wonderful promises. But as the days passed my heart began to shrink within me. Roy didn't change a bit. In fact, now that I shared his secret, he seemed to get worse. I lost several jobs because he'd hang around the kitchen door to take my tips as fast as I made them. Then one night when I came home from work he grabbed me and tried to shove the needle into my arm, so I'd feel the way he did.

The Cure

"I'm leaving you, Roy," I said the next day after the dope had worn off. "It's been bad enough with you taking the stuff, but trying to shove it into my arm, that's different."

Roy's mouth fell open in disbelief. "Honestly, Mary, I didn't do it? Did I?"

"Just as sure as you're alive. You won't quit it and I'll have nothing to do with it. I'm sick and tired. Six months I've tried to make a man of you. What's happened to you, Roy? How can a man with your nerve give in to a habit? You fought the whole world for this freedom, now you're trying to throw it away. Well, you can throw it away by yourself. I'm going home to Carolyn."

"Oh, no, baby. You can't leave me! I can't live without you. I couldn't get snow. They'd pick me up. I'd burn for murder."

"Then you'll have to burn. I'm through, I tell you. I'm tired of paying for dope with sweat and blood. You're not the man I married! He was sweet, and good and tender. You're a demon of hell fired with that poisonous venom. You're not fit to be the father of your own child."

Sobs were racking his body as he pleaded, "I'll quit, Darling, I'll quit. I'll do anything if you just won't leave me. I'll never take another jolt."

"That's getting to be a broken record, isn't it?"

"Here's all I got, honest. I won't ever touch it. I'll lay it here on the dresser and it'll be here when you come home from work. I've got nothing to live for without you. We'll get Carolyn just as soon as I get straightened out. Will you forgive me if I prove to you I can? I know I'm an addict. I'm not fooling myself, but I'll quit it or die trying."

I wondered if he could lay off it, just one day. He had been taking two or more jolts every day recently. It was time for me to go to work. I didn't say anything except that I was going to work. I felt like I should just keep going, but I couldn't help but wonder if he could leave the deck on the dresser for eight hours while I was gone. One day more wouldn't matter and I needed it for my fare home. I was almost happy in my own heart during the day. I was giving him one more opportunity and I knew he couldn't resist. I felt like I was going the extra mile. Tomorrow I would be on my way to Carolyn.

The room was dark when I returned. I was remembering what had happened once before when I had entered and switched on the light. I hesitated with my hand on the knob, then I heard him. Heard him moan and then heard something thudding against the wall.

What I had seen before when I switched on the light was nothing compared with the writhing mass I now saw on the bed. He didn't even realize the light had been turned on. He was deathly white. Blood oozed from his skin in a dozen places where he had dug his flesh with his fingernails. All this was glossed with sweat. Every muscle in his body seemed in torment. He rolled on his stomach and gripped the head of the bed until his knuckles were white, then he shook it like an animal in a cage.

I ran to him crying, "Roy! Roy!"

The deck lay on the dresser, untouched. "Roy, I cried, pulling him over, can you hear me?" He looked at me with glassy eyes that saw nothing as he cried out in pain. I threw my arms around him and his fingers dug into my flesh, bringing blood.

"You've got to do something," I cried, jumping from the bed. "I'll get a doctor."

"The doctor's on the dresser," he moaned, "but I'll die before I'll touch it. You can't leave me, I'll die!"

I had never known there could be a torment like this before. I watched in horror as he shook and writhed and then lay still and exhausted, only to repeat the performance a few minutes later. Once he was still so long I was afraid he would die. His eyes stared without seeing and his mouth hung half open. He was pale as death and I was wondering if he was still breathing when he went into another spasm. I couldn't stand any more.

"Roy, Roy, darling, can you hear me? I won't leave you, I promise I won't. I've never lied to you Roy. Take it. You've got to have it. I'll stay with you, Roy. We'll break it off slow, like you broke the dopies in prison."

He reached for it like a dying man. I fell on the bed he left and hid my face in the wet pillow. I couldn't see him take it. We couldn't talk. I had built my own little dream world and it had toppled.

When he had finished I changed the sheets on the bed and bathed his wounds. He looked at me like a sick dog one had befriended. He didn't get wild nor talkative. I said he must have food and went to prepare it. Before I returned he was asleep. I lay beside him far into the night . . . thinking . . . thinking . . . thinking.

The next morning we had a good talk. We made plans. All the long summer and fall we had looked at and longed for the beautiful mountains which lay just out of our reach. Now that the tourist trade was over I had been watching advertisements in the papers. Cabins could be rented for almost half price. Maybe we could. Although it was early December, mineral baths were still being advertised in the Box Mountains, near Los Angeles. Maybe it would even snow. I could count the snowfalls I had seen in my lifetime on my fingers. "Oh, if we only could."

"If we could only what?" Roy asked with real tenderness.

"If we could only get a lonely little cabin in the mountains by one of those mineral springs," I said. "Why you could take hot baths in a walled off part of a pool and fish for Rainbows in the clear, cold water downstream. That's what the paper says. Some of them are only an hour's drive from downtown Los Angeles."

"Yeah, that would be heaven," Roy answered, "but how could we get the money. Waitresses don't make that kind of money. Maybe I could go to work."

My heart leaped with joy at the very thought of his mentioning work. "No, darling, no. You have your part to do. First you must help yourself. After that I intend for you to take care of your daughter and me. How does that sound, honey? I worked nights and went to school four years while you were in prison. Why couldn't I do it a few days now? I could get a job in a night spot. I know my drinks now," I said thinking of the short time ago when I had ordered a martini from the kitchen and ravioli from the bar. "My family never drank, not even at Christmas, and nothing but beer was ever legal in Texas, so I was really as dumb as they come."

"But how? How could I help?" Roy asked with enthusiasm.

"Yours would be the hardest part," I continued. "We can do it if you cut yourself off dope entirely. Do you think you could work out a little formula for yourself like you did for the dopies in Huntsville and cut yourself off in ten days? If you could I believe I could scrape up enough money for a week in Box Mountains. Would a week without dope make you sure of yourself again? Could you do it? I'd be with you every minute."

"Sure I can do it," he assured me. "It won't be easy, but having you with me all the time when I have to do without it, I could make it. My formula will be easy to work out with ten for a denominator. Ten more days and I'll never take another jolt. But how do you think you can manage the trip?"

"I'll keep working days, and I'll get a night job. I've never worked in a night club but it won't be for long. Just ten days and then my husband can start taking care of me."

It was with real hope and enthusiasm that I set out to find

work in a night spot. I was really scared at first, but I caught the hang of it before the first night was finished.

Roy bought five decks of snow which he had all figured out so he could cut himself down to nothing in ten days. He stuck by his guns and I could tell he was doing his part. On the third day after we made our little pact I put down a $10 deposit to get the cabin reserved, the rest to be paid in advance when the wonderful day came for us to take possession of a little corner of heaven for a week. I was already picturing fresh, crisp vegetables cached in a crystal, cold stream flowing back of the cabin and rainbow trout freshly caught. How wonderful and extraordinary to bathe in a hot spa, bubbling from the heart of the earth, and then becoming a part of the cold stream. The spring was walled off from the rest of the stream, the advertising agent had told me. It was nature's own bathtub with miraculous curative powers. I could close my eyes and vision the hot spring cleansing Roy's pores of the last vistage of dope. He would feel so good and clean he would never want to touch the horrible stuff again.

I never worked so hard, and by the time seven days were past of working day and night I felt like I could use a little rest at the cabin myself. Every day we were living on one of my salaries and putting away what I made at night. I was trusting Roy with the money and our pot grew. It was easier now that it didn't go for dope.

Eight days passed and I was jubilant. Roy was sticking to his part of the bargain. I had wanted to surprise him with a fly rod or an automatic reel, but it looked as if I wouldn't be able to make it. It would be the most wonderful surprise in the world, but many fish are caught without fancy equipment.

One day to go, finally, and then came the tenth day. I was so nervous and high strung that I couldn't be still a minute. If I could just make enough for that rod and reel, but chances looked slim. I hadn't made too much during the day and I was never sure what I would make at night. I had to keep doing something. I had to keep moving.

While I was filling the sugar bowls during the slack time in the cafe, I spilled some sugar down in back of one of the leatherette cushions of a booth. I tried to wipe it out but it was too deep in the crack for my cloth to reach. I removed the cushion and found it badly in need of cleaning where it fitted against the back rest. Then I decided I would clean all the cushions on my station while I wasn't busy. Then it happened. I found, beneath one of the cushions, a $20 bill. That was a fortune to me at the time. It meant I could buy the rod and reel I wanted so badly for Roy. I know I should have turned it in, but it may have been lying there for weeks and I felt sure no one would ever know to whom it belonged. My desire for the rod and reel won out so I stuck it into my pocket.

I hadn't been going home between jobs because I didn't have time to make it on the street cars and I couldn't afford taxi fares, so I had just been eating luxuriously in order to catch a few moments of rest before catching a car for my evening job.

This afternoon I didn't stop to eat. I dashed out of the cafe the minute my time was up to get that wonderful rod and reel to make our stay in the mountains complete. I just couldn't keep the secret. If I hurried I could buy it and catch a taxi home and show Roy. This would make the last night much easier, because this was the night he was to do without dope. Just the thought of it made me nervous. I had to surprise him. I had to help. What a wonderful thrill I had for him. This would be his Christmas in advance. I could just see him trying to practice with it in that small room while I spent my last night at work. Maybe I would be lucky my last night, too.

I told the taxi to wait for I hardly had time to make it from one job to the other, but I had to surprise Roy. I hit the door with a joyous cry of "Surprise! Surprise!," but it was I who received the surprise.

How quickly can one's heart fall from the peak of expectancy to the darkest depths of doom. One look at Roy's glossy eyes and that half crooked grin did it for me. I had flown from the taxi to the house but my feet were like lead as I dragged back to dismiss the cab driver.

Roy didn't even know I was in the room. He kept saying over and over, "I'll die without it! I'll die without it!"

I ran to where I kept our savings hid for the week at the cabin. He had bought more than one deck, but a major portion of the money was left. I opened his suitcase which was already packed. I couldn't find anything suspicious.

''She'll never know I have it. She won't be home before two in the morning,'' he continued. ''I won't take any of the deck I got hid, but I got to have it along, so far away from everything in a cabin for a week.''

So near and yet so far, my heart cried out. I knew if he had it hid in his things there was nothing I could do. My defeat was final. Somehow I had known it all along, but I couldn't make myself give it up. I couldn't stop loving the father of my own child.

Suddenly I was crying. My own child needed me too, of this I was sure. Tears streamed down my face and splattered to the floor as I sat the prized rod and reel in the corner.

I went to my suitcase which was partially packed. It all seemed so much like a dream which I knew was too good to come true, but it made such a bright spot in a drab life that I couldn't turn it loose. I knew what I must do. I was in no condition to work that night and I no longer had the heart for it. There was enough money left for my ticket home. Sobs shook my thin, tired frame and I seemed very cold. The face I saw in the mirror when I tried to apply a little make up looked old, very old for a young mother.

I would leave enough money for Roy to eat on a day or two. I wondered what he would do with the rod and reel. Like the few other nice things I had been able to buy him, it too would be hocked for dope. Somehow the thought didn't bother me. I had gone the last mile. All dreams were dead. There was no future. Roy slept, or had passed out.

Together We Die!

My heart was numb as I packed my suitcase just as I had done so often before. But this time it was final. This was the last trip. The last bond was broken.

I dared not think what would become of Roy. There was nothing to say in a note. When he came to he would see the rod and reel and the receipt for holding the cabin for us. Dope meant more than these. When he came to it would probably be time for us to be on our way to our heaven in the mountains, but I would be gone.

If it hadn't been for the ache in my heart for Christmas with Carolyn I don't think I could have stood leaving him so hopeless, but staying would be throwing my life away with my eyes open. Six years now I had devoted to a lost cause. It wasn't so bad as long as there was hope. I was completely defeated but I had to face my family to see my daughter. I felt I couldn't go on living without her.

I tiptoed from the room, leaving Roy just as he lay. At the bus station I bought a ticket for my hometown and found there would be two layovers on the way, three hours in El Paso and one hour in Abilene.

Abilene! How different things might have been if I had stayed there. I had my college degree and could have been teaching school. Carolyn would have been with me if I had only had sense enough not to try the impossible.

But all this was over now. I must put it out of mind and start a new life with Carolyn. I had plenty of time for thinking things over while enroute.

Finally, two days later, the bus pulled into Abilene. It was during the early morning hours, but I couldn't resist taking a walk past the *Reporter-News,* where I used to work, during my layover.

I had gone about three blocks through the dark and silent city when I heard rapid footsteps behind me. I walked faster, faster, but the footsteps overtook me. Suddenly I felt a gun poked hard into my ribs.

"Where do you think you're going, sister?" a rough voice asked. My scream was choked off. I was trapped, terrified. Then I looked up . . . into the bloodshot eyes of Roy Gregg! My lips fell open with amazement. Roy, here? How could he have found me? He must have wakened to find me gone, guessed where I would head and somehow beaten me here. How could he dare do such a thing? It was the worst thing he could possibly do. After working all night in the town for four years the first cop who saw me would probably sound the alarm.

"Left me!" he hissed. "So you left me! Well, it isn't as easy as that. Don't you know that when the cops pick you up they'll try to pin every unsolved robbery and murder on you? You gonna tell them you tagged along with me to try to make a Boy Scout out of me? They'll give you a medal for that!"

He turned me around and marched me ahead of him through the streets to the edge of town. We came to a tourist court. Keeping the gun on me from his coat pocket, Roy hired the last cabin in the row. Once inside he locked the door, tilted a chair against it and sat down.

"Make yourself comfortable, baby," he said. "We're gonna be here for awhile. We got lots to talk over."

I walked over to the bed and sat on it, not caring much what happened. Roy began to talk in a rambling manner, about the prison, about his childhood, about anything that crossed his mind, but mostly about his plans for the future.

"I got big things in mind, baby. I got plans to bust that prison wide open and set my buddies free. Then I'll have a gang that nothing can stop. We'll be riding on top of the world . . . you and me."

Delusions of grandeur, I thought. I wondered if taking dope did that to the brain.

"I know I've never done much for you," he was saying, "but from now on it'll be different, because we're going to live my way. A couple of good jobs and we're on easy street. There's no turning back for us, baby. Our names are on the same marker. We go out and make history together, or we die here together." He pulled the gun from his pocket and aimed it straight at my heart. "Make up your mind."

I thought of Carolyn and of what Roy had just said. Maybe he was right. I had nothing to look forward to but a prison sentence. Maybe our names were on the same marker, and there was no turning back . . . only death. Could death be so bad?

But face to face with death, I was desperately frightened. My sins seemed so small for so great a retaliation . . . all committed to help the man I thought the world had wronged.

Six years I had wasted for a lost cause. Now it was to cost me my life. Strange, but now that I was to pay in full it was difficult for me to see what I had set out to accomplish. My intentions were good and my purpose had looked noble in my own eyes, but how could I have been snarred in such a web? My strength was sapped. I no longer felt a desire to fight. My former weight, one twenty-six, had dwindled to ninety-seven. I was a skeleton with just nerves hanging on. I cried without provocation and uttered a mute scream at the slightest sound.

Yes, I was sure my child would be better off without a mother than with one in the pen or crazy house. Perhaps her memories would be pleasant if she never saw me again. Certainly I had no intention of bringing more suffering into the world, more crime and blood shed. No one but an inexperienced fool dreams of glamour in connection with crime. What did it matter which way I died? If I could only embrace my daughter once more. She was mine, but I was the one who had made the choice, I was the one who must pay.

"I'm ready," I whispered, looking long and hard at Roy. "Go ahead and pull the trigger if you want to. I don't care."

I closed my eyes and braced myself for the bullet as he leveled the pistol at my head. If it would only be over quickly. "Please God," I prayed. "Make it quick."

Four seconds, five, six . . . then a long sob filled the room. "I can't do it," Roy said brokenly. "My aim's not very steady. You do the honors. I'll go first."

I hid my face in the pillow. After a long silence I opened my eyes to see Roy fumble in his pocket and bring out a hypodermic needle. He prepared himself a shot. The needle sank into the tender flesh, then slowly he pushed the plunger. In a matter of minutes his face began to relax.

"A little shot of this won't hurt you any," he remarked. "Makes it a lot easier."

"It's robbed me of every dream I lived for," I bitterly remarked, "I don't see why I should embrace it in death. I'll die hating it."

"But you won't look very pretty," he remarked as I burst into a new flow of tears. "Go wash your face and put on some make-up. You wouldn't think I was doing you a favor. Comb your hair real pretty and spread it out on the pillow."

How could he carry on such banter in the face of death? Dazedly I followed his instructions, knowing morphine would give him courage to finish the job where he had faltered a few minutes before.

Dope is the very soul of the devil, I was thinking as I applied a little lipstick. Not being able to find my comb I pulled open the dresser drawer, through habit, I suppose. There lay a Bible. I picked it up and fumbled it curiously. "Gideons" was stamped on it.

I heard Roy laughing. The dope had taken effect and he was laughing at the irony of the situation. The joke seemed too good to end abruptly.

"It won't hurt you none," he was laughing. "Read it!

I hesitated, but could think of nothing to say.

"Read it. It won't hurt you none," he repeated. "Maybe it will carry you to heaven in a chariot of fire. This is your last chance, kid. Better catch up on your readin'. Read all you want. I can wait. Our rent's paid up for a week. You're not going any place. You're going to die. Death's pretty permanent, they tell me. You still got time to change your mind."

Mentally I recalled some of the passages I knew as a child. Once, when I had dreamed of becoming a foreign missionary, I was very familiar with its passages. How well I knew the laws of God and the ten commandments, many of which I had broken.

I thought of the first commandment, "Thou shalt have no other Gods before Me."

I had forgotten God. In my struggle I had depended upon love as an indestructible force. I had wanted to do right, but with my own motivation, which stemmed from the love of man, not God. I had wanted to prove to the world that it had made a big mistake, that the man I loved was not a criminal.

Roy seemed engrossed in his own thoughts so I climbed back into bed with the Bible. I had little desire to read. How well I knew the old passage, "As a man soweth, that shall he also reap." Yes, I had sown destruction. Now I was faced with the harvest of my errors. I laid the Bible aside.

"Go on and read," Roy was saying. "It's your last chance. Better be sure you're finished."

I don't know why, but I picked up the Bible and opened it to the New Testament as he again leveled the gun at my head. I came to that verse in the eleventh chapter of Matthew: "Give not that which is holy unto the dogs, neither cast your pearls before swine, lest they trample them under their feet, and turn again and rend you."

What are the pearls of life? I thought about the passage for a long while.

Once I had possessed the pearls of life, and I had cast them before swine. Surely virtue is one of the pearls. My thoughts swirled back over five years, to the time when Roy was first sent to prison. It was then I threw away my first pearl. Our baby was only two weeks old when that fateful trip started. Perhaps I should have died then. Why should I relive it now? Where does sin really begin?

I guess the events leading to my greatest and most foolhardy sin began the day Roy was carried to prison. I was so young and ignorant. I can still see that barred truck and remember my desperate loneliness.

Alone, Afraid and a Fool

As that caged truck pulled slowly away from me, as it carried my husband to prison over five years ago, the bars through which I caught the last glimpse of Roy's face seemed to pull the remaining hope and strength from me like magnets. I had never been so utterly alone before. I wanted to cry out, "Take me! Take me to prison with you! At least in prison there is shelter and some kind of food. That is more than I have on the outside!"

The two-week-old baby in my arms tugged at an empty breast. Dazedly I crushed my darling daughter to me, picked up a battered suitcase so crammed with diapers that there was room for only one change of clothing for myself, and drifted in the direction the truck had taken. I had been given a choice by my parents, my husband or my home.

Before I realized what I was doing a man pulled up and offered me a lift to where I was going in his car. I can never forget that astounded look on his face when I told him I was going to Huntsville. He thought I was only walking a few blocks and could hardly believe his eyes when he saw how young my baby was. The man looked at me like he thought I had lost my mind, and didn't hesitate to tell me that he would gladly take me and my fine, young baby home if I would only tell him where I lived. But to let me out on the edge of the highway to thumb a ride! "It's unthinkable!" he said.

Unthinkable, perhaps, but not to one who was forced to such a choice. My own mother had said she could never love a convict's child. How could anyone keep from loving an innocent baby?"

That's how the chain of events began. My heart would not listen to reason. I hated my own mother and I hated society. I hated my mother because she had said my child would be better off if it were born dead. I hated society because the man I loved had been given an unjust sentence. I must free him. I must follow him to prison . . .

Roy remained engrossed in his own thoughts as my own sinful past flashed back as if on a screen. I hated reliving it, but . . .

I was back at the edge of the highway. Texas is a big state, a very big state when you're afoot and broke. Let it suffice to say that my trip began in West Texas on Thursday, November 22, and by Saturday I had covered over 500 miles and was in Huntsville waiting for the prison gates to open Sunday afternoon.

If there is any place on earth with a harder heart for a prisoner's wife than a prison town, I never found it. Huntsville was fairly small and everyone seemed instinctively to know why new women were always showing up on Saturdays and Sundays.

While enroute to Huntsville I managed to spend Thursday night in a depot, pretending to wait for a train. Friday night I spent in a bus depot, but it was different in Huntsville. I went to the union depot but was promptly informed that there were no trains out that night. I sneaked into the bus station, was looked at skeptically, then informed that after 11:20, when the last bus pulled out, the station would close for the night . . .

Roy now seemed in his own element. My thoughts continued reliving this horrible trip with my two-week-old baby . . .

Sleeping on a bench in a depot hadn't been exactly restful, especially with Carolyn whimpering of hunger and in constant need of dry diapers. My art of drying diapers in a depot wasn't easy and I would scarcely recommend it now. The only lines I had were the partitions enclosing commodes. These had to be dusted and the jar from opening and closing was a constant hazard.

Feeling greatly in need of a good night's sleep for myself and my little Carolyn, I looked the downtown area over as I stepped into the chill dark outside the bus station. My baby was only seventeen days old and the trip had been a hard one. I had to find a bed. About a block away was a big, white colonial looking place with a hotel sign hung out. I had heard of people making beds and scrubbing floors for a place to sleep, so I decided to ask for a room. I will never forget how small and scared I felt as I walked up to that desk.

No one was there, just a sign reading "Push the Button." I pushed and a middle aged woman with a frost bitten face cracked open a door and demanded to know what I wanted without even bothering to enter the lobby. Surely a child could have detected the sincerity of my voice as I asked to work for a night's lodging, but it didn't faze her.

"We don't keep that kind of girls here," she barked at me and slammed the door in my face before I had a chance to say more. Then she again opened the door a crack and yelled, "All you women with men here at the prison are just alike. I can spot one of you a mile off."

"What kind of girl?" I wondered. Tears coursed my cheeks as I left the hotel. I had never spent but one night in a hotel in my whole life. That was the night Roy and I were married, only fourteen months before this happened, but it seemed like centuries now that I was so soon to die.

I wanted to forget it before I died, but I kept remembering. Remembering a nineteen-year-old mother who was but a bewildered child on that night. A child who felt like a yellow pup whipped for no apparent reason.

All I wanted to do was find a place to hide, a place to bury my empty and aching heart until tomorrow when I could see my husband. Surely this would make things right. I stumbled along, not realizing where I was going. I was just trying to get away from it all. Several times I had to put the battered suitcase down to shift Carolyn who slept peacefully, cradled in one arm. She was so sweet, such a little darling.

The load was getting too much for me when I saw what looked like a college, and across from it there was a park. Later I found out they were Sam Houston State College and park. I crossed the street, actually the highway to Houston, to a stand of tall pines. The only pines I had ever seen in West Texas were very small ones at Christmas. Trees were wonderful and I loved them. A tree is always a friend in West Texas, but there you have to plant and nurture them. These were so real, so tall, and there were so many of them that I seemed to be in a very strange world. I pushed my way into the pines to where the moon scarcely peeked through the branches and sank at a bench. Soon I realized I was cold and hungry. I got up and pushed deeper into the park, away from the highway.

I was frightened, afraid of the deep darkness underneath the pines, but I kept telling myself that just this one night and then I would be able to see the one I loved. He could tell me the way. Nothing else mattered but seeing him.

I came to a long table which must have been placed there for picnickers. The branches of the big pine it was under drooped so low that they formed a sort of curtain around it. I had found my bed, a concrete slab. I sat the suitcase on the bench beside the table and one by one I took out every diaper, except one, and wrapped it around Carolyn, like a cocoon. The last one I tied on my own head. I took out my only change of clothing, a suit which I hoped would look presentable tomorrow, held it and shivered a moment, then pulled it on over my much-too-lived-in skirt and blouse.

I took off my shoes and tried to wrap my feet and legs in the short coat I had brought along. Late November in East Texas is warm, but it can get mighty cool for sleeping out at night. I wished for a pillow, the stone was so hard, but I had little energy for wishful thinking. The only other thing I remember was giving Carolyn credit for being an optimist, for how else could she have gotten any satisfaction from tugging at an empty breast as she lay cuddled in my arms. I was so glad she was too young to remember.

I was cold and numb when I awakened. It was still gray-dark. A heavy dew had fallen and my hair felt damp through the diaper I had tied around my head. My hunger became acute, and among other daylight sounds I heard the rattle of bottles. On the other side of the park I saw a white truck pull up and stop in front of a huge, rich looking brick house. I stepped from beneath the sheltering pine. When the truck pulled away I saw what looked like several bottles of milk showing white from the shadows on a side porch. I had never stolen, but hunger does something to a person's conscience. You begin compromising with it, at least I did, asking how people living in such a fine home would miss so small a thing as a bottle of milk. How much it would mean to my baby and me. Why, they would even want us to have it if they only knew. I must forget it.

I unwound the wettest diapers from Carolyn, hung them over the back of the bench to dry and told myself everything would be O.K., but my mind was still on those milk bottles across the street. Before I knew what I was doing I found myself edging toward that house, baby in arm. It was not yet good daylight. I slipped across the street, stepped quietly up to the porch, slipped one bottle between Carolyn's body and mine, then pushed another under my coat and pressed it to my body with my free arm.

I must have squeezed Carolyn a little too tightly, for she let out a little cry and my heart stood still. I pressed her closer to my breast to try to stifle any sound and dashed across the street to the shadow of the pines. No light flashed on in the house, so I relaxed a little . . .

Yes, I thought as I lay on the bed in the tourist court now with a gun pointed in my direction, another commandment I had broken, "Thou shalt not steal." I wanted to forget, but couldn't.

Never had milk tasted so good. I gulped down the first quart. I wanted to share it with Carolyn, but she was so tiny. This was her birthday. "Just wait a little bit," I consoled as she whimpered. "Mommy will have a surprise for you."

My courage rose with the sun. I fancied my baby smiled at me as she nursed, but it didn't ease my conscience too much.

When she had finished I took a wash cloth from the practically empty suitcase and wet it at a nearby hydrant. I held it close to my heart until I felt it was warm enough for her bath. She must be pretty and clean to see her father. Church bells rang. It was the Sabbath. I said a little prayer in my own heart, asking forgiveness for stealing the milk and for a way to gain Roy's freedom. Perhaps the prayer was a sacrilege, for I drank the rest of the stolen milk. I almost popped, but I just couldn't waste it.

I was first one in line at the prison for a pass. I shall never forget how those dull, gray walls looked as I approached the prison for the first time. There were guards stationed in little guard houses atop the wall every few hundred feet with mounted machine guns. A cold shiver hit my spine. It was the most foreboding place I had ever seen.

What is a visit like inside prison walls? I hope you never know. Enroute to the prison there had been a million things I wanted to talk to my husband about, but now that I was there we just sat staring through the cage at each other, hardly able to speak at all.

Finally, when we did come out of it, Roy had a plan. I must go to Austin, to the Board of Pardons, explain the situation and see if I couldn't get a parole. The pardon could come later. Surely, under the circumstances, a man would be given a parole to earn a living for his wife and baby. When they were shown what a farce his trial had been with a state-appointed lawyer who was so intoxicated he was worse than no defense at all, when they found out he had been given the limit on a first offense, surely he would at least be granted another trial.

How could I go to Austin without money? Roy had it planned. I was to go to a hotel, tell them that part of my luggage got set off the bus in the wrong town and I would have to wait for it to come through. This way I would not have to pay my hotel bill until my luggage arrived and I checked out. Without luggage I could walk out of the hotel whenever I got ready without paying my bill. It scared me to even think of such a daring plan, but I said I'd try. I had to find a place to stay, and I couldn't forget what happened when I tried to earn a night's lodging honestly. I wasn't sure whether my eyes were watering and my nose was sniffley because I was with Roy or because I had caught a cold.

Our hour to visit was up before I had time to think. Then I was walking out the highway again with Carolyn in one arm and the suitcase in the other. At least I didn't have so far to go this time, just about 150 miles. With luck I might catch a ride all the way and make it before midnight. It was around three in afternoon. I didn't know what I'd do if I got caught out on the highway after dark, and I certainly didn't feel like spending another night in a park or depot.

Roy babbled a little to himself and let the pistol lay across his knees. We each seemed in our own world of thought.

Some Call Them Whores

As I lay on the bed with the pistol still aimed in my direction I thought of the most shameful sin of my life. If Roy had asked me then if I was ready for him to pull the trigger, I think I would have said, "shoot," but he was still talking to himself and I was reliving the chapter of my life I would like most of all to be able to forget. Neither one of us seemed to disturb the other's reverie.

I was in Austin before ten o'clock that night. The fellow who gave me a ride said he was going by the Capitol building. I shall never forget how that big, gold dome gleamed in the floodlights that made it the most beautiful building in all the world to me. A couple of blocks from the Capitol I saw a cheap looking hotel and asked the man to let me out. He had been very nice all the way, even asked me if I needed money. I refused.

I don't think the hotel clerk believed my little story, I was a poor liar, but he called the Negro porter to take me to a room. It was barren, not too clean and very small, but it did have a bed with white sheets and any kind of bed was a luxury to me. The only window in the room seemed to hang over a streetcar line and the cars waked me up before dawn. I had never slept near a streetcar line before, in fact, I had never even ridden one.

Everything was strange to me except my hunger. Carolyn was still asleep as I gathered her into my arms, crept down the stairs and through the empty lobby. I walked toward the nearest residential section, found what I was looking for, slipped a couple of milk bottles under Carolyn's blanket and headed back to the hotel. Stealing was easier this time. Luckily the lobby was still empty.

After I had drunk my breakfast I started washing clothes. What luxury! Hot water and soap at the wash bowl. The bath was down the hall, but it was the first real all-over bath I had had in almost four days and it was even more wonderful than the bed.

Carolyn and I were waiting when the Board of Pardons opened. We waited . . . and waited. There were many waiting. A secretary took my name, but I had no appointment so I had to wait my turn. Jim Ferguson, or rather Ma Ferguson, was governor of our state and many sought pardons. Jim had been impeached during his term as governor, one of the allegations was the selling of prison pardons, but his wife, Miriam, had run and was elected.

As the day wore on Carolyn grew restless. There was a girl sitting across from me in the office whom I thought I had seen at the prison. She grinned and winked at me and I was sure. She had been there during visiting hour the day before. She didn't seem to have an appointment either, but she wore such fine clothes that I was sure she must be from a rich family and would have no trouble at all.

Neither of us got in the Board of Pardons that day. As we left the office at closing time she offered to help me carry the baby.

"What's your old man in for?" she asked as we walked down the long corridor.

I told her and finally worked up enough nerve to ask if it was her husband or brother she was visiting at Huntsville and what he was in for.

''My old man,'' she replied, ''he's in for paper hanging.''

''Paper hanging!'' I repeated with astonishment. Why would they put your husband in prison for hanging paper?''

She laughed and patted me on the back. ''You got a long way to go, kitten,'' was her only explanation. ''Where you stayin'?''

I told her and she gave a little whistle of surprise as she asked, ''What room?''

This seemed even more of a surprise, because I was in the room next to hers. This gave me a little feeling of elation, but she did not look pleased at all. Maybe she thought I would let the baby cry.

''I guess I'll be seeing you tomorrow at the Board of Pardons,'' I suggested as we reached the hotel.

''Oh, I don't know,'' she remarked casually. ''A person just can't sit and wait. Anyway, I can tell my old man I tried. Unless you got money, kid, you're just fluffin' your duff.''

As we walked through the lobby the Negro porter approached us and addressed my companion, ''There you is, Miss Betty. Where you all been so long? I'se been lookin' all ober for you. They'se a man here been gettin' powerful impatient . . .''

''Break it off, Apple Blossom,'' Betty retorted. ''How come this girl is given a room in the wing on second? I thought that was reserved.''

''Yessum, but yo see, I wasn't for sho . . .''

''Wasn't for sure, you simpleton, now get her room changed, but quick,'' Betty commanded.

I blushed in shame. I thought I had found a friend, but now I was sure she thought Carolyn would bother her, or was she afraid I would hang around and embarrass her? I knew my clothes were quite modest, but I didn't think they looked that bad.

I was ready and anxious to move when Apple Blossom knocked at the door a few moments later, but he said there wasn't another room available and that I might as well stay in the same room another night since I would probably be leaving early in the morning when my baggage arrived, anyway.

What a fool I was! If I had only had sense enough to understand Betty's real meaning I would never have stopped until I reached home. But I didn't know. I didn't want to think of the dreadful sin that followed. Why must I think of such dreadful things in the face of death. The pearl I threw away for the man who was now ready to take my life. I had never told him of the sacrifice. Why should I tell him now? He was too doped to understand. better to die with the secret in my breast. I was ready to die.

I recalled an old quotation, "Every man kills the thing he loves." Did Roy really love me? The Bible seemed easier to understand.

I thought again of the Bible, "Cast not your pearls before swine, lest they turn and rend you."

Those words set down over nineteen hundred years ago, described my situation perfectly. But it was too late before I realized their meaning. I had nothing to live for.

I laid the Bible aside and turned to tell Roy I was ready, but Roy was no longer looking at me. I could tell from that far-away look in his eyes what he was thinking. He was reliving that prison break he had already relived a thousand times. I was reliving my sin.

The Night I Bartered Myself

Do all persons relive their sins before they die? Again I was in that hotel room in Austin. Another day I had spent in the Capitol building, a day of misery. I had coughed so much and Carolyn had fretted so constantly that I think the receptionist finally gave me an appointment for the next morning at ten to see the Board of Pardons to get rid of me. Betty was not among those waiting and I was glad because Carolyn had been so fretful. Apple Blossom had seen me come through the lobby and I was sure it was he who was knocking at my door. It was that same slow, quiet knock I had heard on Betty's door several times the night before.

I opened my door just a crack. "I jes come to see if you all wanted me to check on yo' luggage?" Apple Blossom greeted me with a grin.

"I've already checked and it isn't there," I said, perhaps with too much fear in my voice.

"Yessum, I knows. But don't you all worry too much. I done fixed it up wid the man at th' desk. I done tole him you all had me check on it and it would be here in the morning for sho."

I did not understand his sudden generosity in defending me but felt it was backed with sinister meaning when he continued:

''Isn't you all jes a little lonesome all by you'self? I'm not tryin' to get personal, but if . . .''

I slammed the door closed in no uncertain terms.

Evidently Betty was coming down the hallway because I heard her pounce upon Apple Blossom before I got back to my bed.

''If you knock on that girl's door one more time,'' I heard her saying, ''There won't be a hair left on that wooly noggin' of yours. Now why wasn't her room changed?''

I didn't hear the rest because I heard Betty's door close. They spoke in subdued tones. In just a moment I heard the door open again and I knew Apple Blossom was leaving.

I couldn't help but wonder why Betty left her room so often. At first I thought it must have been telephone calls, but I didn't hear the telephone ring. She couldn't eat that often. Why did Apple Blossom always speak to her quietly before she left? I was too tired to reason. Another fit of coughing sapped my strength and I slept restlessly.

I don't know how long I slept but it was dark in the room when I heard a knock at my door. I listened, then it sounded again. It was that same slow, low knock I had heard on Betty's door several times. I didn't move. Then it sounded again. Maybe I could pretend to be asleep.

Then Apple Blossom's voice sounded through the door as he said:

''I been hearin' yo' baby fret. I been wonderin' 'bout gettin' somethin' for yo' cough.''

He sounded sincere and I opened the door. ''Don't you all go worrin' about th' money. You can give it to me when yo' feels better. I hopes you'll forgive me for gettin' a little confidential, but there's a man done been seein' you come through the lobby that sho done took a powerful likin' to you all. You know, I hesitates to tell yo' all this, little mother, but th' nice man gone give me a good tip to do it and you all knows how hard money comes these days. Forgive me fo' askin', but ain't you all jes a little bit lonesome. The man done got more money than he know what to do wid and he powerful generous.''

I sprang to the door and closed it in Apple Blossom's face again. Why should a man whom I didn't know want to give me money? Suddenly the soft knocks I had heard on Betty's door made sense. I had read of women who took money from men for favors, but I had never seen one before that I knew of. Betty didn't look like I expected that kind of woman to look, I was thinking as I drifted back off to sleep.

It was hours later when that fatal knock came. I jumped up thinking it must be morning, but it was still dark.

''Pardon me, Miss, but I wants to speak to you all for jes a minute,'' Apple Blossom's voice came again through the door. I was wonderin, Miss Mary, ifen yo' would talk jes one minute?'' I was wondering how he learned my name when he continued, ''They'se a man here want's to see you.''

''I don't know anyone here and I don't want to see anyone,'' I replied through the door.

''Yessum, but this man is different,'' he continued in a very confidential tone. ''Open the door jes a crack and I'll tell you all, he's from the Board of Pardons.''

This opened my door and the porter told me that the man was a member of the board and wanted to see me before I went back tomorrow. I didn't know how Apple Blossom knew where I had been going or how the man knew I was staying here. On second thought, I had left my address at the desk, maybe he had seen me, but why was he looking for me. Deep within me there was a warning, but how could it hurt just to find out what he wanted? Perhaps he had seen me sitting and waiting for the past two days and really did want to help. Was it possible?

''He might be able to help you all a powerful lot,'' Apple Blossom said as if reading my thoughts. ''He said you couldn't talk about such things in the lobby in front where anybody could hear, so he's waitin' in room 316.''

''Tell him I'll be right up,'' I said bravely as Apple Blossom left with a big, white grin.

I looked at my baby, asleep, blessed little darling. Why should I disturb her? I would only be gone a minute. She was too small to roll off the bed. Her rest seemed peaceful now and there was no fire in the room. Trying to justify myself, I left her for the first time in her short life.

The door was ajar when I reached 316. I did not recognize the man inside, but I had paid little attention to the men I had seen go in and out at the Board of Pardons. He was dressed in a dark suit, middle aged, stout, and I fancied he looked the part. He handed me his card. It was from the Board of Pardons.

''I've come to help you,'' he said as he indicated a chair. ''Noticed you in the office. A girl like you doesn't stand much chance without a pull. Suppose you tell me all about it so I will have the case cut and dried when you get in.''

I told my story and he seemed very sympathetic. Then he asked me about money, if I had it, as he edged closer and closer to me. He patted my hand in a fatherly manner.

''You know,'' he remarked thoughtfully, ''it takes lots of money to handle these things, but it could be managed. You really love that man of yours, don't you? Just how much would it be worth to you to have him back? You'd give the world if you had it, right now, wouldn't you.''

I quickly replied that I would as I clutched his card. ''I know you probably don't have the money right now,'' he remarked, ''but maybe we could work it out.''

''Do you really think so? I asked with great hope. ''It would not take too long, if my husband was out to help me. Tell me how it could be done. But first I've got to run and see if my baby is still asleep.''

''Take your time,'' he smiled.

When I returned he seemed different. He came very near, too near, just to talk, so I just asked him to tell me how we could help Roy. If some kind of deal would let him wait for the money.

''You're a beautiful young mother,'' he said. ''A man is lucky to have a wife like you waiting for him. I can help you.''

''But how? I asked as he drew me uncomfortably close. I wanted to run. I wanted to slap his face, but I listened.

''It's going to be a long, hard row without anyone helping you,'' he said, ''and why shouldn't I help you. Why, I could get a parole for him so easy. He wasn't even given a dog's chance.

I tried to pull away from him but he drew me closer. and said, ''Of course it would take money, but you've got something that's worth more than money to me.''

His nearness nauseated me and all the world seemed in confusion. I was so alone. Perhaps Betty was right. You did have to have an ace in the hole. Everything seemed to be swimming around me and I pretended I didn't feel that ugly kiss.

''Your husband will be out in less than a week,'' he consoled. ''I knew you were a smart girl. No one will ever know. I'll have everything ready when you get to the office tomorrow. Just give them the card I gave you and ask for me. I'll take care of all investigation expenses. No one will ever be the wiser.''

I felt a clutching hand slide toward my breast and a warm kiss on my neck as reality faded. Suddenly it seemed I was smothered by an octopus, a slick, slimey octopus that pinned me down and started consuming me, at the breast.

When I came to I was again in my own room. I don't know how I got there. Carolyn was on the bed beside me. The light was on. I was clutching a card in my hand so tightly that it was all wadded. As I looked at it it suddenly seemed to change to blood. I dropped it with a scream.

I was hot, hot and sticky all over. I wasn't sure what had happened but suddenly I felt unclean, unfit to lie beside my daughter. I got to my feet, but fell against the wall. I tried again and did stay on my feet. I staggered down the hall to the bathroom. With all my scrubbing I still felt dirty. My sobs were uncontrollable as I returned to the room.

I fell across the bed. Finally my sobs gave away to a steady flow of tears. I was a traitor. I had been a fool. Not even my husband would love me now. I had thought we could pay for the man's service with money when Roy got out. I had never passed out before. It was all a dream, a terrible dream. Everything would be all right in the morning. This couldn't be real. If tomorrow would only come. Tomorrow! Tomorrow! Tomorrow!

The sun was bright when I awakened. I ran to the window and looked at the clock on the jewelry store sign across the street. It was 9:29. Within 31 minutes I was due at the Parole Board I thought of the night before. It had been a horrible nightmare. Suddenly my eyes caught the crumpled card on the floor beside the bed. It was true! Tears of rage came to my eyes, but this was no time for crying.

Hurriedly I dressed myself in the only change of clothing I had and turned to Carolyn. I hated to waken her but this was what we had been waiting for. Quickly I sponged her off, promising her a good bath when we got back.

I was breathless when I arrived at the office, but I need not have hurried. When my appointment was thirty minutes overdue I timidly handed the card I had so shamefully acquired the night before to the receptionist.

Within a few minutes I was told that the board could see me. I didn't know how I could face the man who gave me the card, but I had to have my husband back. Maybe the card had gotten me in. My face was hot and I felt as if every man in the room was looking straight through me.

I sank into the offered chair. An elderly man with white hair looked at me curiously and asked,

"Who gave you this card, young lady?"

I looked about the room but none of the faces that swam before me resembled the face of the man who had given me the card the night before.

"I . . . I don't see him," I said.

"There must be some mistake," the elderly gentleman said sympathetically, "you have my card but I am sure I have never seen you before. You look pale. Do you feel well?"

I said I was all right and he explained, "I don't know how you came by my card, but so long as you have gone to the trouble of getting here we may as well see what we can do for you. Better let me hold that baby while you tell us your problem.

I told my story and they all listened.

''How long has your husband been in the prison?'' one of the board members asked.

''This is the tenth day,'' I answered feebly.

''Ah, you should have been told,'' the white haired man said with real sympathy. ''We never consider a case of this kind for parole until at least six months of the sentence has been served. Come back to see us then. You'd better get this baby home,'' he said as he handed me Carolyn. ''She's too young to drag around.''

Let Me Die, God, Let Me Die!

Just like that I was dismissed from the room. All my air castles came tumbling down. Tricked! Rooked! How could anyone pull such a dirty trick on me? I guess it was easy. Betty was right when she said I had a lot to learn.

But now I had no desire to learn. My baby was crying. My body felt like a ball of fire. I was sure I was running a high fever, but I couldn't tell whether Carolyn was hungry or sick or both. I made my way back to the hotel and the manager eyed me keenly as I went up the stairs. I felt sure he knew I couldn't pay my bill. I would be kicked out today.

I pushed my way into the room and fell across the bed. Once I had a home, a modest one but a good one. My family had tried to tell me. My mother had almost driven herself insane worrying over me. I had ruined her life and the family name. How could I bring disgrace to the ones who loved me?

Once when I was a baby I had been very, very ill. The doctor said I didn't have a chance. My mother said she prayed to God to let me live. She had asked that her will and not God's will be done. This was her punishment, I could hear her saying over and over again. She could never love the baby of a convict who had brought disgrace to the family.

No past, no future, no home. Not even my husband would love me now. How could I have been such a fool? My life was a mistake, all a mistake. Where could I go if I left the hotel? I don't think I could have carried Carolyn and the battered suitcase a block, even if I could get out of the hotel with them. My mother was right. I should have died when I was a baby.

Carolyn was crying. I thought I heard the porter knocking at the door. Maybe some other man wanted to see me. I had seen one man. He could lie and steal that which meant more than life itself, yet he was on the outside. He would never be punished, yet my husband must remain in prison for a smaller crime. Nothing in the whole world was fair. Why should my baby be crying of hunger? My husband was paying the price now, but she still cried of hunger. What difference whether she was born or unborn? Perhaps my mother was right.

How much should we suffer? My lungs burned and I ached all over when I coughed. I was no longer hungry. Carolyn wouldn't stop crying. I could not remember when I had eaten. Was my child to suffer like I had? God forbid! There was no one in the world to love her, my sweet innocent baby. My own mother had said she wished she had been born dead. Perhaps she would be better off dead. She would never have to face the things I had to face. I would not leave her in a world where she was not wanted. Babies went to heaven, of this I was sure.

"Just a minute, darling, just a minute," I tried to console her. It won't hurt long now. Mommie wants to go with you. Help mommie pray."

I heard knocking on the door. They wouldn't put us out. No one could. The door was locked.

"Just a minute, darling, just a minute," I consoled Carolyn "Mommie's got to turn on the gas. We're going to make a wonderful journey. We won't be sick or hungry any more. Hold tight to mommie now. Don't let me go! I've got to go with you! Mommie's been awfully bad. Please, God, let me go with my baby. She's so small!"

Carolyn stopped crying and we seemed to be floating up

toward the ceiling. I was mad at the ceiling for holding us down. I heard bells . . . beautiful bells. The ceiling opened and we were floating high in the clouds, beautiful clouds, soft and silver and dazzling light . . .

I came to in a hospital. Betty was sitting beside my bed. She smiled and rang for the nurse.

"My baby! Where's my baby! I cried in alarm.

"Wait," Betty said in a promising manner. "I'll ask the nurse to bring her to you."

Betty returned with Carolyn and a nurse. The nurse laid my darling in one of my arms and put a shot in the other. I drifted back to sleep.

When I came to again Carolyn was crying.

"This young lady resents being starved to death," the nurse smiled at me.

I was surprised that I had milk for her.

"We've been feeding you glucose through the veins," replied the nurse in way of explanation. "You've been a mighty sick girl. Delirious when your sister got you to the hospital. You don't get over that high a fever and pneumonia in a day."

Betty winked at me without saying a word.

I must have looked puzzled.

"You need all the rest you can get," the nurse said.

"I'll make my visit short," Betty said, reading the nurse's mind. "But I would like to be with her for just a few minutes since she has come to."

As the nurse left the room Betty put her finger to her lip. "Now let me explain," she began. "I told them I was your sister to get you into the hospital. You were out of your head with a fever. I could hear you raving. We had to break in the door."

"But the gas . . . ?" I whispered.

"All in your mind," Betty assured. "Get some rest and keep your mouth shut, Sis."

With that she was gone. Why would she go to the trouble to say I was her sister?

I looked at Carolyn safely cradled in my arm, thanked God and drifted back to sleep. When I waked up again it was dark. I rang for the nurse. I must have been dreaming. My baby was gone and I had to be sure.

When Carolyn was brought back to me and I was sure I had not been dreaming I asked what day it was.

''Two minutes from now it'll be Sunday.'' The nurse replied as she looked at her watch, ''and I'll be off duty.''

''But what day of the month?'' I persisted.

''Today is December 1st,'' the nurse replied as she left the room.

''Then I must have been in the hospital since Wednesday,'' I said to myself. ''Sunday, December 1st. Why this is our baby's third birthday! She's three weeks old today. I gave her a little squeeze and remember wondering if Roy would be looking for me at the prison.

The next morning Betty was beside me asking, ''Are you ready to go home, Kitten?''

When I did get to her room it was December 5th and Christmas was already waiting for us. There was a little tree with all the trimmings and lovely presents for Carolyn and myself.

''Just like having a family of my own,'' Betty answered my unasked question. ''I had a baby once, illegitimate, and they took her from me. This makes me feel like I am having Christmas for her. Take a lesson from me, Mary, you got something to live for. I haven't. Don't ever be like me. You're going home.''

Roy fumbled with the pistol and I bounced back to reality. This time there would be no ''Betty'' to rescue me. Never underestimate the heart of a whore, not this one, anyway.

I'll never forget the day Betty went with me to the prison. It was just before Christmas. Betty had a way of finding out and doing things. She wouldn't believe for a minute that my family wouldn't forgive me, even my mother.

I got to visit Roy Gregg and display our precious daughter. This, to the best of my knowledge, was the last time he ever saw her.

My father was waiting for me, to take me home. This was prearranged by Betty. My mother was contrite and begged forgiveness. She loved Carolyn and took care of her while I went to college. College was my sister's idea. There was no end to her ambition for any of our family. She believed in dignity and culture. She believed in me. Together my sister and my mother helped me. My mother tried so hard to compensate for her cruel tongue that I forgave her a thousand times over . . .

But now I was in trouble again. All their work was for nothing. If I hadn't been such an idealist, or such a fool, a gun wouldn't be pointed at me now. I never had sense enough or good judgment enough to know when to stop fighting. My intentions were always good, but I had always tried to build my skyscrapers without foundation. Again I was reading the Bible.

"And everyone who heareth these words of mine, and doeth them not, shall be likened unto a foolish man, which built his house upon sand:

And the rain descended, and the floods came, and the winds blew and beat upon the house; and it fell; and great was the fall of it."

That certainly summed up my situation. I had thrown away everything holy and built my house upon a false foundation. I half closed the Bible and as I did so I saw the revolver slowly raised.

"Read enough?" Roy asked, "Or have you changed your mind?"

Whatsoever You Ask in Prayer

As I dropped the Bible beside me on the bed it fell open and my eyes were drawn to a strange passage:

"Fear not them which kill the body, but are not able to kill the soul; but rather fear him which is able to destroy both soul and body in hell."

"I'd like to think it over a little longer," I said as Roy again lowered the pistol.

"I thought you would see it my way," he gloated. "It's not easy to say no in the face of a gun. Take all the time you want. Think it over good. I learned a lot in prison, Baby. I'd rather see you wearin' rocks than have them shoveled into your face, six foot under."

In celebration of his supposedly gained victory, Roy again fumbled for the needle. I looked toward the windows. Light filtered around the edges of the drawn blinds. Our vigil with death had lasted all night.

"Whatsoever you ask in prayer," I was reading. Then I began praying, praying like I had never prayed before. Praying for a chance to be a real Christian mother to the little girl who needed me. Praying for a chance to build upon a rock.

I don't know how long I prayed for forgiveness and a chance to live for my daughter, but when I looked at Roy his eyes were glazed and unseeing. Then the gun slipped from his fingers and landed on the floor with a metalic thud. Roy seemed beyond hearing.

The chair which Roy had tilted against the door teetered on one leg for an instant, as his body slumped, then toppled over, carrying Roy with it. This never fazed him. He lay sprawled on the floor, limp. Removing the key from his pocket, I opened the door and ran into the budding light of day.

One Day in Heaven, Almost

I was running . . . running . . . running. Now I was not only running from the law, I was running from Roy, too. The law and the lawless. I was not sure which I feared more. If the law caught me, I would be held for harboring a fugitive, tried for my part in the prison break. But if Roy found me, he might kill me, no questions asked. He was a desperate man, a sick man . . . I knew that.

There are only two sides. I belonged to neither. I knew Roy couldn't live without me. Turning him in to the law would have been the last thing I would have thought of then; but now I can see it would have been doing him a great favor, saved him time, prison time. But how could I have turned to the law, even if I had wanted to, to protect my own life?

My run slowed to a walk. People were appearing on the street . . . going to work. Inadvertently I walked to the little park across the street from where I lived when Roy escaped from prison. I had to think. I sank on a bench.

Oh, how I ached to get back to my daughter. It had been

an eternity since I had heard her voice and felt her arms around about my neck. But could I go? Roy might follow.

Crisp on the morning air, church bells chimed. "Joy to the World, The Lord Is Come. A Christmas carol I loved, but there was no joy within me.

Christmas! Would my darling have to spend it without her mother? I thought of her fifth birthday, the one I spent on the desert thinking I would never see her again. There had been no present, no word from me.

How long could a child love a mother, one so young as she, when that mother had disappeared from the face of the earth? perhaps she had forgotten me already. Maybe my mother had tried to let her forget me. There was nothing her little heart could understand about my life.

The ache, the longing, the yearning were unbearable. I knew that going to see her was the wrong thing to do, but nothing short of death could stop me now. There was nothing in the world except my longing for her.

Tears streamed down my face as I got up from the little bench and walked down the familiar street toward the bus station. What if someone who knew me saw me now? What if Roy came to quicker than I thought. It was a chance I would have to take.

I called the bus station. I was lucky. In only a few minutes I could catch one for home and my darling . . . but I didn't dare just go in the station and wait. I window shopped . . . for a Christmas present for Carolyn. I hesitated in front of a bookstore window, thinking how she had always loved poetry. I went in. I found a wonderful book of illustrated poems. There were some of her favorites in it. I bought it. I would have given her the whole world if I could have bought it with my heart; but the few cents I had left were slightly inadequate as a down payment.

I saw no sign of Roy when I ventured back to the bus station. He would probably be knocked out for hours, I hoped, as I climbed aboard. I thumbed through the little book in my hands, but my mind was reading only the past . . . the last time I had heard my daughter's voice. "Mommie, Mommie, I have a new doll. When are you coming home, Huh? Can I have a birthday party, please Mommie?''

When at last I was in my own home town again, my heart pounded messages like a jungle drum. Outside my parent's house, it seemed to stop. I was afraid to go in.

Then I saw Carolyn through the window, putting tinsel on the tree. Looking out the window, suddenly, she saw me. She screamed, ''Mommie! Mommie! Mommie!'' and raced for the door.

She looked like a Christmas angel as she flew toward me with outstretched arms, her long, golden curls stretching behind her.

I crushed her to me and she kept crying, ''Mommie . . . Mommie.''

Then she broke from me suddenly and raced for the kitchen.

''Grandma! Grandma! I told you my Mommie would come for Christmas!''

My mother walked into the hall with a plate of goodies in her hand. At sight of me she dropped the plate. ''Oh, for the faith of a child,'' she breathed.

I whispered, ''Mother, maybe I shouldn't be here . . . but I had to come . . .''

Mother went on as if she hadn't heard me. ''When I thought you were dead, Carolyn kept saying over and over you'd be sure to come for Christmas because you missed her birthday party. We wouldn't believe her and tired to discourage her in the thought.''

My father came in then. ''I've left Roy for good,'' I said, answering his silent question. ''Once he had the makings of a good man in him, but prison ruined him. He's not the same man I married.''

''Get some food on the table, Mama,'' was my Father's only reply.

I must have looked pretty shabby, as well as hungry, for my mother replied, ''The clothes you left are still in your closet. I'll have food on the table by the time you get bathed and changed. Looks like the kind of life you chose wasn't so glamorous after all. I've always told you . . .''

''Let's not talk about it, Mama, let's just be thankful she's home, alive. There's only one thing I want to know,'' Father said as he turned to me. ''Where's Roy. Will he follow you and cause trouble?''

How could I tell him? If I told my family Roy was only fifty miles away and on my trail? Why should I ruin Christmas? I had so dreamed of this day of happiness. Surely he would be afraid to come to my father's home. Why should they be looking for us . . . any more than they had been since our trail grew cold, unless . . . ?

''I've left him for good,'' was my truthful reply. ''I hope I never see him again.''

''I want to take a bath with my Mommie,'' Carolyn cut in, ''I want to get dressed pretty for Santa, too. Did you know Santa is coming tomorrow, Mommie, did you?''

''Yes, Darling, yes,'' were the only words I could manage. Lifting her from the floor drained every ounce of strength from me.

''Santa is coming tomorrow, Santa is coming tomorrow'' . . . she chimed over and over as I drew our bath. Somehow in my muddled brain they always came out ''Roy is coming tomorrow, Roy is coming tomorrow.''

It was time for the evening meal before our baths were finished. I was reluctant in giving up our private session for I had had only half my fill of kisses.

When the evening meal was finished my father turned on the radio as the women folk headed for the dish pan. Christmas carols peeled from the living room, ''Peace on Earth, Good Will toward Men.''

This is what home should be, I thought as Carolyn pulled up a stool to stand on and told me she was her grandmother's little helper when it came to drying dishes.

''We interrupt this program to bring a flash from the news room,'' a voice burst suddenly, ''A laughing bandit has just held up a filling station on Sycamore Street in Abilene. An undetermined amount of cash has been taken. Stay tuned for details.''

I know I must have turned pale; but mother didn't seem to catch the announcement.

"A laughing bandit," the flash had said, and in Abilene. That one adjective, "laughing," struck fear into my heart. Roy had always laughed and joked when he had robbed, even the first time.

"In Abilene." Those words, too, struck home. He had had time enough to come out from under the influence of the heroin and probably needed more . . . Or was he getting money to come after me?

Carolyn had finished drying the dishes and was again in the living room, dreaming around the Christmas tree. Father had turned off the radio; but something in his face told me he knew.

"Didn't we use to have the tree on Christmas Eve?" I asked. I wasn't sure whether I was speaking for myself or Carolyn. The childish yearning in her eyes was a factor, I'm sure, yet my fear of tomorrow was overpowering.

"Yes," Mother answered, "but I thought we'd wait until the other children come in tomorrow with the rest of the grandchildren. I love to watch them open the presents."

"Please, Grandmother, couldn't I just open one little package tonight," Carolyn begged.

"Well, maybe," grandmother hesitated.

"Oh, goody!" Carolyn cried for joy, for she knew her grandmother's weakness. "I did want to open the big one Santa brought me most of all; but now I want to open the one from my very own mother."

With squeals of delight she extracted the Nursery Rhymes from the wrapping. "Oh, goody, goody. Read to me, Mommie, read to me."

"But we haven't had a chance to talk," my mother admonished. "I spend half my time reading to you. Couldn't you let it go until tomorrow? I want to talk with your mother."

"Let's sing," my father suggested . . . in an effort to change the subject. "Come to the organ, Mother. This is Christmas Eve."

The organ had always meant so much to my daddy. He wasn't willing to see it go when pianos became the fad. He liked the organ so much more. Since I was Carolyn's age I remembered the family gathering around the organ at night. Sometimes we put on little programs.

When I was Carolyn's age we lived in the hills of north Georgia, where there was no entertainment except what came through the church. The organ had come with us to Texas during the oil boom . . . as well as the habit of gathering about the organ in the evening.

We sang all the Christmas carols we knew. Daddy told Carolyn a story about the first Christmas tree he ever cut, when he was very young. Mother didn't feel like reciting poetry, so her granddaughter filled in with "The Night Before Christmas."

"Surely Grandpa's gal rates another package for that performance," my father urged. "The one Santa brought her."

A white, cuddly teddy bear brought stars to her eyes.

"Could I sleep with it?" she begged as father reached for the Bible.

After the scripture I retired with Carolyn to her room. She begged me to read from her new book, which I did until she drowsed, with teddy bear cradled in her arms.

As I lay staring into the night I heard my father turn on the radio for the ten o'clock news cast. This was his custom. I was glad Carolyn was asleep, as I strained to hear.

Panic gripped my heart as I heard them start off on a story about "The laughing bandit strikes again. Must be stocking up for a Merry Christmas," the commentator ad-libbed. "A good description of the bandit is now available, since both victims got a good look at the hold-up man. The bandit is described as fairly short, about twenty-five or twenty-six years-of-age, blond, wavy hair and a perpetual grin. Fingerprints have been sent to Austin. Local authorities now have a lead. Witnesses say pictures shown them of an escaped convict, Roy Gregg, matched the . . ."

I heard father curse as he turned off the radio. He rarely used profanity.

Stark terror struck my heart. Carolyn slept. I had to talk with father.

Pulling on my clothes I reentered the living room to face him.

''Looks like this will be his next stop,'' father commented. ''I'll kill him if he comes here, so help me.''

''That's a job for the police,'' mother cried hysterically as she burst in, pulling a robe about her night-gown without bothering to put her arms in the sleeves. ''They'll watch the house. We'll be disgraced again, and on Christmas.''

''And if they find out you're home, daughter, they'll come for you.'' father commented. ''There's a law against harboring criminals.''

''He might try to kill us, or take Carolyn,'' mother wailed in horror.

''I've got to go,'' I said in a scarcely audible tone. Could I take my daughter?''

''Take Carolyn! Take her away from us!'' Mother shrilled. ''And you without a job . . . with the police looking for you? Are you out of your mind? She stays here. ''I'll turn you in first. Why did I ever pray to God to let you live?''

''Now, Mama,'' daddy cut in. ''There's enough to face without that. We can't send Mary to prison just because she's a hard-headed fool. We can get police protection for Carolyn, if we have to, but we've got to get Mary out of here until this blows over. Get packed!'' he commanded.

While mother cried I threw a few of the dresses left in my closet into a much battered hand bag. Carolyn slept, peacefully. A smile tugged at the corner of her lips. Would I ever see her again? Would I ever possess my own baby? I had to steal just one kiss . . . one kiss to last an eternity.

''Now the police don't know for sure,'' I heard father reassure mother. ''They won't know until the fingerprints have been checked. No one should bother tonight. I won't be gone long, but I think I should drive Mary to Ranger. She can catch the Sunshine Special out. They would notice her here . . . might even try to hold her. I never thought I would work against the law,'' I heard him break into a dry sob, ''but my own daughter . . .''

Mother was white with fear. "What if he comes tonight?" she moaned, "While I'm alone with Carolyn?"

"Call the police, and use this" father admonished as he strode to the closet and dug out the twelve-gauge. "You know how."

I saw mother head for Carolyn's room, with the shotgun, as I heard my father start the motor of the old family car.

For a man who would never lie nor misrepresent anything, my father was making the supreme sacrifice.

"Now you stay away until he's dead or back in prison," my father advised as he handed me what money he had. "Stay on the train as long as you can, at least to Texarkana. God bless you, and take care of you," he added in a broken voice.

The world went numb again as the train pulled away from the station, leaving all I loved behind. Behind in disgrace and sorrow. I hid my face and pretended to sleep.

Perhaps I should have died. Why didn't I let Roy kill both of us in that tourist cabin? Why did a prostitute save me five years ago? My mother was right. My baby would never have a chance in life. People wouldn't let her live. If it wasn't for Carolyn I could die in peace. When I prayed in the tourist cabin I asked to live for my daughter. When I prayed out on the desert it was Carolyn I wanted to live for. Now I realized that she was better off without a mother at all . . . yet she loved me and I couldn't hurt her . . . not on Christmas.

I tried to pray, but I couldn't find anything to pray for. I couldn't pray for Roy to live, I couldn't pray for him to die. Should I pray for him to be caught? To be tried for murder? To burn?

The answer finally came. Just pray that no one gets hurt. Just pray to God there is no violence.

It was morning when we pulled into Texarkana. Christmas morning. I wondered how Carolyn would feel when she bolted upright in bed, remembering it was Christmas. Christmas morning, and her mommie not with her. I felt a traitor, even to myself. How long does a child trust? For most persons it was Christmas, I hoped, but for me it was crucifixion.

I wondered what was going on at home? Would Roy dare go to my father's home? I had to find out. I needed a newspaper.

All I could find was a local paper. It told nothing of Roy. That was good. Everything was quiet, I hoped.

''Merry Christmas, Carolyn,'' I said over and over to myself, as if she could hear. ''Merry Christmas! Merry Christmas to everybody!'' I repeated as I broke into tears.

Capture

Time . . . time . . . I thought desperately. If I could only get far enough away fast enough, before Roy was positively identified . . . before he was caught . . . before I was caught . . . before he caught me, or before the police caught me or him. Everything spun around in my mind.

I moved from city to city, from paper to paper as I read of six more armed robberies by the laughing bandit. These robberies would be added to the murder rap which Roy would have to face when caught. He knew he faced a death sentence because of the prison guard John Grayson's death.

Roy was the only convict participating in the break to escape with his life. What could matter to him now? He said he would never be taken alive.

"Please, God, don't let him hurt my family. Don't let him kill anybody." I should have killed him myself, but I always take the hard way out.

When apprehended I knew I would be sent to prison, Roy was right. I could expect no mercy. They would never believe I had fled with Roy because I thought I could make a good man of him, a reformed man, maybe even a doctor.

What a fool! I would have no defense. What Roy was doing would make things immeasurably worse.

Then the most horrible thought of all struck. They would think I was still with Roy, living off blood money, as he had wanted me to do.

Robberies and more armed robberies by the laughing bandit. Why couldn't the police catch him? Now there were seventeen. He was in Dallas. Why didn't he leave Texas? He was still looking for me! He still hung near my hometown, thinking I would be back. He might snatch Carolyn.

There's only one thing I can do, I thought. I'll go to Dallas and turn myself in to the cops. When they smear my mug on the front page of the newspaper Roy will know I'm in Big "D," in jail. He'll have no reason to go to my hometown.

I was in St. Louis. If I tried to turn myself in so far away from Texas they might not know the story. I might not hit the front page, here, or Roy might not see the paper. I had to get back to Dallas. My money was all but gone. I'd thumb a ride. What if I was recognized enroute?

Keeping up with Roy's whereabouts was no trouble. He was a continuing headline. He jumped from Dallas to Fort Worth, from Fort Worth to Abilene . . . closer home. THE LAUGHING BANDIT! THE LAUGHING BANDIT! He was bound to be mainlining, heavier and heavier. I had to get to Texas. If I could just get as close as Dallas, then turn myself in as the Laughing Bandit's wife, surely the story would hit every Texas newspaper.

I wasn't covering ground fast enough. I would hitchhike at night, too. Most of my rides were with truck drivers, and they were nice. They fed me and did not try to force themselves upon me. But trucks were slow. I would have to try a car.

I was lucky, I thought. I caught a salesman going into Oklahoma City. He said he planned to travel all night. But it was his hands that did the traveling. I had a fight that would have lasted all night if I hadn't been able to break away. I lost time. He was fat and easy to out-run; but I had to hide in the woods until he gave up the search and drove back to the highway. I was deathly afraid to try for another ride . . . in the middle of the night, but a truck driver picked me up and he was nice.

My progress was too slow. I would never make it back to Texas in time. I would have to turn myself in here. It was close enough. They would know.

"Just drop me off at the police station," I told the truck driver in a casual voice.

"So someone did rape you," the truck driver commented. "I thought that was your trouble, judging from your clothes and the scratches on your arms. I wish you luck, kid."

"But no one raped me, just tried." I said.

"Then maybe you are making a mistake, turning him in. You'll just be hurting yourself more, ruining your name in your own hometown. Why don't you take my advice and keep it quiet."

"But I wasn't going to the police because of the attempted rape. I'm going to turn myself in. I'm a criminal."

"You a criminal! Come, kid!" he laughed. "Tell me about it while we eat breakfast. They tell me the food's pretty bad in the jail here," he said as he pulled up at a truck stop.

"But I'd rather go on," I said meekly, having my mind made up and impatient with the delay.

"Then just five minutes for a cup of coffee," he said with firmness. "I don't care what you've done. I need a cup of coffee, and you look like you could use one. You won't loose any time. I'll drop you off within a block of the police station . . . but durned if I want to get involved."

"It won't involve you," I promised. "No one except myself."

We walked in.

"See the headlines," a waitress commented as she handed the truck driver the morning paper, "They've finally caught the Laughing Bandit."

I drank my coffee, too weak to say a word. And the truck driver ordered breakfast . . . breakfast for two.

"It's a shame such a good-looking guy as him could turn

out so bad,'' the waitress commented as she brought our bacon and eggs. ''They say he's wanted for murder.''

''Yeah!'' the truck driver grunted. ''Too bad he didn't get killed. Would have saved the State the trouble and expense.''

I couldn't say a word. I was afraid to reach for the paper, it might be a dead giveaway. Maybe the truck driver would put one and one together.

''Feel better?'' he asked as we again headed for the truck. ''The world's never so bad . . . on a full stomach. ''Do you still want to turn yourself in? You just don't look like a criminal to me. If I thought you had done something bad . . . like that Laughing Bandit's wife . . . helping him in a prison break and probably living it up now . . . I'd turn you in myself.''

''She must be a tough one,'' I commented, adopting Roy's tactics in an effort to throw him off trail. ''Maybe as tough as Bonnie Parker,'' I tried in an effort to change the conversation.

''Never could figure a woman,'' he muttered. ''How one could love a man like Clyde Barrow or that Laughing Bandit is beyond me.''

''They're bound to be as bad as the men,'' I said hatefully. ''Maybe I'm not so bad after all.''

''I knew it was nothing,'' he smiled. ''Always was a good judge of character. Now if you'll just tell me where you want out . . .''

''The next red light will be fine,'' I said as I wondered how near the police station was. ''I can catch a street car home.''

''I don't mind taking you, no trouble at all.''

''Maybe not to you,'' I added (delighted that I had learned to resort to Roy Gregg's light banter, or just plain lies when in trouble) ''but I spent the night with a girl friend. I'd have a little trouble explaining a truck driver to my father.''

''Or to you husband?'' the truck driver added as he raised a knowing brow. ''Good luck, you'll probably need it,'' he concluded as he applied the breaks for the light.

When I hit the sidewalk I felt like I had just escaped the noose. But when I got my own copy of the paper and locked myself in a rest room to read, I wondered.

I read the fine print. Roy had been taken in his sleep, in a hotel room in Dallas, a doped up wreck of a man.

"Where is your wife?" an officer had asked.

"I must have been out!" they quoted Roy, "if there was a dame in my room without me knowing it."

They found no evidence, but felt certain the drag-net set for Mary Gregg would finish the story.

If I was caught now, with the heat on Roy, I may never get to be with Carolyn again. The police would never believe my story. I could never prove I was going to turn myself in. I had even lied to the truck driver.

I didn't want to go to prison. I didn't want to implicate my family. I knew I would get five years . . . plus . . . plus whatever they could hang on me.

Suddenly I was cheating, cheating strictly for myself. I didn't want to pay for my crime. If I did I may never get my daughter back. I'd rather be dead than go through life without her.

I'd hide. I'd kidnap my own child when the heat was off, if I had to. Nobody could keep my child from me, neither the police nor my parents. I'd been a fugitive before.

I knew I couldn't hit the road, not without money. It was a sure way of getting caught. Maybe I could try my old trick, it worked in Phoenix. I'd rent a uniform and look for work as a waitress. Just as soon as I had the fare I'd go far away . . . to New York City where there would be plenty of cafes for me to work in . . . a week or two at a time . . . until they demanded my social security card.

Before the trials started I was in New York. I frequented big news stands where they sold out-of-state papers. Roy was finally brought to trial.

They grilled him, cross questioned him, asked him over and over about my part in his flight. He denied that he had ever seen me.

They could produce no evidence. In all those fugitive months no one had been close enough to identify me positively. No one who could have identified me got close enough to us during our flight.

I wondered if they would be unmerciful enough to put my parents on the stand . . . my child.

"But you were seen with a woman while you were an escaped convict," the prosecutor accused. "What has become of your wife. Where is Mary Gregg? If she is innocent let her prove where she has been the past nine months. Why couldn't she be reached with a subpoena? Is it because she knows there is a warrant out for her arrest? Where is Mrs. Mary Gregg?"

It was here that Roy showed his magnanimous heart and clear thinking. Whether he did it for me or for his daughter, or for whatever reason, the fact remains that this was his reply:

"Where is Mary Gregg?" Roy echoed. "That's what I'd like to know," he threw at the court with a spark of his old banter. "I've been looking for my wife ever since I escaped, but I've never found her."

"What?" roared the prosecutor. "Are you trying to tell the court that you have never seen, nor been with your wife who disappeared from this very town with you after the break? Do you expect this jury to swallow that?"

Witness after witness was called to the stand. No one who knew me had seen me since I had disappeared. Several officers thought they had seen Roy and me at a distance; but none of them had been closer than shooting distance. None of those who were even that close knew me. There was only one officer who could have identified me, and that was Ray Hilton, the officer who first picked Roy up. He knew both Roy and me; but he had not seen us during the time we were fugitives.

Because he knew us both, had seen me both before and after my baby was born and had a better chance of recognizing us than anyone else . . . he was put on our trail. Yet he had never been close to us during our flight.

"But you were seen with a woman while you were an escaped convict," the prosecutor accused. "Twice, when you were shot at, a woman was with you. You were with your wife when you were shot from a stolen car near Tucson. She was still with you when you were shot from a freight near Phoenix. There are at least half a dozen officers who can testify to the fact that you were with a woman on both occasions. Do you deny that fact to the court?'' the prosecutor roared.

''Does being shot at while with a woman necessarily make that woman your wife?'' Roy countered.

This brought the house down. The judge pounded with an unheeded staccato. When the court finally did settle down he suggested they get to the business at hand.

Roy was given 99 years . . . in addition to the 20 year sentence he was already serving. He was tried in other counties. The total rolled to 173 years. He was returned to prison.

My name vanished from the papers. Perhaps there was not enough evidence to bring me to trial . . . even if brought into custody. The court had it's man. Maybe it was appeased.

Gradually I worked my way back toward Texas and home. I had to see my daughter. Because of Roy's magnificent lie I felt fairly safe. I wished I could have thanked him for it. I felt sure he must have done it as a benediction to our love.

In a strange way Roy's statement was true. We had never found each other at all.

A great burden was lifted and my heart was almost light as I neared home. I told myself that I would find work in my own town and make a home for my daughter. God had been good to me. I would humble myself, if need be, in seeking another chance at a new life.

You Wouldn't Let Me Live

Perhaps my story would have ended here if society would have let it. If this were fiction, my daughter and I could have lived happily ever after. But this is not fiction.

I should have known better. Six years earlier, when I first returned to bear a prisoner's child, there were those who felt compassion and would have forgiven my mistake. Now I was a 'gun moll.' I had helped a man escape prison. I had deserted my own daughter!

People looked at me as if I were some kind of animal. Heads bent and tongues wagged until I was out of sight on the street. I was stared right out of church. I was no longer the hometown girl who had wanted to become a missionary. My church work seemed forgotten.

Detective writers came to town and asked for me. Rumor had it that I had helped with the bloody prison break. That I was waiting with guns. That I staged the break. That I was at least partially responsible for the death of eight men. I couldn't stand the pressure.

I seemed to be a criminal and child deserter to almost everyone except my own daughter. To Carolyn, I was an angel mother who came to visit on special occasions. Since I never lived with her, as most mothers live with their children, I guess her childish heart never demanded that which she had never known.

Jobs opened in my hometown, but not for me. I had to leave home to find work. My parents wouldn't let me take Carolyn with me. This could never be, not until I had a good job and a good home for her.

I found a good job, several of them, but I still had a lot to learn. The cops who had been on mine and Roy's trail couldn't quite give up the fact that I was on the outside and the courts had seemingly forgotten I had harboured an escaped convict.

Every time I got a fairly decent job close enough to home that I could see Carolyn often, the cops caught up with me or someone recognized me. Tongues wagged, and I was out of work again. I was even accused of instigating crimes that took place after Roy was returned to prison. What had happened before was my fault, but so help me, the public won't let a person with a record live.

For once I confided in my parents. I wanted a good job, and I wanted my daughter, but there was no future, not for Mary Gregg. Together we planned. My older sister was a teacher and believed in higher education. She wanted me to go back to college. Bless her, I'll always feel she taught away from home because of my troubles, but she never failed to come up with helpful suggestions. She thought I could get my credits transferred from McMurry College in Abilene to Texas Tech in Lubbock, in my maiden name. My whole family would help, if I divorced Roy Gregg immediately. By the time spring semester started, it would be no lie. I could take the family name back.

The transferring of my credits in my maiden name was a false pretense, because I did not have it back yet. It hurt because I had compromised the family integrity so many times with my escapades. But just one small, white lie, which I would make come true, then I could get on the straight and narrow again.

My mother and father loved Carolyn so much now that there

was no doubt as to who would keep her. In fact, it bothered me. they loved her too much.

I wrote to McMurry and had my credits transferred to Texas Tech in my maiden name, pretending my divorce was already final.

I still had a few days I could spend with my daughter before the spring semester opened. Going back to school, as a decoy, to change my name in hopes of securing a teaching position hardly seemed fair, but I was driven to it. Tech had a good journalism department. A little graduate work in writing would be easy enough.

Of course I would have to hold down a job, one in a cafe, but Lubbock was a big town and perhaps no one would know. Meantime I would look for a teaching position. Even if I couldn't find work by fall as a teacher, my journalism experience should enable me to hold down a good newspaper job.

Joyfully I told Carolyn that by the time school started in the fall she would get to live with her mother. Tearfully I told her that mother would have to leave again; but only for a while. I explained that Mother would have to work and go to college again so she could become a teacher, like her sister. Then when she was seven (seven was the school age then) she could come and live with me. Maybe she would go to the same school where I would teach. Wouldn't that be fun?''

The Letter

My heart was light as I raced with Carolyn to meet the postman. Only one more day with my precious child before I left for Lubbock to start back to school. True, it was a week early, but I had to find work and get settled before the spring semester opened. I not only had to find work, I would have to fit my working hours to my school hours. This would probably mean night work again; but it didn't matter. It would only be for a few months.

Meeting the postman was an old habit of ours. Mother had managed, while I was away from home, to get a subscription to Jack and Jill, a child's magazine, for Carolyn. She loved it . . . even if mother did have to barter four old hens and two dozen eggs for it when food was hard to come by, it seemed worth the sacrifice.

Carolyn squealed with delight when she saw a small magazine in the postman's hand. I no longer expected any mail, but strangely enough, there was a letter addressed to Mrs. Roy Gregg. It was in a plain white envelope, postmarked "Huntsville."

"Any mail?" I heard my mother call.

Quickly I concealed the letter. No sense hurting my family again, or start them fretting, I reasoned. Maybe he was protesting the divorce. Maybe he had a lawyer, it wasn't his writing. I'd read it later.

"My Jack and Jill, my Jack and Jill," Carolyn announced with delight, having no interest in the other letter.

"I'm glad you're still here to read it to her," my mother stated as we entered and she returned to her work in the kitchen. "It takes half my day when her magazine arrives. Sure will be glad when next fall comes and she learns to read for herself."

"Read this one to me first, Mommie," read this one first." She urged as she pulled me to an armed chair where we could both sit.

I read words, never knowing what they said.

"But Mommie . . . you skipped a page," Carolyn complained.

Impatiently I read the little stories.

"Tell you what," I finally suggested, "You work the puzzle, then Mommie will come back and read the magazine all the way through."

Who could the letter be from, I wondered as I locked myself in the bathroom. It wasn't Roy's handwriting . . . yet it had no legal return either. Should have, if it was from a lawyer. I hadn't heard from Roy since the trials, but I didn't expect to, either. Hastily I tore it open:

"Dear Mrs. Gregg,

I don't like to tell you this, and Roy didn't ask me to, but he's in trouble and he can't live much longer without your help. There's other boys here, too, needin' help on the Eastham No. 2 farm.

Don't come here, but go to Dr. Jason. He's on the prison board. Don't tell him who sent you, but tell him there's some boys out here needin' medical attention bad.

I know you don't see Roy any more, but if he ever needed you, he needs you now. I know you once loved him. I know you'll remember me, too. I'm Capt. Grant, the one who let you talk overtime and mailed extra letters from Roy to you when I could. That's how I know your address."

The letter was signed, "Capt. A. N. Grant."

How well I remember the guard who had been good to us. My hands crushed the letter desperately.

I cried in anguish. I can't go! I have no husband! He's my husband in name only. In my heart he's dead. I have his baby. She needs me. I owe Roy nothing. Nothing!

All through the day it was hard to hide the turmoil in my soul. I tried desperately to be cheerful with Carolyn as she chattered away. Soon she would be in school and learn to read for herself, she told me over and over. And she would have lots and lots of books. She was going to live with Mommie when she started to school. I had promised her.

Finally she lay asleep beside me. Deep into the night I fought with myself. I just had to make good! I couldn't change my plans now. I had promised my daughter . . .

Why did the letter have to come? Why now? Why must something always have to happen in my life just the opposite to what I expected or wanted. Why couldn't the letter have gotten lost? Why was I home to receive it? Perhaps if I had not been at home my parents would have opened it and torn it up. I had promised that nothing from the prison should ever touch me again.

Then I thought of Roy and how he had lied to save me from a prison sentence. "I never saw Mary Gregg," I could almost hear him saying. "In all the months that I was a fugitive I kept looking for her but I never found her."

In my own heart and mind I had never committed a real crime, at least no crime for personal gain. My only crimes were committed to protect the man I loved, the man I thought the world had wronged. Now he might die, without my help. This would be murder in my own heart. And the others . . . could I let men die if I could help?

Maybe it was all exaggeration, but I had to know. I could not refuse just one trip to be sure. I doubted that Capt. Grant, a man on the side of the law, would have any reason to lie.

Just one trip and no more. I wouldn't even see Roy, just the prison doctor. Then I'd go to Lubbock as planned, with time to enroll for the spring term of college.

"Mommie will be back for Easter," I had promised as Carolyn's arms tightly encircled my neck the next morning. "Don't forget that Easter bunnies are better to little girls who help their grandmothers. Just a few months now, until school starts next fall . . . and we'll go together. Won't it be wonderful? Mommie will start teaching the day her Darling starts to school!"

I bade my parents good-bye. I left, saying nothing of the six-hundred mile detour I must make to go to the prison.

When I arrived in Huntsville on that gloomy Saturday afternoon, little did I know that before I was through I would play a part in the smashing and cleansing of one of the rottenest, most bestial and corrupt prison systems in the United States.

I tried to call Dr. C. W. Jason, Jr., as he was listed in the telephone director, as soon as I arrived, but received no answer.

I would have to wait. I walked toward the park, across from the college, the park where I had slept on the concrete table with Carolyn in my arms when Roy was first sent to prison, six years ago.

Six years, and it was not enough that I should be left in peace. Now they wouldn't even let Roy live.

I dug out the letter, thinking of Capt. Grant, a rare guard, one with a heart. A guard who treated prisoners as if they were human beings. He always gave Roy and me a little break when he could. Many times, after Roy was sent to Eastham No. 1 Farm, he let me talk with my husband almost two hours, rather than the allotted one. He never seemed to hang on every word of conversation.

EASTHAM NO. 2! For the first time the words jumped at me from the letter. Eastham No. 2? That's where the incorrigibles were kept. Roy had been on Eastham No. 1 when I had visited him . . . so had Capt. Grant. I knew that the No. 2 farm was somewhere back of the No. 1 farm, but I had never been there. I had heard it was a tomb for the living.

It wasn't fair. Roy had never killed anyone. Why had he been put with the perverts, the criminally insane, incorrigibles and murderers?

And why was Capt. Grant there? Did Roy's prison break from the No. 1 farm have anything to do with it. Was Capt.

Grant demoted, too? Certainly no one would ask to go to the No. 2 farm. Roy had repeatedly said it was worse than No. 1. Could the Captain be ranked for letting prisoners write too many letters or talking overtime with their visitors?

The clouds grew as dark as the questions on my mind. I must try again. I had to reach Dr. Jason.

By the time I got to a phone it was raining. Dr. Jason was out of town, I was told by someone whom I assumed to be his wife. She said he wouldn't be back until tomorrow.

Impatient with the delay, I rented a little hotel room. From it I could see the red, prison walls. I could see the guards in the little towers atop the walls. My mind flew back to the time Roy had described Raymond Hamilton's break from the death cell. Clyde and Bonnie were already dead. Why, oh why did Roy always try to help someone else?

If it hadn't been for that break, Roy would never have been ranked and sent to Eastham No. 2. He would have left the prison a free man. His parole was so near. Call it circumstance . . . call it fate . . . but that's the way it had to happen for Roy and myself.

If there was ever a trap, one of us always managed to get into it. I closed my eyes and covered my head to cut out all conscious sights and sounds. Tomorrow I would see the doctor and he would surely investigate. There were other sick men who couldn't be overlooked. The doctor would take care of this, then I would be on my way to Lubbock, my conscience at rest. I would never see the prison again.

The next morning I waited for what I thought was a decent hour to call. It was still raining. A sleepy voice informed me that the doctor had not yet returned. Would I leave my number?

It was early afternoon before Dr. Jason reached home and returned my call. I told him my story and asked him if he would go to the prison farm to see about these men. When he asked my name and I had to tell him Mary Gregg, Roy Gregg's wife. I think he was quite skeptical. Where had this information come from? The doctor seemed to appreciate me, even less, when I told him I couldn't reveal the source of my information.

He reminded me that it had been raining hard and that it

was useless to try to visit the Eastham No. 2 farm when it was muddy. In fact, it was practically a physical impossibility. Yet, if it would make me feel any better, he would go, just as soon as he thought he could get there.

Why, of all times, did it have to be raining, I thought in desperation as the telephone receiver clicked in my ear. It might be too late when the doctor arrived at the farm. Maybe he didn't believe me at all. Maybe he would just let it slide. How many prisoner's wives called to gripe, I wondered? I could see his side of the question. If I only had more proof, then I could get the doctor to make it. I must have conclusive proof, but how?

I walked through the rain to the prison walls to ask Warren Bailey for a pass to the Eastham Prison Farm No. 2 to see Roy Gregg. He refused it. Sunday had always been visitor's day, so I asked why the pass was refused.

In the first place, I was informed, Roy was in solitaire and allowed no visitors. In the second place, I couldn't get to the prison farm, even if I had a pass, the road was too muddy.

Hell Hole Of Texas

It was then I told the warden that I wanted to see my husband because I had heard he was very sick. I was asked how I had received such information. Men in solitaire are not allowed to write. I refused to answer his question and Warden Bailey stuck with his refusal to give me a pass.

I went back to town and started calling members of the prison board. I didn't have much luck getting in touch with them. Most of them lived in other cities and I didn't have the money for long distance calls. Finally I did get Mrs. C. A. Leonard, secretary of the board. She promised to call the warden and call me back in a few minutes. When she did call back, I was told I would be granted the pass if I returned to the prison walls.

It was mid-afternoon when Warden Bailey signed the pass. I had the feeling it was givin to me because those concerned felt I would never make it to the farm. Visiting hours are over at five and I had more than forty miles to go. Much of the distance was mud . . . mucky, sticky gumbo.

My money was dangerously low for renting a car; but I could think of no other way of getting there. From Huntsville to

Midway I had about thirty miles of poor pavement. From the one-station town of Midway I turned east on a sand road so corduroyed that I never knew whether to brace myself for the next encounter with the top of the car or to stiffen my neck in hope of avoiding another bruise from the steering wheel. This road was luxurious compared with the black mire I hit nearing the river bottom.

Twice I crawled from the car into the mud and walked through the slime in search of someone to pull me out. Each time I found a shanty inhabited by Negroes. No Negro seemed to own more than one mule and I was informed that it would take more than one mule to pull me out. I had to sit and wait for one Negro to go off in search of another one with a mule.

I didn't know what to expect. I was afraid to think. Roy had told me of the difficulty in reaching the Eastham Farm, where the incorrigibles were housed. It was never meant for a sentimental public to see.

It had stopped raining, but the dark pine bottoms were gruesome. It was impossible to see over twenty-five or thirty feet on either side of the road. I had a feeling that the world had closed in on me, leaving me in a hole where the sun never shone.

I must have broken the speed record of a snail, because a wagon caught up with me and was traveling behind me when I got stuck the third time. Two young men, clad in dingy, white ducking, climbed from the wagon and approached the car.

''We're trusties from the Ferguson Prison Farm,'' one of the men informed me as they both removed their hats and held them politely as they offered their services.

''Isn't the Ferguson Farm just across the river from the Eastham No. 2 Farm?'' I asked, remembering Roy's description from his stories of the prison break. ''Are you going there?''

''Yes'um,'' one of the trusties answered. ''We're goin' there and it is across the Trinity from the Eastham No. 2 Farm. But to get to the Eastham you have to take the ferry and I ain't sure the ferry's crossin'. The river's high. Out of banks in places. We'll pull you to the Ferguson Farm if that'll help you any.

We're in the mail wagon and it's the only vehicle running along here now that the road's so bad.''

I don't see the Ferguson Farm,'' I said. ''How far are we from it now?''

''Why, it's just about a quarter-mile down the road. Don't you see that clearin'?''

A guard met us at the gate. I felt a little absurd, in a car pulled by mules, but I was at the farm and that was good enough for me.

The trusties unhitched the car. They refused pay for their services. I was thankful, considering the status of my pocketbook. The guard looked at me as though I was crazy when I told him I wanted to go to the Eastham Farm.

''Ye can't git no further in a car. Who air ye and who air ye goin' ter see?'' he demanded.

The guard's English, if it could be called such, was poorer than the prisoner's. I produced the slip from Warden Bailey, but the guard looked at it with a blank face. He passed it to another guard who was now at his side. The newcomer gave a ''no thank you'' look and carried it into a squat gray house which must have been the office. Evidently there was someone inside who could read because the guard came back and said that I had the proper permission from Warden Bailey.

''This here ain't no time to go acrost. The river's up an' the ferry's dangerous,'' the guard warned. ''Even ifen you do get acrost, you got nearly two miles to go afore you git to th' Eastham Farm. You can see hit from here.''

The guard pointed his finger. In the gray distance I could barely distinguish a group of low, gray buildings.

I asked how they got to the Eastham Farm in this kind of weather and was informed that the mail was carried over there twice a week on a mule. I asked if I might rent a mule and was informed in no uncertain terms that they were not allowed to permit such going's on. I said I would walk.

The guards and trustees hauled me as far as the river in the wagon. When I looked at the river they asked me if I was ready to return.

So this was why Warden Bailey had given me the permission! Even if I got to the river, he probably thought I would never have the nerve to cross.

The river was muddy and swollen. It was laden with occasional logs. The ferry was an old wooden affair, dependent upon a wire cable. The convicts pulled it across by hand.

I knew they would think I would be afraid but by now, in my life, I had forgotten what being afraid meant.

"This here girl wants to git acrost th' river," one of the guards addressed the two convicts who were puttering around the ferry. "Think you can get 'er acrost?"

All the while I was watching a nanny goat that was standing near the edge of the ferry. She was watching the logs in the swirling current as they were carried down stream.

The trusties agreed to take me across the river and wait for me on the other side. They would wait and bring me back for a dollar each crossing. Ordinarily they would have charged twenty-five cents each crossing, but today it would be dangerous and unusually hard work getting across.

The guards warned me again against crossing and seemed quite angry at my being fool enough to disregard the elements. I think they were wishing I were a convict, then they could handle me.

"We're not responsible fer anything that happens if'en ye cross th' river agin' our advice," the guard cautioned. "Warden Bailey wouldn't 'ave give' ye the slip if'en he had seen th' river."

I didn't bother to tell him that Warden Bailey regretted my being here as much as they.

"The only way to git to Eastham camp after ye leave th' river is to walk up one 'o them turn-rows," the guard warned as the trusties started pulling the ferry across.

Miraculous how far that cable would give without breaking. The old raft, it would come closer qualifying as a raft than as a ferry, capered like a game fish on the end of a line. The nanny goat stood periously near the edge of the bobbing raft, wholly unconcerned except for an owl-like turning of her head as she watched the logs rush downstream.

Being a woman, my curiosity finally made me ask, "Isn't it

dangerous for that goat to ride so near the edge of the ferry?''

''She rides every time the ferry crosses and ain't never happened to a mishap yet,'' one of the trusties informed me.

An abrupt yank on the cable brought me to an undignified sitting position on the wet boards which topped the logs. The goat maintained perfect balance and remained wholly undisturbed. I kept my mouth shut.

The guards were still watching when the trusties unloaded me on the other side of the river and helped me up the slippery bank.

''Keep right up that turn-row, Miss, till you get to the end of the field. Then take the one to your right and it will lead you right to the prison yards,'' one of the ferrymen instructed.

I could not see the end of the turn-row, but I knew it was a mile long. The field looked five miles long to me, but I had no intention of turning back now that I was within reach of my destination.

A few steps from the river bank my right shoe was sucked off by the black mud. I dug it out, draining the water to make room for my foot again. I clenched my toes so tightly against the soles of my shoes in an effort to keep them on that my toes soon became cramped. I relaxed them and lost another shoe. This time I took both shoes and hose off as I felt the mud ooze between my toes. I debated whether I should keep these now oddly shaped balls of mud, that had once been footwear, or throw them away. I might look a little queer, on my way back to civilization, barefoot.

I wondered what time it was as I made my way down the long turn-row, barefoot. Maybe it was already past visiting hours. Would I get to see either Roy or Capt. Grant.

The so called 'turn-row' was a sort of wagon trail at the side of the field. To my left was a field, to my right trees and brush, back of me the river and Ferguson farm, and in front of me I could see the low gray buildings would have to be the Burnin' Eastham, as Roy often spoke of it. From Roy's descriptions I could picture the convicts being run out on these turn-rows before daylight to work in the cotton or corn fields.

Long before I reached the right angle, to turn toward the

squat buildings I could feel eyes peeled my way. At the turn I wiped my feet with my muddy, tattered hose, and threw them away. Shoes, however muddy, were a comfort.

As I drew near I could see little towers on top of some of the buildings, where I knew machine guns were housed. I felt one angle in my direction.

One building was not barred. The porch on it was occupied by several men who wore scabbards and gun belts fastened around pudgy bellies.

"I've come to visit Roy Gregg," I ventured to the guards eyeing me, "I'm his wife, Mary Gregg. I have a pass."

"It's way past visitin' time, Ma'am. Besides that, Spider's not allowed visitors. They should 'av told you."

"But I've come a long way," I refuted, still grasping desperately for some fragment worth the sacrifice I had made. "Who is in charge? May I speak with him?"

"Capt. Grant's in charge. I'll call him, Mam, but it won't do no good. That's orders from the warden."

Nervously I waited for Capt. Grant to appear. What could a man do under such circumstances. What could I say to him? He had written in his letter that I was NOT to come to the farm. One wrong word. . . .

"I hear you're Mrs. Roy Gregg," the captain clued me in with no sign of recognition as we reached the guard's quarters. "Visiting hours are past. Anyway, your husband is in solitary confinement. Didn't they tell you that at the Walls?

My heart sank. Capt. Grant had always been so good to me. I had no business coming to the farm. It was the doctor I was supposed to get. I was helpless, insofar as explaining the circumstances. Maybe the same was true with him. There were plenty of eyes and ears around.

"Isn't there any way?" I pleaded as I stalled for time, hoping some of our gun-studded audience would move along.

"Those are the warden's orders," Capt. Grant said with finality.

I had no words. I couldn't have spoken then, even if I did, for fear of betraying him. There was nothing to do but leave. All this trip for nothing.

''By the way,'' Capt. Grant said as a sort of second thought when I turned to leave, ''would you mind postin' a mail order for me in town? Been no mail out of this place for several days and things don't look any better. My wife's afraid this birthday present won't get here in time if it keeps rainin'.''

I took the Sears Roebuck envelope he handed me. As I did his eyes held mine for a brief instant, speaking to me. They conveyed the message. The envelope was loosely sealed. I could hardly wait to get out of sight to confirm the unspoken message.

It was from Roy, written in the semi-darkness of solitaire. It was hard to read, but harder yet to believe. I had to get help, he pleaded. There had been many self-mutilations. George Barton and Irvin Darden were in the morgue at the Walls and they needed medical attention, quick. Clark Thomas had been in the morgue sixteen months.

In the morgue? I shuddered. The morgue is for the dead. Sixteen months? Impossible . . . or so the public would think.

I knew Clark Thomas. He had been sentenced from my home county. I had no sympathy for him because he was a murderer. Yet he was a human being. How could they put a man in the morgue before he was dead? I didn't understand. It didn't make sense.

I read on, ''there is much mutilation, conspiracy and graft going on at the prison. The mutilations are staged in an effort to draw the public's attention to our hopeless state. We are beyond helping ourselves; but if I can stay alive long enough and can get help, I can break this place wide open with the evidence I have. For God's sake, get us some publicity.

''Go to the newspapers,'' he wrote. ''Keep on until you find someone who will listen. If you can't find anyone any closer, go to Dallas. Harry McCormick is with the *Dallas Morning News* now. Since you've gone to him before, surely he will listen again. Tell him things are just like they used to be, except worse. I don't know whether his newspaper will go along, but I believe he will help. Get someone out here in a hurry. Our lives depend upon it.''

McCormick was a well-known police reporter, known for

his exclusive stories and exposés. He had previously been with the *Houston Press.*

Vainly I sought help from newspaper to newspaper. The story sounded too fantastic. The prison had been rehabilitated. The story was dead, and so was the *Houston Press* editor who had fought with Harry McCormick once before for prison rehabilitation.

War had broken out in Europe. That was the story the public wanted.

I went to Dallas to see Harry McCormick. He had believed the information I had funneled him from Roy in the past, but would he want to face the fact that his hard fought crusade might not be won. Would he go?

The first crusade had all but cost McCormick's life. Roy was on Eastham No. 1 and smuggling out stories to ''Mack,'' as the convicts called him, when Clyde Barrow chopped off a little toe for publicity's sake. He was still there when Clyde and his brother, Buck, were released as well as when Raymond Hamilton, early running mate of Clyde and Bonnie, was imprisoned. Ray bragged that Bonnie and Clyde would come for him. They did. A guard was killed during the break.

Many bank robberies later, Raymond Hamilton was recaptured and sentenced to the chair for the murder of the guard killed during his break, despite the fact that another of the convicts, Joe Palmer, admitted killing the guard himself. Ray contended he had never killed anyone and was sentenced to die because no jail nor prison could hold him. He had seventeen escapes to substantiate his claim.

When Hamilton's death sentence was read, he bragged openly to McCormick, who was near him in the courtroom, that he would escape the death house and give ''Mack'' the story of a lifetime. No one had ever escaped the death house in the Walls at Huntsville. Ray did.

While every cop in the nation was ordered to 'shoot on sight,' the nation's most wanted managed to get a message to McCormick. Mack met him at the designated spot on a lonely road. Ralph Fults, also an early team-mate of Clyde and Bonnie, was with Ray. He was one of the convicts in the break in which

Clyde and Bonnie featured. But Ralph, like Joe Palmer and Raymond Hamilton, had split with Clyde and Bonnie.

During this "impossible interview," when Raymond picked McCormick up, Ralph sat watching, in the back seat of the car, machine gun ready, in case the cops should show. After driving most of the night, while Ray related his story, they returned Mack to his own car. They laughed as they tied and gagged him. Raymond plastered Mack's windshield with fingerprints, to prove who did the "kidnapping."

As agreed, Harry screamed that he had been kidnapped by Raymond Hamilton, escaped from the death cell. He failed to mention Ralph Fults, of course, who was still a fugitive. But Mack did tell Hamilton's side of the story, and well. Unfortunately he was unable to prove it until after Ray's electrocution. Raymond Hamilton never killed anyone.

It was on the night of Ray's electrocution that prison officials tried to trap Harry McCormick. They made promises and offered bribes to both Ray and Ralph, if they would say that Harry came to them of his own free will, rather than being kidnapped by them. Neither squealed.

Did McCormick know the old vanguard was again in power at the prison? He had been told once that there was a slab in the prison morgue with his name on it. Would he go? Why should he become involved again? The public thought his crusade won.

Never Underestimate Harry McCormick

I never felt so small as when I entered the big city room of the *Dallas Morning News*. Everyone was so busy no one seemed to realize I was alive. I just stood there until I spotted Harry McCormick in a far corner. His desk was among dozens in the room. He looked up.

"What th' hell are you doing here, Mary," he blurted out as I approached his desk. Unwinding his gangling thin legs and stubbing his ever-present cigarette he stuck out his hand. "Did you want to see me? Here, take my chair while I hunt another."

He took off his horn-rimmed glasses, which had been added since I last saw him, and retrieved a chair. Tall, gaunt and ruggedly handsome, Harry was the friend of the guy who needed him, always.

"What's on your mind?" he asked, realizing perhaps that no one ever came to him except when in trouble.

"Roy," came my expected answer. "He's at the Ham, in 'sol'."

I handed him the letter. He read it through quickly, all

eight pages, then turned back and reread a portion of it before he said a word.

Soon he was firing questions, fast and to the point. Many of them I couldn't answer, especially those concerning prison personnel and the transfer of guards.

"I don't think my newspaper will handle this," he said as my heart sank. "You see, besides being almost two hundred miles away from the prison and there being plenty of war news to hit the front page, the *Dallas Morning News* has always been a conservative paper. I'm not sure I could talk my editor into it. But Royal Roussel of the *Houston Press* might," he added as I breathed again.

"Can it be soon?"

"It will have to be," he replied understandingly. I wanted an excuse to go to Houston, anyway. Maybe Royal will carry the torch. Could you help us, Mary?"

While I was in mental debate with myself Harry explained.

"Although I am no longer barred from the prison, I am not the guest of honor, especially since Dave Nelson died. (Nelson was the new prison manager who did so much toward re-habilitation, then suffered a heart attack.) But Roussel might go along since he did some work with "Mefo" and me (Mefo Foster was former editor-in-chief of the *Houston Press*) on our crusade to clean up the joint. I'm not in close contact with the prison anymore, otherwise I would not ask you to help."

There was a sinking feeling within me, but it was too late to turn back. Harry did not know, of course, that it was over with Roy and me. Neither did he know that this move would jeopardize my getting my own daughter back.

"You mean you'll go to Houston? It may be too late already."

"I'll go," he assured. "Meantime I'll have to depend upon you to get this information from Roy Gregg and whatever contacts there are now. I'm no longer on the grapevine. I'll let you know what Royal thinks, he's editor now. I'll need this letter, of course. We'll have to check it out. What is your address?"

"Just write me general delivery," I stammered, "Mary Gregg, General Delivery, Lubbock, Texas."

The truth would have taken too much explaining.

When I finally got back to Lubbock I started collecting mail under two names. At the college I was Mary McLeod, but at the downtown post office I was Mary Gregg.

By day I was a coed. At night I was a waitress. Whenever I managed for a week-end I was a mother for a day, as I visited Carolyn and my family, never telling them, of course, that I was enroute to the prison. Thus I started smuggling information from the rottenest prison in the nation, unless Louisiana or Georgia tied for the honors during this time.

Letters came. As pre-arranged with Roy Gregg and Harry McCormick, I made copies of the letters and sent them, not to Harry McCormick, but to McCormick's wife at their home address. The *Dallas News* did use a portion of the material, but it was Royal Roussel who really took up the battle. Later I carried some of my material directly to Roussel. I attended classes at Texas Tech, spasmodically.

Easter I made a visit home, to see my daughter, but only enroute to Huntsville. I lied again, spending only a brief time with my family. Although it was spring vacation at the college, I was also a waitress. I told my parents I had to work, even though I had managed to get the time off from the cafe. You can bet I took every precaution not to mention the kind of work which would occupy most of my time during the Easter holiday.

Graft in the Texas Prison

This part of the story may be difficult to understand. Certainly the conditions mentioned do not prevail at the Texas prison today. Later the rehabilitation program was resumed under the directorship of J. R. Everett. Yet few persons know the story back of the headlines.

It is hard to comprehend the vastness of the Texas Prison System, chiefly because it is spread over so vast a territory.

There is the main unit in Huntsville, usually referred to as "The Walls." During the 1940s there were fourteen farms spread over hundred of miles in south and east Texas. The Walls and some of the farms were easily accessible. Those were the ones the public saw. But behind them were the swampland farms of the Trinity River bottom. Unless personally concerned, most persons were unaware of their existence.

Because of this, it was easy to hide a convict who had mutilated himself. He could be shipped out to another farm before investigators arrived. In like manner the prison system managed to keep brutal guards. If their sadistic action attracted too much public attention, those who regained power after the death of Dave Nelson would transfer rather than fire the guards.

Hands, feet and even legs were chopped off, yet the convicts were fighting a losing battle. However hard the prisoners tried to stay in the public spotlight, prison officials managed to thwart their efforts.

As too much attention was called to one farm, the men mutilating were shipped to other farms. Before reporters could arrive for evidence there was none, or just enough to make the story look highly exaggerated. This is where Roy Gregg's camera and tip-offs as to when and where mutilations were to be staged helped win, or at least focus public attention and action when and where it was most needed.

There were many types of graft in the prison system.

Most prisons have a good behavior plan worked out. This plan can knock years off a man's prison sentence if he keeps his nose clean. Every prisoner leaving the institution is given mustering out pay. In the Texas prison it was $50. During the Depression this was a lot of money, especially when it could be multiplied many times monthly throughout the vast prison system, and over many years.

The deplorable condition at the prison was no secret. For many years many persons had been trying to get at the bottom of the mess. In the early 1930s, Governor Dan Moody introduced a bill which was defeated. During the Raymond Hamilton, Bonnie and Clyde era, W. C. Windsor, then chairman of the State Prison Board, stated before the legislature that: "The Texas Prison System is the greatest University of Crime in the nation."

During the earlier crusade, McCormick and "Mefo" Foster had pointed out that the prison system, which had previously operated at a profit, now robbed the taxpayer's pocket, although the prisoners themselves were half starved. Public attention had also been called to the existing brutality and 'slave labor,' yet no one knew enough, nor seemed to care that these same practices were merely arrested, not eradicated.

Roy had been able to tip me off several times as to when and where mutilitations were to take place. I made sure the press was on hand for photos and stories, yet this was not sufficient.

I honestly believe it was the captain's open rebellion which caused that seething volcano, which had been rumbling and hissing from the thirties to the early forties, to explode.

It happened because Capt. Grant didn't like to see his men robbed of their mustering out pay. When a prisoner, who was supposed to be gaining his freedom, failed to board a bus which carried such prisoners back to civilization, Capt. Grant wanted to know why. The prisoner told Grant he had promised his $50 to get his overtime restored.

He had lost his overtime because of a fight, a fight where he never hit a lick. In other words, he had been framed, as many prisoners were, and he lost his overtime for good behavior. He then had to promise his $50 mustering out pay to get the overtime restored. When he was freed, before turning in this "legal fee," a collector was appointed.

Grant was furious. He had seen many prisoners framed, robbed and stranded. He demanded that the convict who was being freed to be given his bus fare to Huntsville and that it be deducted from the "legal fee." You may be sure that Harry McCormick and the *Houston Press* got the story.

Without advance notice, Capt. Grant was demoted and transferred to the Wayne farm, where the Black prisoners were kept. To cover up, guards who had worked under Grant at Eastham No. 2 were made to sign statements that prisoners were served coffee in the fields, that beer had been found in the kitchen, and that prisoners were allowed to buy and eat candy.

Roy Gregg wasted no time in getting the information to me. These are extracts from his next letter:

> "On Feb. 15, 1940, nearly 30 days ago, the Eastham Prison farm underwent another change of management and a radical change in policy. After fifteen months under an administration that handled the affairs of the convicts and guards alike, with tolerant, broad minded efficiency, it is once more under the management of a group of men who have time and again been fired, blackballed and transferred around over the vast prison system for practicing brutality in all its hideous forms upon an unfortunate

class of human beings who are helpless, without recourse to violence.

"Some fifteen months ago these same guards were transferred from the Eastham prison farm for acts of violence that startled the whole nation and focused the spotlight of public disapproval upon the whole system. Instead of complete dismissal they were only transferred to another unit of the system to continue their sadistic outrages with impunity. These arrangements were made through the efforts of an influential politician who is paid a monthly salary as a legal advisor and bondsman to the system's executive personnel, including the guards. This salary is paid from a fund accrued from each guard's monthly wage.

"However stern the prison system's rules governing punishment, they are considered too lenient under these people's administration. The barrel, the sweat box and leather, including 20 lashes a month, isn't capable of attaining the intended goal when administered by men whose only aim is to cow into submission a class of men who find themselves unfortunate and foolish enough to be under their jurisdiction. To get a good start they want a man or two killed to scare the rest. They have made a statement to this effect.

"For fifteen months these same convicts have worked and cooperated with the new management successfully, with minor infractions of the rules, therefore no brutality. In fact, they have proven beyond a reasonable doubt that they could be handled without even stern discipline, only to be rewarded with a shift in farm management which has not one motive other than exploitation and sadistic cruelty. Let's take these convicts into consideration. As a whole, they are convicted felons who have been classified and segregated to the Eastham as incorrigibles. Individually they are only unfortunate men who have each found justice through incarceration. They are human, however foolish."

Sometimes I had to agree with Harry McCormick that Roy Gregg should have been a lawyer, judging from the way he pleaded his own case and that of his fellow prisoners. I felt Roy would have made a good writer, and much of the material he sent me was published, word for word, yet Roy's one and only ambition in life was to become a doctor. I still believe he would have made a good one, if he had not become a victim of circumstance during the depression. His first mistake was made in an effort to help me. Perhaps that and his sworn statement that he had never found me during the time he was a fugitive kept me funneling this material to the press.

> "Brutality is condemned by society," he wrote. "Still these men have recourse to violence as a last resort, and then only after their plight has been minimized by the skeptical eye of their own free fellow man and ignored by executives who could, by their opinion and censure, adjust such a situation.
>
> "Since the prison manager transferred Capt. Joe Baker back here there has been an average of two mutilations and self inflicted wounds a day. The proof of this statement remains to be seen.
>
> "A timely investigation would expose the whole sorry mess. Two of the men who cut their legs off were shipped immediately to the Wayne farm and a half dozen or more with broken arms are in The Walls, also some of these have burned themselves severely with lye on the buttocks to evade the twenty lashes. One cut his hand completely off. He is in The Walls. Most of these here on the farm have broken legs, broken arms and lye burns. From all indications there will be more mutilations should Joe Baker, John West, Gordon Taylor, W. W. Bailey and O. B. Simpson have their way. To these convicts the two captains, warden, prison manager and the Right Honorable Senator Taylor form a syndicate of terror, and rightfully so. But why?
>
> "Each and every man who has mutilated himself to escape punishment or to evade a few days work under these slave drivers found such measures unnecessary under Grant. Mad Maniaco spent fifteen months under Capt. Grant with a clear record. There have been only a few minor infractions of the rules and no brutality. But two days after Capt. Joe Baker returned to power every privilege had been forfeited without cause. A stern set of rules was put into effect.
>
> "The Captain let not one man of the thousand here on Eastham misunderstand his policy and immediate in-

> tentions. The convicts are at a loss to explain this sudden change in management, much less the unwarranted change in the policy of the Texas Prison Board who define the policy of the executive personnel. To me it is indeed a sad event because I have been elected by the manager to partly shoulder the blame for his failure to come into a complete slave-like submission, (if so) a majority of these men would really be on the spot, for sure. Today some one gave the man a list of names that they claimed were agitators. So I guess there will be more mutilations tomorrow. If so I will write and let you know with the names of those who have already mutilated.
>
> "I have made a home made camera and got two rolls of film. I will send you pictures of guys and their mutilations, stabbings and suicides since these captains were transferred back in charge here. . . ."

Both the *Dallas News* and the *Houston Press* published stories on the brutality and the mutilations at the prison; yet neither was ready to stick its neck out in accusing Sen. Gordon Taylor and the prison officials without positive evidence. This would be asking for a liable suit.

When given tips from Roy, we did manage to get reporters to the prison. Roy was as good as his word about getting the film out, and for a home made camera the shots were better than expected. If they had caught him, I am sure it would have meant his life.

His next letter really frightened me. He wrote:

> "Today I was interviewed with ten other men for agitating so maybe I will be reclassified and punished. If so, then I am going to mutilate myself and mutiny to stay out of the field. I hope not, though. You should know from my letters that I wouldn't dare agitate anyone against Joe Baker and John West."
>
> "Baker is supposed to have a trusty chained out somewhere, trying to get out of him some details about smuggling. How true it is I can't say; but for God's sake, be careful.
>
> "Capt. Joe Baker's slogan is 'More lead and lashes.' It

has caused more hate, misery and sorrow than crime has for me.

"The building tenders were given orders by Joe Baker to kill any man caught mutilating or agitating. Six hours later his No. 1 building tender, Ray Gordon, had been stabbed. He is in The Walls now. Baker has told every man that he would kill anyone caught helping get rid of Sen. Gordon Taylor and the prison manager.

"The feeling of these men is hard to describe. It is a cross between desperation and baffled resignation, because as convicts they have seen Taylor win out time and time again with his little dictatorship.

"Capt. Baker's pet killer is 'Machine Gun' Kelly, a vicious maniac from hell. His mind seems to register only the blackest of expressions, judging from his talk. He told me that if he didn't kill me that he would 'suck my dick'. He must want to because that was several days ago and I am still alive."

Just reading this letter was embarrassing enough, but it describes the desperateness of the situation, thus I have quoted it verbatum.

Roy did manage to obtain a letter from Senator Taylor, demanding the $50 mustering out pay from a short-timer for restoration of his overtime. But like similar letters from him, it was not on a Senate letterhead and did not bear his signature. Royal needed a letter with the Taylor signature.

Time seemed suspended. Only the days on the calendar moved. My grades suffered. My journalism teacher cut me down to the lowest passing grade. He talked with me, saying he didn't understand. My stories, when I got them in, were the best in the class. I should be making all "A's." Several times I had been absent without apparent reason.

How could I tell him that my news stories were making continued headlines? It hurt me to feel his concern. I have never had a journalism professor as good as Cecil Horne, and I told him so. I told him how much passing the course meant to me, and that there was something which I couldn't tell him that required a great deal of my time. I even told him that I was working for a "cause." He believed me, of this I feel certain, for my grades came up.

A few days before school was out a letter came from Roy, saying that he could get that "all important" letter. Senator Taylor, after ten years of graft and virtual control of prison personnel, had finally become careless. In an unguarded moment he, or his secretary, had written a letter to George Watson, demanding $50 for restoration of his overtime. Through some inexplicable error, he had signed it. A letter on his Senate stationery, and with his signature was what had been needed for months. Roy was hot to get it, and wrote it had been promised.

I went to McCormick with the news.

"For God's sake, Mary, forget it," he pleaded. "I never thought you would go this far. Even if Roy managed to get this letter in your hands you'd never get out with it alive. They've turned the prison inside out. Everyone is watching for that letter. Stoolies are planted everywhere. Unless we can get Watson out before the letter is published, he will be killed."

"He will, anyway, if they don't find the letter, won't he?"

"Or maybe he will be kept alive until the letter is found . . . or published."

"Then how?" I asked.

"Only one way, I guess." Mack said thoughtfully. "And that's have someone from the press waiting at the prison the day he is scheduled to come out, or maybe have some sort of outside protection arranged. The letter should be published simultaneously with his release. They'll demand it and the money, or he won't come out, not alive."

"If Roy has it, I'll get it."

"No! For God's sake, no. You've a baby to think about. She's a pretty big girl now, isn't she?"

I exhibited the ever-present photo.

"It's a promise, you'll forget the letter? I don't know why I ever let you get mixed up in this deal. You have a fine family, Mary, and a real opportunity in life. Don't throw it over now, You've gone for enough. There is a point of no return."

"You've risked your life many times doing prison stories,"

I refuted, ''and you have a good wife and fine young son who need you, too.''

''But I get paid for my stories. It's my job.''

''Reporting is your work, Harry, and you do get paid for it, but you seem to have forgotten how ''Mefo'' (Harry's crusading editor) begged you not to risk your neck on these prison stories. In fact, he told you NOT to go for that interview with Raymond Hamilton while he was an escapee from the death house. Every cop in the nation was ordered to shoot on sight. If either Raymond or Ralph had told the truth on the night of Raymond's execution, you probably wouldn't be here now. You didn't get that kind of money, not enough to risk your neck over and over.''

''But this is a man's world, Mary. Look what happened to Bonnie.''

''It's too late to scare me out, Harry. Your ten-year struggle, as well as many lives will have been thrown away if we fail now. What would make you think they would ever suspect me, anyway?''

''The very walls have eyes. You know this as well as I do.''

''And if Roy Gregg hadn't lied, saying he'd never found me while he was on the outside, I'd be on the inside. You know that, Harry.''

''Females!'' Harry said in way of parting. ''Never have any sense when it comes to loving a man, not even a convict.''

I didn't bother to tell him I was divorcing Roy. He thought I was nuts enough as it was. I had to get back to school. This was dead week, as the week before exams is called at college, when all other activities are stopped for study. If a student ever needed to cram, I did.

Only one more week of school, and still no letter from Roy. I was worried about that more than my grades.

On the night before I took my last exam I received a telephone call. I never saw the man who put in the call and he did not identify himself. He merely stated that he was in stir with Roy and had come out on clemency.

''Roy has a letter,'' he stated, 'THE LETTER', but no one could come out of 'the joint' with it and stay alive. Roy says that if you have the nerve to walk into and out of the prison with it, the whole batch, from senator to prison manager, warden, and guards would be fired. It's dynamite.''

''But how can I get it?'' I asked with alarm. ''They know me! I would be watched.''

''The only way is to walk in and out, at night.''

''At night?'' I gasped.

''Roy says to wait in the bushes at the end of the turn-row. The one you walked up when he was in trouble, on the edge of the field, between the Ham and the Ferguson farm.''

How well I remembered, and reminded my informant that the turn-rows were a mile long.

''Near the river,'' he said, at the end of the row, where it does the right angle. There's a good covering of brush. Wait in that. Cross two sticks about 10 yards ahead of the turn to signal you are there. They'll trot the hoe squad out and they'll be alongside that patch of brush before good daylight. Roy will throw the letter to you in an empty tobacco sack. Be sure to stay out of sight. Stoolies are planted. Walk all the way, through the trees down by the river, and only after dark.''

What a sentence. I felt exiled.

''Oh, yes,'' he cautioned, ''Roy will be looking for you Sunday. That way he will know that you will be waiting before daylight on the turn-row. Give no indication of any kind of communication. Leave the prison area, all the way. Take the Greyhound bus out of Lovelady, get off near the Trinity River and wait until after dark.''

''But who are you,'' I blurted as he seemed to be ready to hang up the phone. ''How do I know this is not a . . .''

''Good girl! 'Spider said that if you doubted, just say that you are to transplant his American Beauty Rose, whatever that means,'' he said as the receiver clicked.

It meant a lot. It was the same code which Roy had used when he broke from the prison. It meant that it really was a message from Roy.

I don't know how I got through my exam the next morning. I knew I would have to quit my job at the cafe. I had missed too many shifts already. This would be my last night as a waitress. I would hardly have time to make it to Huntsville, via home. I had to see my daughter, our daughter, before this last venture. My family must think I had only taken a day off from the cafe.

Friday afternoon I was on the bus. One day at home with my family and Carolyn. Saturday I had to leave, to go back to work, I lied.

I headed out of Ross toward Lubbock, as far as Abilene. There I crawled off the bus and headed east, instead of north.

Sunday afternoon found me back in the chicken-wire coop called visiting quarters. A guard sat in the aisle, which separated the visitors and convicts, further than arm's reach. Others were visiting. This made it easier for Roy and myself. Our eyes did most of the talking. But there was one fellow in that coop who seemed to be waiting for a visitor who failed to show.

Roy talked about Carolyn and the weather. I had no idea what he was saying, but his eyes kept talking. He pulled out a Bull Durham sack, rolled a cigarette, and sort of tapped the bag with his fingers as he pulled the string taut with his teeth. His eyes never left mine during this operation. This sack was what I was to look for.

But the eyes of that con, the one waiting for a visitor who never showed, seemed constantly focused on Roy or me, or on both of us at the same time. Suddenly his eyes seemed haunting. Was he. . . . ?

Roy seemed to be reading my mind, over and out. Without so much as a glance in the direction of 'those eyes,' he winked ever so slightly and came on with the banter.

"Did you transplant my American Beauty Rose?" he asked as visiting hour closed.

"No, but I will, just as soon as I get back," I promised, letting him know for sure that I had received the message.

"I know it will be a real beaut. The most beautiful," Roy grinned reassuringly as the convicts were marched from the coop.

Visiting hour was up. I crawled on the shuttle which would take me to Lovelady, where I would wait for the bus, as instructed. My mind recorded every landmark. There was no way to get lost, between the river and the road, but the Eastham No. 1 farm, must be given a wide berth, as well as the community of Weldon and some Negro shanties. The Eastham No. 1 and No. 2 Farms were across the river from the Ferguson Farm. They formed a sort of triangle, with the mile-long turn-row in between serving as a base. Just the thought of penetrating this triangle gave me the creeps.

I had another hour to think about it, while I waited in Lovelady for the bus. I hoped the driver would think me a native when I asked to be let off in the middle of nowhere, about halfway between Lovelady and Trinity. I hid underneath a secluded pine near the river until almost dark. Spanish moss hanging from the cypress trees gave me the creeps, especially when there was air enough for antimation. I waged war with the insects and later put on the dark slacks and jacket I had brought along in a little shopping bag.

After dark I emerged on the side of the little road, if you could call it that, which staggered toward Weldon and the prison farms. I would have to stick close to either it or the river. The road seemed the lesser of the two evils, and less likely to be inhabited with watermouth moccasins. I would have to skirt the farm houses because of the dogs.

As the darkness deepened I felt as if I was walking into a tomb, my own. I made a wide circle back of the first two shanties. Underbrush tore at my clothing. Mosquitoes were unmerciful. Hidden roots and berry brambles allied with the mosquitoes and my fear of snakes. My mind was paralized with fear. I just couldn't penetrate deeply enough, between these houses and the river, to escape the trained noses of the dogs, which every squatter seemed to have. Fortunately they seemed to keep them tied up, I hoped. There was a $100 bounty on capture of an escaped convict, and I hoped neither dog nor man would mistake me for one. I had counted the houses on my way out. I had made it back of the first three. I saw no more between the third and the community of Weldon. I had to chance the road.

Walking in deep sand I slithered along in breathless silence. It was dark, very dark. The air was sticky and damp. I could hear myself breathing and my heart pounded as if trying to escape my body. I was all but running.

Suddenly the moon broke through the clouds and a host of shrouded ghosts were before me on the roadway. I thought I was losing my mind. Then I remembered the graveyard. It sprawled on a mound in a bend of the road near Weldon. It looked as if there were more people here than in town. I wondered if it was really peaceful. How would it feel to be dead?

At least I knew where I was. I didn't know how long I had been walking; but it was seven miles from the highway to Weldon and the graveyard was fairly close to town. From Weldon it was one mile to the No. 1 Farm and another mile further on to the No. 2. Farm, The Ham.

I didn't see a light in town. I don't know whether this was good or bad. It must be near midnight. I didn't have a watch, couldn't afford one. I skirted half a dozen houses in Weldon and started the long mile to the Eastham No. 1 Farm.

What if someone in the prison saw me? At least they couldn't get out, I surmised, not sure whether the thought was comforting. I would have to give it a wide berth. I didn't know whether there were any dogs at either of the Eastham farms. When Roy had told me the story of his escape, he said they got the bloodhounds from the Ferguson farm, across the river. I hoped they kept them all there.

Now to give the No. 1 Farm a wide berth. The going wasn't so bad as the brush. I stayed along a fence row, near the creeping, crawling vegetation which reached inside the fence here and there for a little open space. I didn't dare walk through the field. I had to blend with the underbrush.

Finally I was back of the No. 1 Farm, heading for Eastham No. 2. Again the moon broke through. This time I saw the real tomb, a tomb where men are interred for their misdeeds while yet alive. I was wet with cold sweat. What if this was a trap?

I knew there were some two thousand prisoners and guards near me; yet I was never more alone. There were more across the river, and dogs. A bird flushed from the brush and I was just sure a stoolie was swinging an ax toward me. I fell to the ground, trying to choke back the dry sobs. I don't know how long I lay there. Gradually my fear subsided, at least to a degree that would let me think.

This couldn't be a trap. Roy's words had told me that this very afternoon, or was it a century ago? The worst part of the trip was behind me. I was less than a mile from my destination. Nothing had harmed me . . . unless I caught malaria from the mosquitoes. At least I wasn't snake bit, not yet. It would be after daylight when I started back, yet there wasn't too much comfort in this thought.

What if I were caught. I would be killed, no doubt, and no one would every know what became of me. Again I thought of Carolyn. Why did I always have to be such a fool? I would turn back, now, before I got the letter.

"Coward," I accused myself. "Go through all this then turn tail and run?"

"There is a point of no return," I seemed to hear McCormick saying.

The battle waged within me, and I must admit I said a few prayers.

"This time, God," I promised over and over, "if you will stick by me I'll never turn from the straight and narrow again. If it is right for humanity, please help me to get this letter. This one letter, God, and I'll spend the rest of my life trying to make amends to my daughter and my family. I'm so alone. Please, God."

Strength and some courage returned. At least I had regained self control and some composure. I must follow Roy's instructions. Now, before daylight. I headed for the rendezvous, the turn-row between the ferry and the Eastham No. 2 Farm.

When I reached familiar ground the world seemed less strange and hostile. I couldn't go too near the building. I would cut through a patch of brush and hit it about a quarter-mile away. I stopped and looked at the prison building, a real tomb. In my heart I felt there was someone with me. Roy must be lying awake in his cell. I was not alone. Roy and God knew. I hoped no one else did, not those eyes!

Soon I broke through the brush to the turn-row. The other fields had cotton; but this one corn, and it was high. I felt I could walk on the turn-row itself, between the corn and the brush, with comparative safety. As I kept walking I felt I was getting uncomfortably near the sensitive noses of the bloodhounds across the river.

Through the darkness I saw where the turn-row made a right angle. The brush nearby was quite thick. This had to be the spot. I looked the situation over. Yes, this is where Roy had mentioned the squad slowing as it turned the corner.

I must do as I was instructed, now, and make the cross with branches. I thought of breaking off fresh ones; but this would make noise. Rotten ones would have to do. Since the field was dry rather than muddy this time, I knew I must leave no tracks. I did break off a small branch heavy with leaves. I must brush out my tracks.

Using the brush to eradicate my footprints, I walked back up the turn-row a distance I figured to be ten yards, stepped out to the edge of it, crossed two fair sized limbs, and brushed out my tracks as I again ducked into the woods. Now I must wait.

Because of my afternoon visit Roy would assume I would be here; but he must know positively before parting with the all-important letter. My crossed branches were certainly large enough for him to see, even in moonlight. I felt sure this must be the right spot. From his instructions I could figure no other place. It had to be right.

The clouds grew heavier. What if it rained? The men might not come to the fields at all. Please, God, no, rain, not now.

My scant preparations finished, I hunted for the thickest part of the brush nearest the corner of the turn-row. I needed rest, but I mustn't sleep. I took a mashed sandwich from my shopping bag. Maybe I could eat a bite. It helped me stay awake, but it stuck in my throat and felt like a rock in my knotted stomach. I wondered and wondered what time it was. It seemed the sky was a little lighter in the east, or was it my imagination?

After an eternity of waiting in the damp chill of the predawn hours, the prison lights came on. Now I could see both the Eastham Farms as well as the Ferguson Farm across the Trinity.

Suddenly I heard the baying of bloodhounds and tensed. The barking ceased. It was merely the dogs awakening, too.

It wasn't good daylight when I heard the men leaving the buildings. Fog curtained the Ferguson Farm across the river. The rising fog seemed to be spreading, I hoped. Carefully I glanced about me in the underbrush, making sure I had left no tell-tale footprints.

Now I could hear voices and curt commands. The men were headed toward the fields, but I could not see them. The fog was thicker than I thought. The squad sounded closer, but I saw no one. Abruptly the head and shoulders of one man appeared. He seemed floating along. It was eerie. Then I saw the head of his horse. It was a guard. Only the guards rode. The men trotted alongside. Miles didn't matter, not to the guards.

Then the heads of a file of convicts rose from the fog. I hadn't realized the fog was so thick, so near me. The coming light of day added to the distortion. The line of heads floated toward me. I was glad for a momentary break in the density which showed me there were bodies, too.

Some of the men were in white. They made their own clothes from white ducking in the prison shop, this I knew. A few of the prisoners wore stripes. Those wearing stripes were the ones who needed closer watching because of infraction of prison regulations. I knew Roy would be in stripes. He had been when I had seen him on Sunday afternoon. He would be in the second squad. This I had been told. I strained my eyes.

I spotted his glide long before I could see his facial features. A sudden tautness in Roy's gait made me realize that he had seen the sticks. As he came closer I felt his eyes were directly upon me, even though I was praying I could not be seen.

Roy slowed down and I held my breath. He was rolling a cigarette. He emptied the tobacco sack and slung it in my direction, lighting the cigarette almost simultaneously. I could see the tenseness in his face as he cupped his hands and the match flared momentarily. Quickly the guard rode alongside and reigned his mount.

I had moved! The brush shook! The guard had seen! This was it! The secret was out!

"Hurry it up, you God Damned lazy bastard," the guard shouted as he cracked a whip in Roy's direction.

I sighed with relief as the guard clucked to his horse and resumed his former position, at a safe distance from the cons.

The fog was so heavy I could hardly see the sack. As the last guard turned his back to me, making the right angle at the turn-row, I wanted to dash out. I forced myself to wait until I could barely hear their swearing.

The fog didn't feel as thick as it looked when I crawled from the brush to the turn-row. I dared not stand up. It was thicker near the ground, yet it seemed a thousand eyes were upon me. Snatching the sack I scrambled back on all-fours like a long haired rabbit in a prairie fire. I had to get out of there. The fog would have to cover. Clutching my treasure I plunged for the brush.

I had the letter. The letter which would nail Sen. Gordon Taylor to the cross. The letter demanding $50 from convict Watson for the restoration of his overtime. The letter which finally caught Sen. Taylor during an unguarded moment . . . the letter which bore his signature. The letter which caused all the search.

With the coming of daylight my fear subsided to a degree that I could live with. The cargo which I carried was far too precious to lose through an unguarded moment. Carefully I picked my way through the pine forest where wood chopping crews from Eastham No. 1 had left evidence of their logging. My breath came easier as I hit an old logging trail. All convicts on the farms were busy with crops at this time of the year and I reasoned, rightfully, that they would not be in this area.

I made good time now because I could see the ground where I was walking and fell into fewer traps. The sun was my friend, too, and I headed due east into it with no fear of getting lost. The river was on my right, the road to Weldon on my left and the highway straight ahead. About an hour past the Eastham No. 1 Farm my logging trail ended. My pine forest without too much underbrush was studded with more and more of those moss-back cypress. This meant the swampland of the river bottom. I hated swamps; but I didn't dare the road, now that it was daylight and I had the letter. A few yards past the end of the logging trail I sat down beneath a magnolia tree for a breather, and to think. Finding this wild magnolia made me feel better. The blossoms were large and fragrant. Too bad their beauty was lost to the world. Clasping one of the creamy white blossoms in my hands, I bowed my head in a silent prayer of thanks. The worst of my ordeal was over, I hoped.

While I rested I carefully loosened the draw strings of the tobacco sack and extracted the carefully folded letter. The letter itself didn't say much, in so far as I was concerned, just demanded that Watson leave his $50 mustering out pay with a clerk in the prison office on the day he was released. Other unsigned communications had carried a similar message. But this one was on the senate letterhead and bore the signature which made it the most important document in my life. I must get it to Harry McCormick.

Folding the letter very carefully so as not to make more creases, I put the letter into the pocket of the light jacket which I was wearing to protect myself from the underbrush and mosquitoes, extracted a safety pin from my purse and pinned the pocket closed.

Nearing the highway I secluded myself underneath the protective curtain of an old moss-back, as the trees heavily draped with Spanish moss were called, and changed clothes. Carefully I unpinned the pocket, extracted the letter and hid it deep within a zippered pocket of my purse. Again in a dress I discarded the mutilated slacks and jacket in some thick brush. My muddy oxfords would have to stick with me a little longer, until I was closer to the road. When I was within seeing distance of the highway I took my slippers and hose from the bag. These were its only contents now, save for my dirty blouse which I had saved for this purpose. Dipping the blouse into a little stream which flowed into the river I washed my face and applied a little make-up. After washing my feet I threw away the blouse and oddly shaped balls of mud which had once been fairly decent school oxfords. Wearing a dress, as well as hose and high heels, I felt sure no one would suspect that I had spent the night in the swampy bottomland. Clutching my purse as if it contained all the gold in the world I cautiously crept out to the edge of the highway, when no car was within seeing distance. I timed it just so, when I heard a big truck groaning in the distance.

I had to be lucky, and was. When the truck driver stopped to pick me up I explained that I was walking into Lovelady to catch a bus to Dallas. My prayers were answered. He was driving a through truck on this run and insisted that I ride with him. Within an hour we stopped for breakfast. I was starved. I insisted on paying for my own meal but the truck driver would have none of it.

Once in Dallas I wasted no time in calling McCormick. He left the News office and came to the Walgreen drug store from which I had made the call, almost immediately. Never could a man have been more grateful, or relieved. I told him that I felt fairly positive that I was not being followed. It would have been impossible. Besides, if they had known, I would have been slain in the woods rather than being allowed to escape with the letter.

Here Harry agreed with me. I did not tell him about "those eyes."

"This does not mean that they won't suspect, or put a tail on you later," Harry cautioned. "Now promise me to get out and stay out of this mess. I'll take the letter to Royal myself."

"But do you think he will use the letter right away?"

"He will more than likely have it photostated, ready and waiting. The timing will have to be just right. First we use the first letter you sent, without the signature. Taylor will deny it, naturally. Then, boom with the killing blow, when we're sure it won't cost Watson his neck. We'll be ready and waiting when he comes out of prison, or at least when he is supposed to emerge. No one will get his fifty bucks. We'll have a photostat of that letter, just waiting for them to stop him. We've got the kingpin this time."

"Are you sure?"

"Absolutely. We've had an investigation committee on other types of grafts. This signature is all that is needed to clean house, from Senator Taylor, right down through the prison management to the guards. Just keep your nose clean."

Never was I happier to make such a promise.

"And change your address," Harry warned. "Don't even let Roy know where you are. A letter from him, however innocent, could trap you. Just get out and stay out of this, You've done more than your share. Take good care of yourself and that baby," he reminded as he stuck out his hand in way of confidence and goodbye.

My work at the prison was done, but I was afraid it was too late to make good my promise of teaching. How could any professor recommend me, considering the classes I skipped and my poor grades. Besides, I was afraid to go back to Lubbock. Prison eyes could be glued on the 'Mary Gregg' mail box.

Mary Gregg? Who is that. I never knew her, I promised myself with the greatest confidence.

Where should Mary McLeod, the person I wanted to be, live? A boom town? Not too far, and yet close enough home for me to see Carolyn.

Things were opening up in Odessa, a West Texas oil field town. It was booming, not only with oil, but with the bombardier training base going in ten miles from town, between Odessa and Midland. There would be many, many new residents in Odessa. Another wouldn't matter. Who would even notice?

Maybe I could find a job as a reporter, with the war growing hotter. Some of the newspapers in the area had carried reprints of my articles. I felt sure that the editor of the Lubbock *Avalanche Journal* would recommend me because of my stories which they had published. Newspaper work is respectable. I just had to make good my promise. I would apply for a teaching position . . . just so I could truthfully say I had tried. Although I had passed my college work, I knew no justifiable reason for my professors recommending me.

This would be a new life for me. I would let no one from the prison know I was in Odessa, no one. Now I must help myself and get my daughter back. Surely I could find work at the newspaper office. I would use my maiden name. I could never afford to say that I had worked as a reporter in Abilene because the name was Mary Gregg. This name must be dropped, forever. In fact my maiden name should become legal right away, or maybe it already was. Roy had signed the divorce papers. Confirmation would be sent to my parent's home. It would be so good to have only one name again and lead only one life.

My experiences had been nerve-wrecking. Maybe I could soon sleep again without the constant fear that followed me from the time I smuggled the first letter from the prison. There would be over 600 miles between me and the prison. I simply had to sever all ties.

Jailed on a False Charge

I was not discouraged when I did not find work immediately at the Ector County newspaper office when I arrived in Odessa. They talked as if I had a good chance of getting work with them soon. It looked as if one of their reporters might be drafted, and with the opening of the new Army Air Corps things would pick up. I could wait. I had to land this job. I had written my parents I was fairly sure of a good newspaper job in Odessa. That was my excuse for leaving Lubbock. I could never tell them the real reason why. All I could do was tell them I would do newspaper work while waiting for a teaching position.

But I had to eat while waiting for the newspaper job, so I went to work as a waitress at the American Cafe. I had been working in Odessa for over two weeks and had learned to appreciate oil field workers, commonly termed 'roughnecks.' True, they exercised a great deal of 'free speech,' and those without families usually drank and were broke from one payday until the next . . . but they were good, rugged Americans, a new breed. They lived in trailers or flimsy shot-gun houses, but drove fine cars. Hotels and tourist courts were overcrowded.

There were more saloons, honkey tonks (as they called them) than grocery stores.

It was a man's town, no doubt about it. But somehow, between those 'tin hats' (all men working on drilling rigs were required to wear aluminum hats and steel-toed shoes) and iron shoes lay a kind heart.

They were always easy to talk with, and hungry. Soon I knew exactly what most of the men liked packed in their lunches, how to avoid soggy sandwiches, and how they liked their steaks cooked. I knew payday from the weight of my tips.

It was early summer and my 26th birthday had just passed. Mother had sent me what I wanted most, a picture of Carolyn. I was exhibiting it proudly to those who knew me best. I still had over two months to make good my promise. By fall Carolyn would be ready to start to school. I had been promised the newspaper job and filled out a teacher-employment blank, giving my hometown mailing address, more or less just so I could say I had tried.

I was through with Roy Gregg and my old life, truly through. What I had done to help the prisoners was for humanity, not for Roy. For him there was nothing more I could or should do.

With a song in my heart and a cup of coffee in my hand I turned to the cafe counter that morning . . . and looked into the cold, steel blue eyes of the last man in the world I wanted to see less than Roy Gregg.

Coffee splashed over the cup, burning my hand as my glance met Ray Hilton's. He never said a word, but I knew he recognized me. Hilton was the first cop to pick up Roy. The cop who had been at the original trial when I was carrying Carolyn. The cop who had been put on our trail when we were fugitives. He could never forget. He had lost his position as a detective and made a flat-foot again when he failed to find us.

He knew me, and I knew I was in for trouble. What kind I didn't know . . . but trouble. I knew I had best leave town as soon as possible. My chances at the newspaper job were shot with him around.

I wonder what he said to the manager on his way out? The

manager kept looking at me. Under close scrutiny I couldn't remember my orders, and I spilled more and more coffee into saucers. Finally I was on the verge of tears and said that I was sick and going home.

I was packing my bag at the rooming house when a car drove up out in front with four officers inside. Two of them jumped out and ran around the house while the other two burst through the front door without knocking.

''What do you want?'' I gasped as the men flung open closet doors.

''You know who we're looking for,'' Ray Hilton said. ''Where's Roy Gregg.''

''In prison,'' I answered, weak with fright.

''Don't pretend you don't know he's out again.''

''Oh! No!'' I cried. ''There's been no prison break! There's nothing in the paper.''

''This didn't get to the paper,'' Hilton said disdainfully, ''We knew he'd come to you.''

Could it be? Could it possibly be I wondered as the other men continued the search. When they had satisfied themselves that Roy wasn't there, I thought they would leave me alone. Instead Hilton took me by the arm and said:

''Come with us.''

''Why?'' I cried ''Why?''

''Because Gregg is out and we know you had a part in it. He'll bust heaven and hell to get to you . . . so we're keeping you in the Ector County Jail until he shows up.''

''But I've done nothing,'' I cried as I jerked away.

''We know your game,'' he rejoined, ''Why the packed bags?''

I was pushed into the back seat of the car as the neighbors looked on. I wondered if he considered four big men enough to handle me?

When we got to the courthouse I demanded to use the telephone. I wanted to confirm the report about Roy Gregg. I didn't believe it.

They laughed at me and started upstairs . . . carrying me to a cell.

''I demand to use the phone!'' I said very sternly as I held back. ''It's my right. You can't hold me without a charge.''

''Take her on up,'' Hilton instructed the jailer.

''It's a lie!'' I yelled. ''Roy Gregg has not escaped prison.'' I yelled . . . hoping someone who might help would hear. No one seemed moved.

I couldn't be imprisoned like this, without knowing why. I thought of the letters I had smuggled from the prison. Did they know? Was that the reason my room was searched? Would they go back? I couldn't let them lock me up without help. I knew what they had threatened to do to anyone at the prison they caught smuggling.

''You've got to let me use the phone!'' I hissed as I started struggling to free myself. Hilton grabbed me roughly and I started a real battle. He was everything I hated, it seemed suddenly, and I lashed out.

I was hysterical, I admit it, but I was afraid of what might happen if I were locked up. I couldn't sleep for fear I was being watched while I was doing the smuggling. Now that I was finished . . . the last and most important letter from Sen. Gordon Taylor was in the hands of Harry McCormick. . . .

''Oh, God!'' I thought, ''They don't know! They think I have that letter! Someone saw me! Those eyes!''

I slugged and clawed. When they pinned my arms back . . . I bit Hilton's arm. It sounds strange, now, for I have never been a violent person . . . but I turned animal, an animal caught in a trap.

They shoved me into a cell. I grabbed a tin cup and started beating it against the bars, trying to attract the attention of someone on the street below . . . screaming at every passerby to call me a lawyer.

''I'm not drunk nor crazy,'' I screamed when one man stopped to listen, but I'm sure he thought I was. No lawyer came.

I hadn't bothered to notice there were two other women in the cell . . . a Mexican and a white woman. I don't blame these women for being afraid of me, if they were. But that's the excuse that was used for putting me into the padded cell.

There was nothing, absolutely nothing in that semi-dark padded cell, not even a commode. It was too late to yell.

I tried to get hold of myself and think. It wasn't easy. For hours tears of frustration kept forming and I would shake like one with palsy. I couldn't figure out how they could throw me in jail in our own country without a charge and refuse to let me use the telephone, but they did. So help me God, they did.

What would happen to me? Why did they have me here? More than anything else I wished I could call Harry McCormick . . . but I knew that I mustn't . . . it would be a dead give-away. If I could just call Huntsville and find out if there had been a prison break, but I was helpless.

I was near the men's cells. Some of them were turned out into the run-around for exercise. They seemed to pay no attention, but I felt eyes staring at me from one of the cells. Why didn't this man come out? His door was unlocked. He was free to exercise, too.

Suddenly my blood curdled. Those eyes! I had seen him at the Eastham No. 2 Farm. He was in the visitors' "chicken-coop" that last Sunday afternoon I visited Roy. Was he the stoolie Roy had mentioned? Roy and I had talked only with our eyes, true, but maybe he knew.

When the other men were put back in the cell blocks, only one cell door remained unlocked. He was a trusty, and was free to move about the run-around whenever he choose. Only bars between us, but how thankful I was for those bars.

I was afraid to go to sleep. All through the night I sat upright, right in the middle of the cell, practically over the drain which served as a latrine. I was afraid to get near the edge. An arm could reach through the bars and choke me in my sleep. There probably wouldn't even be an investigation. I was in the padded cell, wasn't I?

All through the night I sat in the middle of the cell, trying to think, praying for an out. My foe never moved from his cell at all . . . but I felt his eyes upon me.

I could have been wrong, about the stoolie and his being there to kill me. . . . I'll probably never know. Maybe he wasn't working with Ray Hilton at all . . . maybe Hilton just couldn't stand seeing me free, as long as he chased us and failed. Maybe Hilton thought the state still wanted me and would try me for harboring a fugitive from justice. In his own way of thinking, he may have had a right to pick me up . . . but why had he used a big lie to do it?

What would happen to me now? Would I be murdered, just as my work at the prison was finished and my divorce from Roy Gregg had finally come through? Irony of fate. I'd lived through one night, but they'd probably get me the next, I thought as daylight came.

Nothing could have surprised me more than what actually did happen. After much clanging of keys and the serving of a tin plate of oatmeal, which I refused to eat, the keys were again clanging in the outside door. Men approached my cell. One was the jailer, I knew without looking, for keys rattled. They stopped at my padded cell. When I did look up I saw I had a visitor, a "roughneck," one of the oil-field workers I had served at the cafe. He was R. D. Latham, the roughneck who had been most interested in my daughter's picture.

"I heard them talking about you at the cafe," he offered in way of explanation. "Thought I'd bring you a little handout and see if there's anything I can do."

I jumped at my only straw of hope. "Please call the prison at Huntsville and see if Roy Gregg, my husband has escaped," I begged, "I can't believe it. If he hasn't escaped, then try to find out why I'm here. Get me a lawyer. Make them let me use the telephone."

There was genuine sympathy in his voice as he promised to find out. It seemed strange. I could have sworn there was mist in those pale blue eyes as the ruddy Irishman fumbled a delicate box of chocolates in ham-like hands. He hadn't said much around the cafe, and he must have been nearing forty, but he always seemed pleased beyond words when I put a little something special in his lunch, something he didn't expect.

Later in the morning he came back. Roy had not escaped. He couldn't find out what the charge was against me, so he had hunted up Judge Pilkington, whom he knew personally. After much fishing around the judge said he thought I was there on charges of insanity.

"I told the judge that somebody was crazy as hell," the Irishman stated, "but I told him it wasn't that girl in the cell. I told the judge it was high time someone got to the bottom of this."

I was taken before the judge, but before I reached the courtroom the charges had been made to read, "Disturbing the public peace and resisting arrest." The fine was $14 plus cost.

"Disturbing the public peace!" I cried. "I was at home, alone, when officers rushed in and said my husband had escaped prison. It was a lie! A frame up!"

"Watch your accusations," the judge continued, "Or you'll be charged with contempt of the court."

"I'll pay her fine," Latham said, "but it's a damned dirty deal, pushing a woman around just because her husband's a convict."

"You won't pay my fine!" I blazed in anger. "No one will pay it! Send for a reporter from the newspaper. I have a story, and it's not of a prison break," I fired as I stomped from the courtroom, clicking my heels like pistons. The jailer stayed a respectful distance behind me as I returned to my cell.

In a few minutes, not a reporter, but Mr. Latham and the jailer were again at my padded cell.

"You're free to go," the jailer said as the key grated in the lock. "This man's paid your fine."

"I won't go!" I spat. "I was jailed on false charges. I owe no fine. Let Ector County pay me. I want a lawyer."

"You're coming out!" the sheriff, who had just appeared on the scene, declared in no uncertain terms.

"I won't come out!" I shouted in defiance.

"Please listen to me," Mr. Latham begged. "You're making things worse. You may be right, but you can talk to a lawyer more freely on the outside."

"I appreciate your efforts," I said to the sympathetic Irishman, "but this is America. I was jailed on a false charge. I owe no fine. I want a reporter and a lawyer. I'll wait here."

As R. D. talked with the sheriff I became conscious of eyes

staring at me from behind a lowered newspaper in a near-by cell, gloating eyes. Those eyes!

''Maybe you're right,'' I said to Mr. Latham as he again turned to face me through the bars. ''A jail cell is not the best place to confer with a lawyer,'' I added as I stepped outside.

Outside the courthouse R. D., asked me to lunch with him before going for a lawyer. He might be able to offer a suggestion himself, if he understood the circumstances.

When we were alone I poured out my story to him. I had to confide in someone, and I couldn't help but trust him, even to telling about the letter.

''But if you yell about your imprisonment now, and give the real reason, you would have to give Harry McCormick's name, wouldn't you, to prove there is such a letter?''

''Yes, I agreed, as the light penetrated, ''and it hasn't been published yet. They'd get McCormick for sure. Let them think I still have it. I've waited this long, I can wait a little longer, but I can't stay in Odessa.''

''You can if you want to,'' R. D. asserted, ''I'll get a body-guard for you if necessary.''

''Thanks,'' I grinned at the mental picture, ''but I'm afraid a gun beside me wouldn't be the best recommendation for work. I've got to find a job. No one would hire me here, not now, and I have a child to support. I'll have to leave Texas.''

''So long as they think you have that letter, it would probably be wise to leave. I'll help you.''

And he did. ''I'll drive you out of this hole,'' R. D. promised, ''as soon as it is dark.''

Leaving Odessa, west, toward El Paso, we drove until we hit an oil-field road to the north. Taking every precaution, R. D. stopped, when we had gone less than a mile, and waited. No headlights turned in our direction.

''Maybe I could catch a bus out of Lubbock,'' I suggested.

''No,'' came his studied reply. ''Are we agreed that Denver is the largest out-of-state town that is not too far away?''

''It's big enough for me to work under more than one name, if I have to,'' I answered. ''But then I couldn't hear from my mother about Carolyn. Maybe, if I just give a street address, wherever I get a room, I won't be traced, not before the letter is published, anyway.''

''Then I'll drive you into New Mexico.''

''But aren't you working graveyard tower? You could hardly get back by midnight if you turned around now.''

''Forget it, I'm out on a drunk. They'll pick up some other roughneck, if they can find one sober, to fill in.''

As we drove through the night, we planned. Several times R. D. pulled off on a side road and stopped as we watched for headlights. There was no indication we were being tailed.

We ate breakfast in Hobbs, New Mexico, and I insisted that I had been transported far enough.

''Town's too small,'' R. D. replied as we headed for Roswell. ''Maybe I'll let you off there, maybe I won't.''

Roswell was rather small, and it looked as if most of the persons who lived there were Mexicans.

''You'd be a little conspicious in a bus station here,'' R.D. surmised. So long as I am taking a day off, I may as well enjoy it.''

It was good, getting this far away from Texas. It was pleasant, too. R. D. was very thoughtful, and a very sympathetic listener. Suddenly I realized that all my talking had been about myself. It was evident he didn't have a wife, not in Odessa, because he ate all his meals at the cafe.

''Don't you have a family?'' I asked.

''Not a wife,'' he answered. ''I do take care of my mother, but she lives near Dallas. My father has been dead many years.''

We stopped at a crossroad cafe and ate lunch. No one seemed to be following us. R. D. thought it best that he buy my ticket, when we reached Albuquerque. I insisted that I was close enough now that my funds would suffice, but he would have it no other way. He assured me, too, that he would watch the newspapers for ''The Letter'' to be published, just in case it didn't hit the Denver papers.

Then he really surprised me. How could he, who had probably never been on the lam, think of so many points of caution.

''You take my car,'' R. D. directed, as we pulled up within a block of the bus station, ''and if that bus that's loading, with 'Denver' smeared across the front is pulling out, meet me at

Alameda, about 20 miles north of here. Wait at the bus station, ticket in hand.''

Before I could protest he pushed two $20 bills into my hand and headed for the station. When I again saw him he waved as he boarded the bus.

Not knowing my way too well, I tailed the bus until we were out of town. When I saw a sign, Alameda 18 miles, I watched for an opportunity to pass the bus. R. D. saw me pass. There was a big Irish grin like who threw the overalls, as I pushed by with only a turn of my head in recognition.

I saw no one, absolutely no one, following. Strange R. D. would realize that city bus stations might be watched. Why should he do so much for me? He hardly knew me. Two weeks ago I didn't even know his name, when I first started packing his lunch at the cafe. Now he was taking every precaution to see that I made a clean get-away.

There was little time for thinking about anything except the road. I had to stay ahead of the bus. In Alameda I had just finished buying my ticket as the bus pulled up. A wink was R.D.'s only sign of recognition as I brushed beside him and slipped the car keys into his hand. You could hardly have called this a regular bus stop, except for the little flag being placed outside when there was a passenger.

As the bus left the station I was again in a very lonely world. I couldn't help risking a very small wave as R. D. left the station simultaneous with the bus, but headed back toward Albuquerque. Certainly no one could have helped me more. Perhaps he had even saved my life. I shuddered at the thought of the padded cell and those eyes, those gloating eyes, in the cell adjacent to mine. It was good, realizing they were not upon me now.

The Only Way

With World War II brewing, I doubted that I would have much trouble finding work in Denver. I would have liked to have applied for newspaper work, but I knew I could never hope for any peace of mind so long as that letter, 'The Letter', from Sen. Gordon Taylor, was not published.

The world situation was as shaky as I was. The Battle of Dunkirk was over. The great air battle against Britain began with mass daylight raids. Prime Minister Winston Churchill voiced the determination and courage of the British to endure to the end, but there wasn't much courage left within me.

I had no choice. I, too, had retreated after giving up in Lubbock and Odessa, but I couldn't tell my parents why. I couldn't think of a lie good enough for not getting a newspaper job in Odessa. The summer of 1940 was half gone. My family expected great things from me. Would they give up when I had to write I was again working in a cafe, in another state?

What a blitzkrieg I received in the next letter from my parents. They charged that instead of working closer home, as I should, I continued to move farther and farther away. Carolyn needed me. She needed new clothes and medical attention before she started to school. She had lost weight. She begged for me continually as she thought of school opening soon. It was not right to break promises to a child. It was quite evident that I was nothing but a gadabout. If I really wanted my own child I would have to settle down. They loved her and did not want to see her hurt. She belonged to them. They had raised her.

I cried a salt lake. If I could only tell my parents why I had to leave Texas, but I couldn't. I had promised to have nothing more to do with Roy Gregg or the prison. If I told them, I might never get my daughter back at all.

I resolved to work harder and send more money home. For the next six weeks I would hold down two jobs. I'd worked night and day while going to college. Surely I could hold down a daytime job in a cafe and a job in a night club. I hated drinking and the passes made at a cocktail waitress, but I had to have my daughter.

Why wasn't the letter signed by Sen. Gordon Taylor published? Surely they could not hold Watson in prison much longer. Could they have ranked him again? Maybe he was even dead. I couldn't write to Roy, but maybe I should chance writing to McCormick. I had to know. Jobs were opening up everywhere. If that letter were only published there would be little point in killing me, just for revenge. Surely I could return to normal living if it were proven that I had been crusading for a just cause.

Holding down two jobs I did make money, good money. As July collapsed into August the calendar bombarded me with the urgency of the date. Only a month and school would start.

I sent money home. More money than they could hope for. Money enough to attend my daughter's pre-school needs. I had paid R. D. the money he put out for my fine and I owed him only one more $10 payment on the money he had given me to buy my ticket to Denver. Faithfully he clipped even the minutest of news from the prison and mailed it to me, but the news we were looking for seemed dead.

From his letters I knew that R. D. loved me. So often he hinted that he would like to provide a good home for me and my daughter. I admired and appreciated him, but he was almost fifteen years my senior, more like a father than a lover. Somehow I translated my hate for the prison officials, cops and the clutching hands of night club patrons into a hatred for all men. Some day I would sue Ector County.

With confirmation of my divorce came another withering letter from home. Money couldn't make up for love. Where was I getting such money? What was I doing? Surely I wasn't making that kind of money waiting tables. Why didn't I get a decent job. I had a degree. The urgency of the war situation left a demand, even for teachers. Time was growing short. Had I applied for a teaching position? School would start within less than a month.

My family demanded the truth, as well as my intentions. It seemed evident that I did not deserve my own child. Decent jobs were opening near home. It was wrong of me to let my sister help me through a term of graduate work, only to be wasted in a cafe. I didn't deserve my own child. They could no longer promise her I would come home. It seemed evident that I had rather continue my fling than shoulder the responsibility of motherhood.

I was desperate. Somehow, in desperation and hopelessness, I came to identify with Britain. Bombardments from home were as ruthless as those of the Luftwaffe. Where could I turn for help? Somehow Winston Churchill's plea to the U.S. seemed to paraphrase my struggle. I clipped it from the newspaper, in fact, I still have it. Whenever I have a tendency to become discouraged I read:

> "We shall fight on the seas and oceans, we shall fight with growing confidence and growing strength in the air, we shall defend our Island, whatever the cost may be, we shall fight on the beaches, we shall fight on the landing grounds, we shall fight in the fields and in the streets, we shall fight in the hills; we shall never surrender, and even if, which I do not for a moment believe, this island or a large part of it were subjected and starving, then our Empire beyond the seas, armed and guarded by the British

> fleet, would carry on the struggle, until, in God's good time, the New World, with all its power and might, steps forth to the rescue and liberation of the old."

I had retreated until there seemed no further stand, no honest one, to say the least. Once I had planned to kidnap my own daughter. This might be the answer, a sad one to be sure, but time was running out.

Feeling I could wait no longer, I was writing Harry McCormick, asking what had happened to The Letter, when I heard the mailman clanging the apartment mail boxes in the downstairs hallway.

There were two letters for me, one from R. D. and one from home. Dreading the one from home, I ripped R. D.'s envelope, which felt quite heavy. There it was! The Letter! The Letter had been published. Watson was free. A wholesale clean-up at the prison was underway. I didn't take time, not just then, to read all the small print about the graft and corruption exposed, and of the firing of prison officials. Sen. Gordon Taylor had been asked to resign. An investigation committee had been at work, since it had been presented with a photostat of the letter, and everything was already set in type, I learned later, just waiting for Watson's release, when the headlines could be written.

Before reading the letter from R. D., which could be only anticlimatic now, I fumbled with the one from home, trying not to read the answer which I felt inevitable from my last plea. I had sworn by all that was holy that I was doing nothing wrong, that I was holding down two jobs, because when school started I wanted to quit one job to be with Carolyn. I would have enough money to come for her. I would bring her back to Colorado with me where no one should ever know she was a prisoner's daughter. I assured my parents that I did love Carolyn, that I had always loved her.

Knowing my parents, I sank in the lone chair at the little table by my lonely window, where the unfinished letter to McCormick was now ready for the waste basket. The first sentence answered my question.

"You are not about to take Carolyn off to another state where we may never see her again," flew the spark from my mother's pen.

"She's ours. Your father and I have given her a good home and love. Since we've taken care of her since she was a baby, I guess the good Lord will give us the strength to carry on. It breaks our hearts to hear her talk about her mother coming home for her to start school. She still thinks you are going to teach. I haven't had the heart to tell her it's a lie.

"When school starts and that's only nine days from now, she's ours. Nothing can take her from us. We didn't want her to have to attend school in a town where everyone knows her father is a convict, but this seems better than what her own mother has to offer.

"How could you have done this to us, Mary? I'll never understand how you could do such a thing to your own child. We've given you every opportunity, even sent you back to college. Teaching positions are opening everywhere, since so many persons have resigned for better paying jobs. Things are booming, yet you have failed us. With your maiden name back I am sure you could get a job closer home. If you were not qualified for anything better than what you are doing, I would understand. What has happened to you? Surely your own child and her welfare should come before anything else.

"It's hard to say this, Mary, but I've talked it over with your father. There's no need of coming home for Carolyn. We won't give her to you. We'll call the police, if we have to. When school starts, she's ours. We're too old for taking care of a child, we know, but she will have the right kind of home. God has punished me for saying I could never love a convict's child. I love her more than I ever loved any of my own. She needs our love. She brings a great deal of joy to your father since he is retired. We could never give her up to be carried off to another state."

The letter was signed by my mother.

My heart was dead, simply dead. It would kill my mother and my father if I kidnapped my own daughter now, even if I could get away with it. I had won a battle and lost the war. Why had I broken my promise and gone back to the prison after filing for divorce from Roy? My victory was short lived. In a fit of defiance I grabbed the newspaper which I had so eagerly read a few minutes previously, and flung it into the wastebasket to rest beside the letter I was writing to McCormick.

I had no heart for reading R. D.'s letter, but I could think of nothing better to do. In fact, I couldn't think. My victory had been my defeat.

"Thanks for your last payment," the letter opened, "but I wish you had kept it to apply on your trip home, now that 'The Letter' is published.

"I know you don't love me," R. D. continued, "but since the letter has been published I feel you could come back to Texas. Things might be better for you and Carolyn if your name was changed. I'm asking you to marry me, Mary. I love you so much that I can't help but feel it will be reciprocal.

"You deserve some peace of mind and I'm asking to make a good home for you and your daughter. I've been looking at some pretty cottages in a quiet section of town with a good school nearby. Why not give yourself a break? If you don't learn to love me and to respect me I would never contest a divorce, if you wanted it later. It would give the public a chance to forget about you and Roy. It would give your daughter a different name. I want to adopt her. No one need ever know her father is a convict. Think it over."

How could I marry a man I didn't love? Certainly I already appreciated R. D. Latham, but marriage was something different. I had never really loved but one man. I could never love another.

Don't be a fool, I said to myself. This is a last and only chance. R. D. is a good man, why fight it? He would be good to me and to Carolyn. That was more than I could hope for, banging around from one cafe to another. No more clutching hands in night clubs. The arms of my own daughter in my own home.

It would be cheating, marrying a man I didn't love to make a home for my daughter, but I would try to make R. D. a good wife. Maybe I would even learn to love him in time. This he understood.

I knew the sudden turn of events would shock my parents, perhaps break their hearts, but Carolyn was my daughter. She wanted me and loved me. They had said themselves that it was not fair for her to have to start to school where everyone knew her father was a convict.

It was a hard decision to make, but marriage seemed better than kidnapping. Certainly it would help me to give Carolyn a better home than anything I had to offer previously. My parents couldn't contest this, not even in court, I reassured myself as I began a letter to R. D.

"Tomorrow is my payday," I wrote R. D. "I will have plenty of money for the trip back to Texas. Go ahead and buy the house, that is, if we can take off the day after we are married to pick up Carolyn. She needs to be in school.

"I appreciate your offer and will try to make you a good wife. I will leave for Texas tomorrow, as soon as I pick up my check. I may call you enroute, since I doubt that this letter will reach Odessa before I do. The urgency to get Carolyn into school necessitates a hurried marriage, so go ahead and apply for the license if you wish."

I should have mailed the letter, but I didn't. R. D.'s getting it before I arrived in Odessa was doubtful, anyway. It didn't matter. Odessa was enroute home.

I caught myself dreaming a little. After banging around for almost seven years a cottage with white curtains and flowers sounded like utopia, especially with Carolyn to love and be loved by. Besides, my parents would soon become reconciled. We would be close enough for weekend visits. Soon they would forgive, seeing her with a good home and the devotion of two parents.

I told myself all these wonderful things over and over, but I didn't mail the letter. It was late. I needed to pack. I would just put an air mail stamp on it and post it in the morning. It probably wouldn't get out tonight, anyway. I would mail it when I went after my check, before I caught the bus.

I was awake before my alarm screamed at me. Hastily I dressed. I hoped this was the last time I would exit from a drab little room with my worldly goods packed in a couple of battered handbags. Although I couldn't get excited about marrying a man I didn't love, I would have my daughter and I could lie down and sleep at night without fear of being stalked or fired because of wagging tongues or failing to produce a social security card.

"It's good to leave this dirty rooming house," I said to myself as I made my way down the hall to the scabby old phone with dozens of numbers scribbled around it on the eroding wall paper. Sometimes it waked me up ringing . . . and ringing. It always seemed to take forever for anyone to answer it.

"This is my last call from this bellowing monster," I assured myself as I put down my suitcases. Removing the letter to R. D. from first place position in my purse, where I had placed it to make sure I didn't forget, I dropped a nickel into the slot and called a cab. I would have the driver wait while I ran into the Blue Parrot Cafe to pick up my check.

Picking up my bags I headed for the hallway steps. I could at least get to where the air was fresh while I waited for the taxi. Reaching the last step I set down the luggage and reached into my purse to make sure of the letter to R. D.

Extracting the letter from my purse I looked at it with an ironical laugh. It was my passport. A means to an end. A way to steal my own daughter, legally. Legally! I laughed aloud at the thought. It might be legal, according to the record, but according to my own conscience it was cheating my own parents. Could it be so bad, marrying a man I didn't love? The stakes were high. The thing which I wanted most in life was within my reach.

It wouldn't be easy, going through with such a fraud, but life had denied me the things it gave to others. My own child was all I wanted, all it seemed I had ever wanted. I had tried to get her the right way, but circumstances always seemed to interfere.

The telephone rang. I laughed. It could just keep ringing. Nothing mattered now. Thanks to R. D. I was now on my way to steal my daughter, legally.

My taxi hadn't arrived. It couldn't possibly get here this fast. At least, whenever I was in the greatest hurry it seemed I always waited the longest. The phone kept ringing. Let it. It could ring right off the wall so far as I was concerned.

''Why don't you give up?'' I said under my breath, impatient with the interruption. A person couldn't even think straight with it bellowing like a threatening bull.

''O.K. Just once more,'' I said through clenched teeth. ''But I'm not chasing all over the building to drag somebody out. My taxi might come.''

''Hello,'' I barked into the receiver. ''Who do you want at this time of the morning? I'm sure they must be awake by now.''

''I'm sorry if I have disturbed sleepers,'' came a businesslike apology over the wire, ''but this is Western Union. We've a telegram for Mary McLeod. Do you have a Mary McLeod living at this address?'' a feminine voice inquired.

''I'm Mary,'' I stammered. ''Mary McLeod speaking,'' I finally managed in a more audible tone.

''Shall I read the telegram, or do you want it sent out?''

''Read it, please.''

''It's dated Monday, Aug. 26, 1940.''

''Please,'' I begged in an effort to hurry her.

''It reads: 'VACANCY IN ROOSEVELT SCHOOL NEAR LUBBOCK STOP WE ACCEPTED IT FOR YOU STOP COME HOME IMMEDIATELY STOP BARELY ONE WEEK FOR YOU AND CAROLYN TO GET THERE'.''

''It's signed mother,'' she added. 'Do you wish to send a reply?''

''Yes,'' I answered in a dazed tone. ''Send it to W.Z. McLeod, same address. Say ENROUTE . . .'' I hesitated.

''You have nine more words if you wish to state which route you are taking and your time of arival,'' she suggested.

''There's only one way, and only one destination,'' I mumbled underneath my breath.

''I didn't understand you,'' she said. ''Which route did you say you would take?''

''There's only one way, the right way,'' I said with strange finality, more to myself than to the telegraph operator.

''But I don't understand you?''

''Excuse me, operator. Let's just say,'' I hesitated as I looked at the letter addressed to R. D., which I still held in my hand. ''Let's just say I'm taking the straight way home, immediately. NON-STOP,'' I added with emphasis, crumpling the letter which seemed my passport a few minutes earlier.

''Is that your message? 'I'M TAKING THE STRAIGHT WAY. . . .' I'm not sure it makes good sense,'' the telegraph operator puzzled.

''Never mind,'' I assured. ''It will to my parents. For me it's the only way,'' I said to the receiver as I tore the letter in half and headed for the taxi.

Epilogue

Fifty years have passed since our story began . . . and still I hide. Not from the law or the lawless, but from you, the public.

My daughter, that convict's daughter, has suffered all her life because of her parentage. When she was in school she came home crying, day after day, month after month, and year after year. Now she is afraid to tell her own children about their grandfather.

Must this stigma last forever? I am not asking society to condone sin, certainly not, but to forget the past if one tries hard enough and long enough to be forgiven, to prove oneself an honest, upright citizen.

Jesus said, "Go and sin no more," but we ourselves are less forgiving. My daughter still bears the cross, the cross that I have borne for fifty years. Will it be handed down to my grandchildren?

However hard I try to convince my daughter that she is not accountable for the sins of her parents, she shrinks, just as I have always done when it looks as if the past might be unearthed. When I told her I was working on this book she wrote the following concerning her childhood:

"I guess having the children in my own home town making fun of me and laughing at me really marked me for life. Their favorite song on the school bus was "You Are My Sunshine" and they sang it almost every day. When they got to the part "I was peeking through prison bars" they would always snicker and point at me. I have spent my entire life trying to prove that I can be a decent person despite the fact that I am a convict's daughter.

"I have never told the children about their grandfather. I have tried to protect them from the shame and humiliation I have suffered all my life. I told my husband about it before we were married because I didn't want to disgrace him later. But I could never tell the children. I don't want them to suffer. They have done so beautifully in school. I've always tried to build up a feeling of pride in the family background because I never want them to be ashamed to go anywhere, like I've always been.

"So if you go ahead with this book, please don't use my name, the family name or our own hometown. What would it do to my husband's business? To our children? To your very own grandchildren? They are so very proud of their grandmother, so trusting." . . .

Yes, daughter, I am extremely proud of my grandchildren, and you too. Forgive this trite statement; but you are my pride and joy. Perhaps this is what I am trying to tell you. You have been the greatest factor in helping me prove my point. You have surmounted circumstance over which you had no control.

I know you worked very hard as a student, housewife and mother. It must have been very difficult for you to finish one of our larger universities in the upper one-and-a-half percent. It is most gratifying to know that your children, that convict's grandchildren, are doing as well or better themselves. You and your husband helped to make it so. You have given them every opportunity I wanted to give you, and a fine home. Through the grandchildren I have lived vicariously the years I wanted your arms around my neck, your hugs and your kisses.

I tried, but I never really had a little girl of my own. I was too busy running, hiding and trying to make a living.

When it seemed I would hurt you and my family less if I were dead I tried to compensate by risking my own life over and over to help those less fortunate, perhaps, than I. I wanted to die, but God wouldn't let me die. Finally I came to the conclusion that maybe my life was spared because I had a story to tell.

A story to warn others that the point of no return can be reached through good intentions. Loving any human being too much and trusting in God too little can lead to one's downfall. I loved your father too much and was too forgiving. In trying to help him I almost lost my only child.

Never condone sin. Watch your own excuses for breaking the laws of God and man. Mine were goodies. I stuck by my husband because I felt that he was a victim of circumstance, the depression. I fled with him and became a fugitive when he was the only man who lived through a prison break. When eight tried and seven died, I felt God let him live for a reason. I was determined to prove to the world that he was a good man. I was sure the world had done him wrong. Maybe so, up to a point, but I became so involved in proving my own belief that I failed to see when my point was no longer valid. Prisons change lives.

Know when to quit. I never did. Know when to re-evaluate and when to stop. Eventually we must face the truth.

Time was when I thought I hated my own mother. But it was my wrongdoing that drove her to the brink, to say things she later regretted. Thank God for good, strong parents. It took a whore to teach me how much I had to be thankful for when I had no desire to live. Parents and God forgive. Others take a little longer.

Perhaps it is good that society makes one prove sterling qualities. But it is bad when so called "society" exiles one who has overcome adversity, shoving him back into the mire.

Afraid of this, dear one, I have postponed publishing this book for over thirty years. I did fictionize a portion of it, while you were in college. The fictionized segment won a first place national award, as well as $5,000.00. That was a great deal of money in those days and I could have stopped teaching school, at least long enough to have a try at my life's ambition, writing. I felt this was my high-tide for writing, but I could never tell anyone I wrote the story because I had to hide to keep from hurting you and those I love. I wanted you to at least finish college with your head held high. . . .

Alaska, for many years my home since I left Texas, has been good to me. Here one does not look for skeletons, but achievement. I love Alaska. I am a leader in my community, and honored as such. I have become well recognized and honored as an author. Am I throwing my status away because I am keeping a promise I made to God so many years ago? If so, what is status?

Winning a national award in writing and telling no one was one of the hardest things I have ever done. I might have gained a little status as a writer by bragging; yet I could have hurt you at that time.

But now that both you and I have proven our point to the world, why must we hide?

Your father was a good man when I married him, a compassionate man. It was I who was weak. I cried because I had no food, no money to see the doctor, no baby clothes for you. He robbed for his unborn child.

How many of us yet alive lived through the great depression? Were you ever hungry and homeless? Did you ever feel as if no one in the whole world loved you? Did you ever hate the law and so called "humanity" because it held you down? Did you ever contemplate suicide?

When I sank to the lowest ebb of my life a whore showed me how much I had to live for. When I thought I hated my own mother she did not hesitate in telling me I was an ungrateful fool. My parents were strong. Betty's mother was an alcoholic; she never knew her father. Her stepfather raped her when she was thirteen; her child, the only thing in the world she really loved and wanted, was taken from her for adoption. As a teenager she was forced to hustle to support her parents' bad habits.

My life was a Sunday School class in comparison to Betty's; yet without her help and advice I do not know whether I would be here today. Betty knew my parents would not turn me down. Perhaps through helping me she was making some effort to compensate for her own sin. In making Christmas for my baby she may have lived one vicariously with her own, the baby she never knew but always loved.

Perhaps through writing this story I can help someone, sometime, somewhere. I could never tell you this story face to face, it's too embarrassing. I could never tell it to my own daughter, to whom I am now pleading.

Take this skeleton from your closet. Why live in fear that someday someone will open that closet door and the sins of the past will destroy the image you have worked a lifetime to develop? Be strong! You have nothing to hide.

Am I talking to you, daughter, to myself, or to both of us? We have both proven ourselves worthy citizens. Let's drag that skeleton from the closet, point a finger at it and say:

"See, we belong to a good world, a world lost to you through your own weakness. You were given ample opportunity and failed. You are the one who was condemned by society to pay the price. A just society does not demand your debt be paid through the second and third generation."

We are human beings, daughter, and as such we can control our own destiny. Circumstance may alter our course, even reverse it, but if we are strong enough we surmount that which is beyond our control. Think not of the past, but the future.

Let's take that skeleton from the closet and give it a decent burial. In a way, all who succeed in life owe their skeletons a debt of gratitude. Perhaps a fitting epitaph from each of us would be:

"YOUR WEAKNESS MADE ME STRONG."